Blood

LANA POPOVIĆ

AMULET BOOKS • NEW YORK

Library of Congress Cataloging-in-Publication Data

Names: Popović, Lana, author.
Title: The blood countess / Lana Popovic.
Description: New York : Amulet Books, 2020. | Series: Lady slayers |
Summary: In 1578 Hungary, sixteen-year-old Anna is elevated from
scullery maid to chambermaid by the young and glamorous Countess
Elizabeth Báthory, falling completely under the Countess's spell until
Anna realizes that she is not a friend but a prisoner of the
increasingly cruel and murderous Elizabeth.
Identifiers: LCCN 2019034842 (print) | LCCN 2019034843 (ebook) |
ISBN 9781419738869 (hardcover) | ISBN 9781683356431 (ebook)
Subjects: LCSH: Báthory, Erzsébet, 1560-1614—Juvenile fiction. | CYAC:
Báthory, Erzsébet, 1560-1614—Fiction. | Countesses—Fiction. |
Murder—Fiction. | Household employees—Fiction. | Lesbians—Fiction. |
Hungary—History—Turkish occupation, 1526-1699—Fiction.
Classification: LCC PZ7.1.P6444 Bl 2020 (print) |
LCC PZ7.1.P6444 (ebook) | DDC [Fic]—dc23

Text copyright © 2020 ABRAMS
Illustrations copyright © 2020 Jen Wang
Book design by Hana Anouk Nakamura

Printed and bound in U.S.A.
10 9 8 7 6 5 4 3 2 1

Amulet Books are available at special discounts when purchased
in quantity for premiums and promotions as well as fundraising or
educational use. Special editions can also be created to specification.
For details, contact specialsales@abramsbooks.com or the address below.

Amulet Books® is a registered
trademark of Harry N. Abrams, Inc.

ABRAMS The Art of Books
195 Broadway, New York, NY 10007
abramsbooks.com

For Taylor Haggerty, who literally makes dreams—and the *best* kind of nightmares—come true.

Prologue

SARVAR, HUNGARY
May 8, 1575

The day our Lord Nadasdy weds the countess, the sky above us is the color of bleached bone.

They say the sky on a wedding day portends the marriage to come. Even my mother, usually so scathing of superstitions held by lesser minds, believes this to be true. *What then*, I wonder as I gaze up, *does this bode for our lord and his mink-haired new wife?* As their grand wedding procession wends its way through our village, the heavens leer down on us, unforgiving and leached of sun. Low on the horizon, where the clotted scrim of clouds breaks open, a mean sliver of crescent moon already perches though it's barely afternoon. It looks as though some divine hand has scored a sharp fingernail into the flesh of the firmament.

A bitter sky, I think, *near as squalid as the day itself*. Even though the year has just rounded into spring, it is unnaturally hot, without a breath of wind to cut the unwashed reek of massed bodies.

The torpor does little to deter the crowd from making merry, jostling and calling out bawdy well-wishes to the newly wed lord and lady. The heave and swell should unsettle me, but it doesn't. I may be little—so small that Peter once likened me to the innermost kernel of a nesting doll, the kind Romani peddlers bring from Russia—but my legs are strong and my elbows sharp. I don't budge even when the countess stands in her open carriage, emblazoned with a dragon crest and drawn by two splendid chestnut geldings, and begins to toss handfuls of glinting filler coins to children in the crowd.

What must that be like, I wonder with a pang of envy in my hollow belly, *to have coffers so full you could dispense with them freely, make them rain down into grasping hands like a shower of minor stars?*

The countess laughs as she metes out this bounty in unbridled peals that easily reach my ears, though I cannot quite make out her features from where I stand. The sound is so inviting and infectious it makes me wish I were close enough to properly see her face.

The basket tucked into the crook of my arm twitches in my grip. I glance down to see owl-round eyes, a brindled face nosing its way out from beneath the swaddle of cloth. "Shh, sweetling," I croon down at the kitten, running my thumb down the silken slope of its nose. It meows plaintively up at me, its tiny, needle-fanged maw gaping with each cry. "You'll be out as soon as we are home."

Before the procession began, I'd been foraging for mushrooms in the woods behind our cottage. Instead I'd found the baker's son, a notorious little ruffian, tormenting a mother cat and her litter nestled inside a former foxhole. He'd caught one of the kittens by its scruff and was holding a flaming stick to its tail, while the harrowed creature twisted helplessly in his grubby grip. I'd cuffed him upside the head and sent him running back to the village, howling at the injustice of being upbraided by a girl.

The kit's tail was scorched, raw and seeping. Rather than letting nature tend to it, I tucked it into my basket to take home, where I'd dress the burn with a salve of comfrey and marigold. I could even make a gift of it to Klara, I'd thought, my heart buoyed by the notion. My little sister was a tender touch, easily moved to tears by an animal's plight. She would love this bedeviled little darling.

The kitten squirms again, overwhelmed by the rumble of the crowd. My own brothers are likely in the thick of it, stomping on toes and driving scrawny elbows into sides as they scrounge for fallen coins. As I think this, I catch a flash of Miklos's towheaded curls, my heart stuttering with alarm. He and Balint are the youngest, much too little to be here; Andras is meant to be watching them. If anything should befall them, Papa would fall upon the rest of us like a thunderclap, unstinting in his rage.

I'm so distracted by the blood-well of my dismay that when the kitten bolts from the basket, I'm too slow to catch it.

It spills over the basket's rim like something boneless and oiled. I fall to my knees to snatch it back, but it vanishes in an instant into a spindly forest of shins and ankles. Scrambling back up to my feet, I begin shoving my way gracelessly in pursuit through the milling crowd. It'll be crushed underfoot if I don't find it, by a wayward boot snapping its spine or splitting its fragile skull. And after what it's already suffered in its little life, I find that I can't stomach the thought of such a brutal end.

Work-worn faces glower down at me as I push past, spewing a fug of liquored breath and indignant challenges at being jostled. I ignore them all, plowing onward. I've nearly reached the crowd's lip when the kitten lollops out ahead of me—darting directly into the path of the countess's chestnut geldings, between their falling hooves.

One of the steeds goes rigid, while the other rears a little, hooves stamping, eyes rolling white with senseless panic. The carriage lurches to a stop, abruptly enough that the countess loses her feet and thuds down to sitting with a startled, undignified yelp.

A chorus of gasps races through the crowd, followed by a silence so deafening that it somehow makes commonplace sounds—the creak of branches, the phlegmy clearing of throats, snatches of birdsong—unspeakably profane. My heart scrambles up my throat, wedges there like a mouthful gone awry. Though the countess is a new arrival, rumor has preceded her. By all accounts, she is sharp even by blue-blood standards, uncommonly quick to take umbrage to any perceived slight.

And I have disrupted her wedding day.

My heart cudgels my ribs as one of Lord Nadasdy's soldiers leaps from his saddle, nimble despite the weight of his armor. He dashes out between the geldings, snatching up the kitten with one gauntleted hand. It dangles pitifully from his fisted grip, tiny limbs flailing as he offers it up to the countess, who has alit from the carriage in a dizzying swirl of damask skirts.

"What would you have me do with the creature, my lady?" he calls out, giving the kitten a careless little shake. A bored, desultory ruthlessness underpins his tone. "Will you suffer it to live?"

The inside of my mouth prickles with trepidation, as if I've been chewing on nettles. Please, I beg silently. *Please don't let her kill it.*

The countess holds her hands out for the kitten, then cradles it to her chest, tipping its tiny face up to hers with a finger under its chin. I can see it go rag-doll limp in her grasp, ears flattening as if it knows its life might well be forfeit. "That depends, I suppose," she muses as she strokes its head with long, pale fingers, each caress prolonged and deliberate. Finally, her eyes lift to spear mine. "On what its owner has to say."

She crooks a slim finger at me, beckoning me closer. I stumble forward on legs like stilts, my knees threatening to give way. My vision shudders in rhythm with every heavy heartbeat. Not even my father's explosive furies have ever left me this afraid.

"Now," she says briskly when I stand before her. "Let us see what we have here."

I dip into a clumsy curtsy, fearing for a breathless lurch of a moment that I will overbalance and tip forward. But I right myself at the last moment, licking my lips as I meet her eyes.

The world beyond us wavers like a heat mirage, until it

seems to vanish altogether. Leaving me alone, marooned, pinioned by her gaze.

Her eyes are captivating, large and lustrous with a distant glimmer, like very deep wells—almost black, even darker than her raven hair. So dark, the pupils barely show beneath the swoop of shadow cast by her lashes. They fix on mine, unabashed in their appraisal, and my insides fist tight with surprise. I know who she is, of course. We commoners know all those who own the lands we occupy only by their leave. Countess Elizabeth Báthory, daughter of a baron, niece of the Polish king. Yet, highborn as she is, her beauty somehow takes me unawares. So formidable and unyielding that it seems to exert its own force. Though she's only a few years older than my thirteen, she already wields it like a scepter.

I can see the answering flicker of recognition as she surveys me in kind. Her gaze trails over my eyes, which are cold and clear as a winter sky, then down the pale sluice of my hair, swept over one shoulder and only loosely braided. A boy whose attentions I spurned once told me I looked untouchable, like something carved from ice. Though my blood runs common as the silty mud of the riverbed, I know my face commands much the same response as hers.

I wait with bated breath to see if it will make her hate me.

"Anna Darvulia," she says in that same speculative tone, a faint dimple creasing her smooth cheek as the corner of her carmined mouth turns up. "The midwife's elder daughter, if I am not mistaken."

Shock knells powerfully inside me. I curtsy again, a bobbing twitch of a movement. "You—you know me, my lady?"

"Of course," she says, tipping her head to the side. "Several of my new chambermaids speak of you and your mother in the same breath. They say you are both healers. Herb women, the likes of which this village—perhaps even all of Sarvar, and Hungary beyond—has never seen." Her face warms appreciatively. "Though they failed to mention you were a beauty, too."

"I'm not . . ." I fumble, a scalding rush of blood filling my cheeks, uncertain whether it's seemly to accept such lofty praise. "They are too kind."

She rolls her eyes playfully, casting me a conspiratorial look. "I daresay few have had cause to describe Margareta or Judit as 'too kind,' baby vipers that they are. Nor does honesty tend to trouble them overmuch. But in your case . . ." She leans forward, takes a long and measured inhale of me. I can smell her, too, the heady spice of some dark, extravagant perfume. "I can smell the truth of it on you."

Her eyes sparkle secretively at the last, and a flurry of tingles suffuses my skin. Could she somehow know about the pennyroyal I stirred into the seamstress's tonic this morning, when she begged me to rid her of the unwanted child waxing in her womb? Her eighth, sired upon her by an uncaring husband, a babe whose birth she is certain she would not survive? I had scrubbed my hands after handling it, but perhaps its reek had somehow lingered in my hair.

"Do not fret, little sage," she whispers as the blood plummets from my face. "Your secret is safe with me. For we are both women, are we not? And some things are better kept between us."

"Dearest Beth," Lord Nadasdy drawls lazily from the carriage. Beneath the carelessness of his tone, I can hear something ironclad and uncompromising. "Must you insist on tarrying further? They are expecting us at the keep."

"Of course, my husband," she replies sedately over her shoulder, but I spot the telltale tightening at the corners of her mouth, a bright bloom of fury in the depths of her eyes. The countess does not take well to being enjoined by a man. "Just a moment."

She turns back to me, gently pressing the kitten into my waiting hands. I clasp it gratefully to my chest, nearly sagging with relief. The countess wheels back to the carriage as three attendants swarm to help her up. Before she steps up, she flicks me a glance over her shoulder—a warm secret of a wink, likely invisible to everyone save me.

But I see it. Just as I see Lord Nadasdy's hand close around her wrist, the skin paling with the force of his grip. I can see how it hurts her, in the way her smile slides off her face.

For all the gold and silver in her coffers, in some ways the countess is just like me.

A woman, with a man's cruel hand around her wrist.

PART ONE: Summoned

Chapter One

The Thorn and the Taint

Three Years Later

"Anna. Annacska. Wake up, my sweet."

I rise from the murky depths of sleep, my hands lifting of their own accord to guard my face. The voice isn't my father's, and the words themselves far too tender to be his. But he's woken me with a slap so many times that my body responds by rote, rising to protect me before I even come awake.

My mother gingerly grasps my hands with one of hers, lowering them. "Come," she says quietly, grazing a knuckle down my cheek. "The countess calls for you."

I blink as the dim outlines of the cottage resolve into

focus, my mother's shadowed face hovering above me. My mind turns over sluggishly, mired in confusion. I haven't seen the countess since the day she returned Zsuzsi the cat into my arms, tossed that glimmer of a wink over her shoulder.

But even so, I have never forgotten the dark pools of her eyes.

"The countess?" I say blearily, dragging a hand over my face. "The Lady Báthory needs *me*? What for? She is not with child, is she?"

My mother glances over her shoulder to the door, and even by the light of the single candle I see the glint of fear spark up in her eyes. "Her man did not say," she replies, keeping her voice to a whisper. I can hear my father snoring in their pallet by the hearth in rattling grunts that might have belonged to the wild boars that charge through the woods in rutting season. He'd staggered in long after we'd already had our dinner, so stupefied with rotgut drink he barely reached the bed. Waking him now would be unwise. "But he insists it cannot wait for morning."

The urgency seeps into me then, lights my belly like a flagon of spring wine. I rise and dress as quickly and quietly as I can, stepping into my coarse, homespun work dress. My mother drapes her own cape over my shoulders to ward against the nighttime chill as I belt my herb bag around my waist. I pause for a moment, turning back to her. "Why me, Mama?" I ask in a voice just above a whisper. "Why did she not send for you?"

She adjusts the hood over my head, tucking a wayward lock behind my ear. "My hands are not what they once were, Annacska," she replies, casting the gnarled knots of her knuckles a rueful look. "Surely the lady would have heard as much."

A sharp rap at the door jolts us both; the countess's man is growing restive.

"Quick," my mother urges as my father stirs, groaning. "Before we wake him."

I press a hasty kiss to her swollen knuckles; even at the barest brush of my lips she sucks in a pained breath. Then I step outside into the bracing night. The countess's man is no more than a hulking shadow under the cloud-cloaked sky, and when he moves toward me it is somehow sinister, as if a portion of the night has snipped itself loose to assail me. I take a reflexive step back toward the shelter of our eaves, my hands clenching at my sides.

It is not the dark itself that I fear, but the men who come creeping under its cover. Though I am often just as leery when approached even at high noon. It seems many of them are not safe at any time in our lord's creation.

"Took your sweet time, girl," the man sneers, lifting his head so the dim light from the cottage spills across the overhang of his brow, revealing the crude-cut features that cluster beneath it. "The lady does not take well to being kept waiting. Let's go."

I hear the reassuring nicker of his horse tied to our fence, her musky smell carried on a breeze already sharp with night-blooming plants; I'm much more inclined to trust this mare than her owner, but there is little I can do about sharing her with him. I slip my foot into the stirrup and move to mount her, but the mare is broad-bellied and tall, and I can't quite sling my leg over. With an irritated grunt, the man clasps me by the waist and heaves me easily up onto the saddle.

He mounts behind me, my back pressed tight against his front as his arms circle me to grasp the reins. To his credit, there is nothing untoward about his touch. And he's called me nothing worse than girl, though "trull" and "twit" and "slattern" roll so easily off my own father's tongue.

"Hold on," he orders gruffly into my ear as I wrap my hands around the saddle horn and tighten my thighs. His breath smells faintly of ale, apples, and dried meat. He isn't drunk, at least. "I won't be putting you back together should you topple off and break your bones."

"I can ride," I retort stiffly. "And mend my own bones just fine, should the need befall me."

"See that it doesn't, for your own good." He spurs the horse into a canter, and soon we flash between the trees and onto the main road ahead.

As we ride across Sarvar's rolling plains, shrouded in night, I find myself tilting my face reflexively toward the sky, searching for the moon. I always know where the moon is, even when I cannot see it for the clouds. The midwife's sight, my mother used to call it, this *knowing*. The moon holds sway over all women, over our monthly fluxes and the cycles of our wombs, waxing, waning, ripening with child. When I was small, she'd take me to the lake with her long after nightfall—only once my father and brothers fell asleep, my sister too little to join us, too. This gathering was not for men, she said.

I'd help her harvest the herbs that grew by the banks, the ones best pulled after midnight.

Before we began, she'd put her hands over my eyes, her rough palms smelling of valerian and yarrow. Back then, her hands were still unmarred by pain, her fingers fine and nimble. "Find the moon, Annacska," she'd whisper in my ear. "Go on—tell me where it is."

I'd tip my face up and scan the sky through closed eyes. And then there it would be—a pale, blazing imprint of an orb, against the muddy darkness of my eyelids. It had a halo to it, like the dark opposite of flame, a corona of tendrils that writhed and pulled. I could feel the way they tugged at everything. At the rippling surface of the lake, the sap inside the herbs we'd gathered in our aprons, even the pit of my own belly.

I told her, once, that I could see it in this way, thinking she could, too. Her mouth had thinned, eyes cinching at the corners. "You're running wild with imagining, Annacska," she'd said lightly, but tension crackled through her tone, like lightning forking through clouds before it struck the ground. "You do not truly see such a strange, devilish thing, do you?"

I'd denied it, frightened by her fear. Most likely she was right, and I only imagined that I could see it because she'd taught me to track the moon so well, to follow its steady progress across the heavens. And the sight did fade as I grew older and willfully tamped it down. But sometimes I still think I spy its echo in the living things I tend to, in uncut herbs and vegetables and even our spavined goat, and especially the ailing who call on me and my mother.

Sometimes I even let it guide my hand to where it is needed most.

I'm so rapt that I barely notice our gradual slowing, the

changing of our course as we trot into another silent, drowsing village, much smaller than my own. The countess's man pulls the horse to a halt in front of a small wattle-and-daub cottage with a straw-thatched roof, so cramped it nearly makes our own look grand. A fat plume of smoke wafts from the chimney hole, and I frown, wondering why their hearth would be blazing in the dead of night when everyone with sense tamps their fires down to embers.

"But where are we?" I ask, misgivings roiling up. "I thought I was wanted at the Nadasdy keep."

"Never said any such thing," he rumbles in my ear. "As to what the countess needs, she'll tell you so herself—she's inside, waiting."

Confusion ratchets up inside me. Why would the countess be here, in this grim hovel? Before I can ask, he dismounts with a thud and unceremoniously hauls me off the mare's back, without bothering to wait for me to attempt the landing on my own. I pointedly straighten my disheveled dress, casting him a glare as I turn to the door. I can hear the faint, high note of muffled weeping from within even before I swing it open.

The inside is stifling with the heat of a roaring fire, candles clustered thick and dripping on every surface, throwing trembling stripes of shadow over the walls. I spot the countess first, on her knees on the beaten-earth floor with her skirts rucked up around her. She kneels beside a low, shabby pallet, clutching the hand of a flush-faced little boy. Her head lifts at the sound of the door, and I'm struck by her salt-streaked face, the skeins of hair unraveling from their complicated twist beneath a net.

"Anna Darvulia," she says faintly, terror and relief coiling together in her tone. "You've finally come, thank our maker. I was beginning to contemplate despair."

I dip into a curtsy, then hasten over to the bedside. "Of course, my lady," I murmur. "Please forgive the wait. He's—this boy is ill, I take it?"

She hooks a piercing look at me, hearing my silent question. "His name is Gabor. He's my son," she adds bluntly. Her eyes alight on me, intent as a falcon plummeting toward its prey. She waits to see what I will say.

I catch my breath; I cannot help it. "Your son," I repeat, careful to temper my tone lest I betray any censure even as my mind races ahead. He is clearly not Lord Nadasdy's son as well, else we would all have been treated to the fanfare that surrounds the arrival of an heir. Besides which, this boy looks to be nearly five, only a little younger than my sister. He would have been conceived and delivered years before the countess's marriage.

Whoever this boy's father is, her pregnancy must have been concealed.

She rolls her eyes skyward, as if she finds my hesitation deeply tiresome. "His father was a peasant," she snaps. "Our farrier's son, back home in Ecsed. I was very young, and he had a winsome face. And a back like one of the thoroughbreds his father broke for us. I—briefly and misguidedly—believed that I loved him. He was disinclined to refuse his mistress, and that is how Gabor came to be. I could not keep him, of course, so he became my wet nurse's son."

"I—I see, m'lady," I stammer, taken aback by how baldly she speaks of this transgression, as if taking pleasure with a man unwedded is her divine right. I'm even more astonished that she would see fit to share her indiscretion with me.

"You wonder of my husband, and why I am being so candid with you," she says, as if she can read my mind. "No, Ferenc does not know of Gabor. No one does, save for myself, my mother back home, and Zorka. And now yourself—only because I need you to understand how imperative it is that he should live." She scrutinizes me for a long moment, lifting an eyebrow. "I trust this will remain between us. Am I correct in thinking so?"

"Y-yes, m'lady," I choke out. "Of course. But, why call for me at all? My mother is the one who—"

She slices through my question with an imperious hand. "She is not the one they speak of, at least not any longer." Her eyes lock onto mine, coal-black, boring into me. "You are. It is known that you're a witch, more deft with herbs than any mortal has the right to be."

"A *witch*?" My voice climbs so high it fairly squeaks, my heart stuttering painfully with the accusation. "My lady, I assure you, I am no such thing! I'm a midwife's daughter, that is all! I've studied with my mother, learned from her as any woman could, not—"

"I question what you could have learned from your mother without ever wielding pen and paper, or consulting the recorded wisdom of the ancients," she snaps, rounding on me, terrible in her fear for her son. "But what you are matters not a whit to me—as long as you can save him. So, tell me, *can* you? Or are you as useless as my lackwit physician has already proven himself to be?"

I wring my hands together to halt their trembling, draw

a long breath. Whatever she thinks of me, her son needs me now, and I will not fail him. "How long has he been ill?" I ask.

Her eyes drop to the boy, and she sweeps a tender hand over his clammy brow, clearing the damp ruck of hair away from his face. The boy whimpers under her touch, pursing his rosebud mouth. He is beautiful, raven-haired and milk-skinned with features fine as his mother's, the stamp of her clear upon him. His father seems to have barely left a mark.

"Just over a day," she replies, her voice dropping to a whisper. "He burns with fever, thrashes in his sleep. Zorka—the woman who raises him—will know more of how it begun."

There is movement by the tiny hearth, from the patch of shadow my eye skimmed over before the countess drew it. A small, unprepossessing woman flinches forward, ducking her head to me in greeting. She must have heard what the countess called me, and I'd wager "witch" holds weight with her.

"He was playing just yesterday, the poor little mite," she breathes, her eyes darting between me and the countess. Her fear is a palpable thing, and I realize immediately that she is terrified for herself as much as Gabor—for what will befall her should this illness claim him. That is why the cottage fairly blazes with light, her attempt at warding off the impending shadow of his death. "And then he began complaining that his feet hurt and his head ached, that his belly was sour. I did not— I should have put him to bed immediately, but I had sewing work yet to be done." She closes her eyes, her lips trembling. "By last night, he was fevered thus. He would not stir when I tried to wake him."

I nod briskly, already shuffling through possibilities. "I will examine the boy, then," I say, flitting a glance at the countess. She nods her permission, her eyes still fastened on him. "Will you fetch me some water, Zorka? And a clean cloth."

Once she does, I scrub my hands thoroughly, rinsing off the dirt of horse and travel. My mother has long since claimed that clean labors unfold more smoothly, so I have made a habit of it even when tending to other ills. Under the lady's avid gaze, I run my hands searchingly over her son. I peel back his eyelids, peering at the red-riddled whites and the pink tissues that line them, lever his mouth open to observe his tongue—white-furred and dry, his breath fanning furnace-hot across my face—and prod gently at the tender nodules beneath his jaw. I listen to his heart and lungs, both blessedly clear, though his pulse flutters like tiny wings against my ear. I then press my fingers into his abdomen, searching for stiffness and finding none.

"Zorka, tell me," I say, firing questions like arrows at her. "What water do you drink? What has he eaten in the past few days? Has anyone else fallen ill?"

As she stutters her responses, a picture forms in my mind, taking on a pattern of its own accord.

"I'll need to strip him," I tell them. Zorka and the countess exchange perplexed glances, but neither questions me. Zorka strips off the child's sweat-soaked nightshirt, fine linen subtly trimmed with lace, lovelier than anything I've ever touched; clearly a gift from the boy's blood mother. I pore over his front, finding nothing but the collection of welts, scratches, and bug bites customary for an active little boy. Puzzled, I have her flip him over, but his backside is no more revealing.

"What is it?" the countess demands, her voice quivering with impatience. "What are you looking for?"

"Perhaps I'm wrong," I murmur, frowning as I slide my hands down his legs. "But there should be— Ah!"

As my fingers skim over his rough, dirt-encrusted soles, the boy shudders in his sleep, letting out a mewling cry. I freeze, then press my thumb into his instep. Beneath the dirt, it's swollen and tender, hot to the touch.

Gabor releases another muted howl, his foot twitching against my grip.

"Oh, what is it?" the countess cries, distraught at his pain. "What is *hurting* him?"

I dip the cloth into the pail of water Zorka brought me, then cleanse his foot as gently as I'm able. He clearly runs about barefoot, which is why I did not see it at once. But when the mud and dirt scour away, they reveal a circle of puffy, reddened skin—with a fat black thorn embedded at its center, pus seeping sickly around it.

The sight would turn many a stomach, but not mine. Nor the countess's, it seems. Instead, she cranes for a closer look, smooth forehead furrowing with interest. "He did say his feet were hurting, did he not, Zorka? But a thorn?" she demands, nonplussed. "A mere thorn is sickening him unto the brink of death? How is that possible, Anna?"

"It is not the thorn itself, my lady," I whisper, my belly lurching with dread as I tilt his sole toward her. "See where these red lines fork away from the wound, like little rivers? The puncture has allowed dirt to enter his blood, taint and sicken it. It festers now."

"Blood itself can sicken?" she asks in bemused, almost

marveling tones. "It is meant to be the sanguine humor, robust and enduring, is it not? But perhaps that is why his cheeks glow so brightly." She tilts her head speculatively. "How strange, that such a taint could bring an even greater beauty to him. I would not have thought it possible."

"I know nothing of humors, sanguine or otherwise, my lady," I say, somewhat bewildered that she would be considering her boy's rosy cheeks. "I'm sorry."

"No matter," she responds with a dismissive wave. "Now is not the time to consider Galen. In the absence of a dead philosopher to guide us, what can *you* do for my son?"

"I'll do what I can, m'lady," I say heavily. "I will prepare a poultice for the wound, as well as a tisane for him to drink. The rest—I fear it will be up to him more than me."

"Will he live?" she asks, somber. "I warn you, do not dare lie merely to appease me. If you do I will know, and it will be the worse for you than any unwelcome truth."

"He will have to fight to live, my lady," I respond truthfully. I would not have lied to her even if she hadn't cautioned me against it; I'm not against a well-advised deception, but I can sense her nose for truth. "And fight hard. But I will be by his side, to help as much as I am able."

She considers me a moment longer, her dauntless gaze holding fast to mine. Whatever she sees in my eyes must be enough to sway her, for she gives a curt nod.

"Do it, then," she orders. "My trust is in you, Anna. You have my leave to do what you must to save him."

Chapter Two

The Fever and the Coin

We hold vigil over the boy through the night, which seems to unfurl like some endless flower, hours unfolding after hours like black petals without end. It is one of the longest I have ever known.

Gabor burns and thrashes, whimpers at my gentle ministrations. His mewls of pain remind me of the sound Zsuzsi the kitten made when that foul little boy burned her tail years ago. It isn't the first time that I've thought it, that cats and babes sound so alike when they suffer. I do my best not to attend to the noise of his torment, tending instead to the poultices, refreshing them every hour. I've crushed honey, garlic, goldenseal, and clove into a sticky paste and smeared it on the wound, and every so often I tip a hot tisane of steeped willow bark and garlic past his lips, though he sputters and flops like a landed fish to evade me. When I must, I pinch his little nose and put my hand over his mouth to make him swallow.

"What a brutal thing it is," the countess remarks, watching me with her avid gaze. "The way you must hurt to heal. Your heart must be hardened like a stone against others' pain."

"I do what I need to, my lady," I respond softly. Of course my heart is not hardened—I feel an answering stab in my own gut each time the boy moans. But it is my conviction, not my compassion, that the countess needs to see while I struggle to save her son.

We watch, and we wait. In the hours before dawn, his fever spikes and I fear that we will lose him. Beside me the countess turns bone-white. She even reaches for my hand as if we are kin, squeezing it tight, desperate for what little comfort I can offer.

Then the boy's fever breaks. He begins to stir, asking Zorka for stewed fruit and milk. His eyes, when open, are exactly like his mother's, black and shining as obsidian. I don't particularly like small children, but he's undeniably appealing. Even barely recovered, he reaches for his adoptive mother's neck and entreats her with kisses, his eyes glinting with sharp curiosity when he looks at me.

"Feed him clear broth, and keep giving him the tisane," I instruct Zorka. "It's foul, he won't want it, but you must insist. And keep his foot bandaged and clean, the poultice refreshed whenever it loses savor. You've seen how I make it, haven't you? I'll leave you enough herbs to last you several days. After that, his body will flush the sickness of its own accord."

Zorka nods vigorously, aglow with relief, her eyes fixed on

the boy. I am heartened to see she loves him for more than just the fact that her life clearly hinges on his well-being.

"Thank you," the countess says quietly when I rise from the bedside and join her by the door. Once the boy woke, she withdrew. Unwilling, I think, to disturb or confuse him with her presence. "Your clever hands have preserved my son. I will not soon forget your service."

"It was no trouble, my lady," I respond dutifully, though I sway on my feet, half-dumb with exhaustion. "It is what I do."

Her lips purse with distress, and she cups my face like a concerned mother or sister, though her palms are like petals against my cheeks, far softer than my own mother's or sister's have ever been. She smells just as I remember, of dark, luxuriant flowers I do not recognize. "You are dead on your feet, poor thing," she croons, sweeping her thumbs over my cheekbones. "I'll have Janos return you to your home. He'll have a purse of coin for you, as well."

"Oh, no, I could not, it isn't necessary—"

"Of course it is, don't be daft," she counters briskly, her hands tightening around my face. "You've saved my son, my own living reflection. How could I leave you unpaid after such a service? Now go, and rest." Her eyes hold mine, gentle but relentless. "You are quite remarkable, Anna Darvulia, with your healer's heart of stone. I hope that our paths cross again, and soon."

I can think of nothing to do but nod.

I barely remember the rough ride home with the sun cresting the horizon, or the welcome weight of the coin bag that Janos drops onto my palm. My father has already lumbered off to his workshop for the day, where he will pummel metal with more enthusiasm than precision, leaving me free to drop into the bed I share with Klara. She nestles against me with Zsuzsi clutched to her chest, her corn-silk hair tickling my mouth, until her warmth lulls me into a dreamless sleep.

Hours later, I wake to flung-open shutters and the glare of high noon slanting in. Rising blearily, I stumble into the main room, where my mother kneads a paltry ball of dough on our cockeyed trestle worktable while the twins chase Klara all around the room, shrieking like demons. Andras is nowhere to be seen; now that he's eleven, most days he apprentices with our father, though he never seems to acquire much skill to speak of.

"Out, you rapscallions!" Mama calls over their piping voices. "Out, or you will have not a bite of this bread once it's done."

"Mama lies," Balint informs Miklos, flicking a devilish look at our mother. "Apu would not let us go hungry. Klara, maybe. She's too skinny already, anyway."

My chest tightens at the look on my mother's face. It's true that our father would hoard the last precious bite to make sure my three brothers were fed, even though Andras can be blockheaded as an ox, Balint a little bully, and Miklos an insatiable glutton despite our scant portions. Father dotes on them despite their faults, calls them his heirs as if they'll inherit some vast fortune rather than a mountain of debt.

Maybe if he didn't swill most of his earnings at the public house, it would be easier not to resent my brothers for plucking the food out of our mouths. But though they are only little boys, one day they will be men just like our father.

Too often, it makes me loath to love them.

Mama's eyes flash, for once, and she cuffs Balint so sharply behind the ear that he recoils, howling. "Mind the way you speak to your mother, and of your sister," she scolds. "You are not so old yet that you'll escape a hiding for your wicked tongue."

Balint races past me with Miklos on his heels, tossing us both an outraged look over his shoulder. "I'm telling Apu!" he hollers on his way out. "I'm telling—"

His voice cuts off as the door bangs shut behind them. My mother and I exchange aggrieved looks, and finally she shrugs, defeated. "Even if he does, what of it? More likely than not, Istvan won't remember by tonight anyway."

"Would be a miracle if he did," I mumble sourly, moving to stand beside her and sifting my hands through flour. Klara slinks under my arm like an overgrown kitten, nuzzling her cheek against my side. At six, she's growing tall, too old to cuddle quite so much; she's sweeter even than Zsuzsi, who has sauntered over to twine between her ankles now that the twin menaces have been banished. But I don't have the heart to refuse her. "Shall I help you, Annacska?" she asks, blinking up at me with her startling blue eyes, the same vivid shade as mine and our mother's. "The potage needs stirring."

I glance over at Mama, who gives a tiny shake of her head and a significant look. She wishes to speak with me alone. "No, sweetling, but thank you for the offer. Why don't you run out to the lake and see if you can cut some honeysuckle for us to have with supper?"

Her face brightens sunnily; there are few things my precious dandelion loves more than to please, but flowers are a close second. She presses an exuberant kiss into my side and flies out the door, the pale banner of her hair trailing behind her.

My mother watches her go, her face suffused with tenderness and apprehension. "We will soon be living on edible flowers, if Istvan keeps losing custom," she mutters, and I can feel the pounding of her concern, the lash of relentless worry. This year's harsh winter and poor harvest has blighted us all, and many of those who once bought my father's metalwork have no coin to give him, little else to trade. "I worry for her especially. She grows so quickly, I can almost see it as it happens. She needs milk and bread and meat, not petals."

Silently, I drop my bag of coin on a flourless spot on the table. Mama picks it up, agape, weighing it on her palm. "The countess . . ." she murmurs, marveling at its heft. "It went well, then?"

"Very well, and even more surprising." I reach for the ball of dough to relieve her aching knuckles. I consider lying to her about Gabor's identity, but decide against it. I dislike deceiving my mother, and she can keep a secret just as well as I. "Her son had taken ill, an inflamed puncture. I brought him through the worst of it."

"Her son?" Mama cocks her head at me, eyes narrowing. "But the countess has no children. We would have heard of her confinement."

I lower my voice, as if someone might overhear even in

our cottage. "Not with her husband, at any rate. This one is a commoner's get. Apparently she bedded their farrier's son."

Mama purses her lips, shaking her head. "I'd heard she was unruly in her youth, but a peasant's by-blow—such brazenness, to enter wedlock defiled. She should hang her head in shame, not flaunt her wantonness to you."

I try to imagine the countess with her head bowed, long neck bent, and cannot. "She wanted me to try my hardest for him, that is why she told me. And it worked out well enough for us, didn't it?" I tilt my head toward the bag, sinking my fingers into the unyielding, salted dough. "As long as we make certain that Father never sees it, it should put proper food in our bellies for at least a fortnight."

"And once it's gone?" Mama asks, her tone uncharacteristically despondent. "What then, Annacska? I can almost smell the winter nearing."

Her hopelessness unsettles me, this chill that seems to have seeped into her bones. I fumble for a solution, anything with which to reassure her. "The countess liked me. Perhaps she will call on me again to tend to Gabor."

"Put that from your mind, Anna," Mama says so harshly my head snaps up. "I've heard talk of her, from the women whose daughters are already there. They say the countess is unusual, uncanny, more given to the flog than any woman should be. Why do you think they are always short of servants at the keep? Even steady coin is hardly worth the risk of such bloody punishment."

I think of the countess's dark, compelling eyes, the silken touch of her palms on my face, her vehement love for her son. No, I do not believe that she would be harsh when uncalled for. Demanding, yes, and intolerant of failure. But not sharp for the thrill of it, not when she loves her bastard son so well. "I spent the night with her, by her boy's side," I say gently, unwilling to contradict my mother but unable to let it stand. "She was warm with him, tender. And kind to me."

"Well, there is a reason why she cannot keep her help, and whatever it is, I would not have you find out for yourself," Mama says crossly. "Besides, you should be thinking of marriage, not of servitude. It's time, Anna. You're of age, more clever with herbs than I ever was, and lovelier than any man could hope to take to wife. You should be wed already, and growing round with child. I see how you dote on your sister. You need a babe of your own."

I wrinkle my nose with distaste, averting my face so she does not see it. Despite her years of catching babes, cauled or stillborn or so monstrously large they rend their mothers open before sucking their first breath, somehow she still loves children above all else. I can't understand it. The last thing I desire is to be split open, to die shrieking and sundered on a scarlet wave of blood, delivering a child that would forever shackle me to my husband, should I have the misfortune to survive. Wed to a man, I would no longer belong to myself.

And my family needs me. They're mine, they are my blood—even my loutish, largely useless brothers—and I will not abandon them when we teeter on the brink of destitution.

"Oh, you've heard how our neighbors' lummox sons talk of me," I say breezily. "They fear my salves and teas as if they're poison or witchcraft, the devil's work rather than medicine. They fear *me*, Mama—save for when they sicken. Then they come calling readily enough. And without a dowry to entice them, I'm afraid you're stuck with me."

"Is that so? And what of Peter Erdelyi?" she counters, lifting a skeptical eyebrow. My mother is nobody's fool, no more than I am. "That boy has loved you since you were both babes. How long will you insist on turning a blind eye to him? You must know he means to propose soon—the village has been talking of nothing else for months."

"Mama, please. You know how idle gossip spreads here. Peter loves me like a sister, no more and no less." I slide the meager loaf back to her, keeping my eyes on it to hide the lie from her. Though Peti has not broached marriage with me yet, it is not nearly so inconceivable as I am making it sound. I haven't seen him in weeks, the longest we've been apart in the course of our entire friendship. Perhaps he's been purposely making himself scarce in an attempt to quash the rumors. "Besides, I can't imagine wedding my best friend. It would almost be obscene."

"Fine, Annacska," she says, relenting. "But if not him, then someone. And soon. That is your lot, just as this family—and these blasted hands—are mine."

I watch her warped back as she wraps the loaf and shuttles it over the embers in the hearth, sighing hoarsely as she straightens. And for the thousandth time I make a vow to myself, a blood oath with my own soul that I will not betray.

This life of hers, of toil and squalor, forever pinned under my father's thumb—it will never be my life.

I will not allow it.

Chapter Three

The Summons and the Nest

When the knock comes, a week has shuffled past, and I have almost succeeded in putting the countess and her boy from my mind.

We are breaking our fast, the seven of us crowded around the table over four eggs, stewed plums, and stringy bread rinds. Mama and I exchange wary looks; the demanding cadence of the knock is familiar to us both.

"What're you waiting for, then, woman?" Father grumbles, hunkered over his plate. "It's sure to be one of your needy lot, come wheedling for grasses and leaves. Go see to it, will you, before their rapping rattles my brains."

Mama rises and hastens to the door. Sunlight spills into our gloom, making me blink like a surfaced mole; Father has demanded the shutters be kept closed so he can cosset his ever-tender head. When my eyes adjust, I make out Janos's strapping silhouette.

"Morning, mistress midwife," he says to Mama, tugging his forelock. "Is your daughter Anna about?"

Grunting, Father levers himself up, shooting me a glowering, suspicious glance. As if I'm some notorious temptress, as if strangers have ever come calling at our door for anything but my healer's hands. "She's here, sure enough," he says, stumping over to the door and shooing my mother aside. "What d'you want with her?"

Janos appraises him with an even, unflinching gaze. "My mistress wishes to retain her services."

Father gawps at him, squinting. "Is that so? And who might your mistress be?"

"The Countess Báthory, wife to our liege. She summons your daughter to serve as her chambermaid. She—"

"Anna? For a lady's *chambermaid*?" Father breaks in, casting a disbelieving look at me over his shoulder. I attempt to school my taut features, still the expectant pounding of my heart. Chambermaid to the lady herself; I can scarce believe it. To lace her stays, dress her lovely hair, sleep in her chambers should she wake in the night with any needs unmet. And if it pays remotely like the night I tended to her son, it would ensure a life so easy I could barely dream of it before it came knocking at my door. "I've never heard such rot. Even if she wasn't lower born than good Magyar dirt, my girl's needed here to mind her brothers."

"The lady offers her a forint every fortnight, should she serve," Janos adds evenly. "A more than generous sum."

The amount momentarily sways my father. His eyes narrow, turn inward as he ciphers the difference this would make, how much food it would put in the remaining bellies once I was gone.

"No," he finally says with a decisive shake of his head, though I can see the subtle flame of avarice leaping in his eyes. What is a forint every fortnight to a woman of bottomless coffers, he is thinking; if the countess truly wishes to secure my services, she will likely be willing to part with even more. How exactly like my father, I think bitterly, to overestimate his own cunning, gambling so readily with all of our fortunes on no more than a whim. "I'm afraid we can't spare her, not for such a paltry sum. We would consider double but no less, not with my wife's hands as they are. If your mistress wants my girl, then she should rightfully pay what the chit is worth to us."

As if my father has ever considered my worth and found it to be so high.

As he moves to shut the door, Janos wedges a booted foot over our threshold, shouldering the door open until it forces my father back a step. The shock is such that all of us go deathly quiet. Even little Miklos, who'd been obliviously singing child's nonsense to himself under his breath.

Everyone in the village knows not to court Father's anger. It takes only the slightest, most passing of sparks to stoke its dry and ready tinder into roaring fury. And once it is lit . . .

Suffice to say that I have never seen another thing so monstrous.

"My lady brooks no refusal," Janos says into the gaping silence, seemingly oblivious to the danger rushing at him headlong. "Especially not from the likes of you. What she desires, she always makes hers in the end. Now tell your girl to gather her things, and save yourself a world of trouble."

"*How dare you*," Father bellows, seizing Janos's fine waist-coat. The fact that the other man towers over him like a mountain—Father is small, a bantam rooster of a man, but hammering iron into submission has left him with a strength much larger than his slight frame—does nothing to quell him. "Threaten me under my own roof, you blackguard? Try to steal *my* daughter? You will take her only over my steaming corpse, you whoreson thief!"

Borne up by the force of his fury, hangover all but forgotten, he heaves Janos bodily over the threshold, shoving him outside. The man stumbles only slightly before righting himself, then lifts his hands coolly to convey he wishes no violence, though I saw how his hand first quivered over his knife belt. He surveys my father, still puffing and blustering, with eyes icier than a mountain-fed spring. So blisteringly cold, my own neck prickles at their subdued menace.

"As you say," he says with deceptive mildness, as if a blizzard were not brewing in his eyes. "But heed me, master blacksmith—the countess has marked your daughter for her own. Which means she already no longer belongs to you."

He turns on his heel and strides away before my father can even muster a reply.

After Janos is gone, and once my father is satisfied that I have done nothing untoward to court the countess's sudden favor—I do not yield the secret of her son, telling him instead that I tended to one of the lady's chambermaids—I am finally left to the roiling of my thoughts. As we grind meadowsweet side by side, my mother steals slantwise looks at me, but does not trouble me with questions. She knows I prefer to keep my own counsel until I have sorted out my mind.

But I am besieged by questions, a flock of them swarming and pecking ruthlessly at me. Why is the countess so intent on pressing me into her service when she could summon me as healer or midwife whenever she desired? What has she to gain from my presence by her side—especially if she is already familiar with herbs in her own right? Why elevate me so suddenly to a position that I could not possibly have earned over the course of one night?

Whichever way I turn it, I cannot understand the shape of her thoughts on the matter. Unless the answer is something less concrete than I can easily grasp, something beyond the clear boundaries of reason. Something that does not cast the expected shadow.

Perhaps the countess has simply taken to me, the way I have to her. But if that is so, why can I not shed this growing sense of menace?

Finally, even my saintly mother reaches the limits of her patience.

"Out with you, fidget," she orders, shooing me to the door. "You'll turn these fine herbs bitter with all your fretting. Let the sun scour your overbusy head."

I squeeze her forearm rather than her hand, and brush a kiss over her wizened cheek, smiling my thanks. With that I am out the door, my basket slung over my arm in case I spy anything worth gathering as I wander.

The world outside opens wide around me, the hues of sky, leaf, and flower blazing vibrant as a peacock's feather. No ill-fated wedding will transpire today, I think, not under this bright and blameless sky. Only the most faithful and loving of husbands will pledge themselves to blushing brides. Though no early moon is visible, I know exactly where it will rise—slightly south of east, above the lumpy hillock we call Boar's Mound, rearing humpbacked on the horizon.

I cast my mind outward as I walk, beyond the cramped confines of my skull. Our patch of woods teems with birds, their unruly songs distinctive to my ear. I hear swallows, larks, and kinglets; nuthatches, wrens, and warblers; even an osprey whistling down with talons extended, seeking the tender flesh of some poor mouse. A fine, brisk breeze weaves itself through creaking branches like warp through weft, and sunlight paws sweetly at my cheeks.

All is well, or should be. And yet my mind stubbornly refuses to still, clamoring of a danger that I cannot pinpoint, and I amble down the path that leads to the village's center, drawn toward the one person who might help calm the churning of my thoughts. Halfway to the village proper, a pale glint snares my eye, tangled among the undergrowth of ferns and rushes that scramble up onto the path. I wander warily over to it, parting the fronds with my hands—to reveal a magpie's domed nest, half-crushed from the fall, a clutch of gristle-twisted skeletons curled together at its center.

I force down bile, my gaze lingering over the six pitiful

heaps of fledgling skeletons, so impossibly fragile they draw tears into my eyes unbidden. Their mother is missing, the larger needles of her bones nowhere to be found. What happened to her, I wonder, leading her to abandon them? Was she killed elsewhere, or somehow injured and kept away from her brood, unable to fly back before they perished of hunger? Or did she simply choose not to return one day, bearing the gift of mother-love and worms?

Something about the nest, the macabre tenderness of it set against the breathless beauty of the day, crushes me with sadness and trepidation. As if today's serenity disguises some dread peril beneath, a wolf's snarl concealed behind a mild-faced sheep.

Dusting off my hands, I head back down the path. Five minutes later I'm behind the inn, Peter's familiar shadow gliding over the leaded windows. Only the innkeeper's family is wealthy enough in our village to afford the luxury of glass, and the fine, long slabs of stone that form the building's facade; the rest of us make do with wattle and daub, and local shale that need not be hauled from a distant quarry. Ducking, I scoop a handful of pebbles and dart them at the glass, biting my lower lip to restrain my grin. The figure starts, then surges against the frame. Though the glass is so thick and milky that I cannot make out his face, I think I see the flash of his teeth right before he knocks back cheekily, flicking his fingers against the glass in a gesture that, knowing Peti, may very well be lewd.

I wait for him, swinging the basket around my wrist, until he emerges from the heavy back door with a basket of his own. Beyond the pleasure of his company, I can always count on my friend to feed me from the inn's groaning larders.

"I thought I heard a little bee flitting against my windows," he teases, flashing that broad grin again. My qualms settle incrementally; he wouldn't smile at me just as easily as he always has if he were intending to propose so soon as my mother suspects. But before my guard drops entirely, I remind myself that affability is just his way. Peter smiles more than anyone else I've ever met. Perhaps courtesy of his easy life, I think, a touch unkindly. With an innkeeper and vintner for a father, he's never known the taste of hunger, the particular torment of too little for too long.

"I thought maybe she could use a little honey," he continues, "and butter. And bread."

My knees nearly go weak at the thought of warm, crusty bread, generously slathered with salted butter. If Peti had his way, he would split all his rations with me, sneaking me food on the sly at every turn. But even his boundless generosity could not possibly be enough to feed an additional five mouths, and I could not live with being well-fed while my mother and siblings grew ever more hollow with hunger.

Still, I refuse to begrudge myself the occasional treat, and I'll be bringing half home to Klara.

"I would say you spoil me," I quip, dimpling back at him. "But we both know I deserve it."

He rolls his eyes skyward, still grinning. "Ah, my honeybee, modest as she is industrious and fair. The clearing, then? Do you have time?"

"I do today. No one seems to be sick or dying, for a wonder, so I have a moment to catch my breath," I say, though the feeble stab at humor curdles on my tongue as soon as it emerges. Do not court the reaper when an ill wind blows, they say. Another superstition that my mother would not grant the time of day. But I am not my sensible mother, and the notion of it expands in my mind, haunting, twisting out of sight like a trailing phantom spotted from the corner of the eye.

Peter's gray eyes sharpen as he notices my turmoil. "What troubles you, Anna?" He searches my face, the exposed skin on my hands and forearms. Over the years, he's seen the worst of the damage my father wreaks upon my flesh. "Has he . . . ?"

I shake my head. "No. Not this time, anyway. It's something else." I incline my head toward the path that wends away from the village proper, twisting into the silvery thicket of beech and birch on the outskirts. "Come. I'll tell you once we're there."

We're sitting by the trilling little brook that runs through our clearing by the time I feel ready to begin.

"Here," Peter says before I can speak, unwrapping a fragrant langos and pressing it into my hands. "Eat first. You'll be the actual size of a honeybee soon enough."

Peter has called me "honeybee" since I can remember, in reference to my love of plants and how unable I am to keep still, my hands and mind ever busy with some task. I am a whirling dervish of activity in comparison to him, who runs slow and steady and dependable as tree sap.

"Believe me, it's not from lack of appetite," I respond tartly. My mouth fills with water at the aroma of the fried bread, cupping sour cream, garlic, and curled strips of crisped ham in its center. "Are you sure, though? You said just bread and honey. Your mother must have made these for lunch, they're so rich, I wouldn't want to—"

"Eat, Anna," he says firmly. "We have plenty at home."

"Even with the harvest as it has been?"

"Even with that. My father has begun selling his ale and plum brandy to Gor, Ikervar, and Szotony, with plans for beyond. We . . ." He hesitates, not wanting to seem like he's rubbing their prosperity in my face. "We're faring well. More than well enough to feed my best friend in the world."

I nod reluctantly, trying to force down the envy creeping up my throat as I take a bite of the bread. It crackles as my teeth cut through the fried meat, then yields with satisfying give, so greasy and chewy that my eyelids slide involuntarily closed with pleasure. Klara will love it, I think, almost as much as the beloved savory dumplings she so rarely gets to sample. When I open my eyes again, Peter is watching me closely, brimming with satisfaction. He offers me a wineskin, and I tip it to my lips and drink deep, letting the rich red wash down the remains of the mouthful.

"Better now?" he asks, amusement coloring his voice. "It's not nectar, but it's the best I can do."

"It's *wonderful*," I say ardently, taking another swallow. It is, tasting of hay and cherries, incomparably superior to the sour, watered-down pig swill we can afford. "You've been holding out on me. This is even better than the usual."

He gives a bashful half shrug. "I tried my own hand at this batch. Apu thinks I have the knack for it—I'm glad you like it. No, no," he demurs when I try to hand it back. "I brought this bag just for you."

"More for me, then." I shrug, tipping it to my lips again. "Tell me, how is Marika doing? Recovered from her tree fall?"

"Oh, she's fine, the ridiculous imp," he replies, his face brightening at the mention of his littlest sister. He dotes on both his sisters, loving them as I do Klara—as well he should, given how bright and darling they are. "Bossing all the rest of us about while her ankle heals. Apu has been carrying her all over creation on his shoulder; she actually pulls his hair to tell him which way to go, the little snot." He shakes his head ruefully, eyes soft with indulgence. "I swear, that girl thinks she was born to be a queen. And who am I to say she wasn't?"

He continues telling me of his sisters and mother, resting on his elbows as I devour half of the bread with unladylike speed—though I should like to meet the well-mannered lady whose belly growls like a slavering pack of wolves as mine does—and swig his fine wine. When I'm done, I wrap up the remainder for Klara and trail my hands in the icy brook to clean them. I wipe them on the grass before I lean back on my elbows, unaccustomed to the sensation of being so full-bellied and drowsy.

"Now, then," Peter says companionably, turning his gray hawk's eyes on me. The sunlight slanting through them brings out the hidden honey in their depths. "What's been preying on your mind, bee?"

I pause, hesitating for a moment. Whatever his intentions toward me, Peter has known me since we were babes; our mothers are dear friends, and we were born within days of each other, my mother going into labor just hours after having safely delivered him. We are both eldest, reared together, washed in the same basin and swapped freely between our mothers' breasts, sharing the same milk.

No one knows my soul quite as he does.

"I delivered the Countess Báthory's son from death, and now she's set her sights on me," I say, all in a rush. "She wants me as her chambermaid, but my father will not let her have me for the sum she's willing to pay. And I think—I know—she will not merely let me be. Between them, I fear they'll tear me in two."

Peter recoils a little, lips parting with surprise. "The countess's son?" he says carefully. "Maybe you'd better tell me how all this trouble found you."

I spill the entire strange tale to him, words tumbling over each other, sped along by a healthy wash of wine. I swear him to secrecy when I explain Gabor, though I know Peter would sooner die than betray my trust even without such prompting. Finally, I come to this morning, Janos's glowering shadow at our door, the quiet ruthlessness of his insistence.

"He frightens me, Peter," I finish, wrapping my goose-bumped arms around myself. "Or she does, I suppose. *Something* has me badly out of sorts, at any rate."

"But does she frighten you?" he asks, dark eyebrows lifting. "Does she, really? It sounds to me as though you rather liked her."

"I—I did, I suppose," I falter, unsure why I cannot meet his eyes. "But even so. Mama needs me more than ever, with the boys so hard to manage. Honestly, sometimes I fear Father would let Klara starve if I were not there to sneak her my scraps. I'm afraid to go, even if it would mean more coin than we've ever had; more likely than not, *he'd* line his gullet with it anyway. But I cannot see how to slip loose of her."

"I can," he responds, and there's something determined in his voice that draws my startled gaze. "I had hoped to do this later, properly, when I had everything ready, but . . ." He ducks his head at this, jaw working as he struggles to master himself. My heart plummets in anticipation, falling like a stone. "But you need me now, not perfection later. So wed me, Anna. The lady couldn't force you to come, were you a married woman. Becoming my wife would keep you safe from her."

I blink rapidly, a prickly tangle of shock and dismay writhing inside me, for all that I dreaded this was coming. I can feel myself blush furiously, the hot scarlet splotch of it stealing up my neck. "So it's true, then," I manage through clenched teeth. "What the entire village has been twittering about for weeks. It seems you've seen fit to share your intentions with everyone but me, Peti. I would have expected better of my best friend."

He winces sharply at the remonstration, averting his eyes. "For that, I'm sorry," he says, low. "You should not have heard it from anyone else. But that was my mother's doing, not mine. I implored her to keep silent, but you know how hopeless she is when she's excited."

The notion that his ebullient mother would thrill at our betrothal, though I am daughter of the village drunk, warms me despite myself. "Even so. That is hardly the point. We're *friends*, Peti. Don't you think you should have asked me first?"

"Just *listen*, bee," he plows onward, his gray gaze slicing back earnestly to me. "Let me finish, now that we're already here. If we were wed, your family would be mine as well. There would be coin, food enough for feasts, plenty of everything. No need for you to worry ever again."

"But your father hates me," I protest weakly, though I'm aware that it is not me his father despises. "And I have no dowry to offer."

"Why would I need a dowry, when I could have you?" he scoffs softly, a corner of his mouth curling. "And you know well enough that Apu hates Istvan, not you. Never you. He simply cannot abide a drunk, not as often as he serves them. Though I have yet to see him turn one with coin away."

"And what of love, Peter?" I ask so softly it's barely above a breath. "What of your heart? Or mine?"

"I cannot speak to yours, Anna, though I badly wish I could." He reaches for my hand, slides his warm, callused fingers through mine in a strong grip. I can see his relief when I don't pull away. "But I have loved you since I knew my own name. There's been no one else, no one that could matter as you do. Would that be enough for you, do you think? At least, to begin?"

Though I've averted my eyes whenever I could, it is no secret to me that Peter has long yearned for more than just our deep and abiding friendship. While he has been content to hope and wait for me, never so much as letting an embrace linger too long, I could not have missed the desire brewing in him—without ever sensing so much as an answering flicker of the same within myself. Now I consider it again, chewing on the inside of my cheek. Peter is more than handsome enough, strong-backed and tall, with a dark tousle of hair, clear-cut features, and those spectacular predator's eyes, incongruous in their gentleness. Certainly he turns enough heads in our village, and likely the ones beyond as well—though I cannot say I have ever wanted to steal his kiss and mingle my breath with his. I have never wanted that from any of the boys who strut about our village with their fuzz-patched faces and cracking voices, playing at being grown.

But he *is* the only man with whom I've ever felt safe. I would not fear sleeping next to him, nor wake with my hands fisted to protect my face. And he does not look upon me as others do, covetous of my charms while balking at my full measure.

And yet, my insides still churn with rebellion. To wed Peter is to belong to him, for all that he would prize me, never to lift a finger to me in anger. And I don't want the gilded cage of such a love, not from him or anyone.

But maybe this time, I can't afford to refuse it.

"I know honeybees have wings, Anna, if that's what you fear," he says, interpreting my hesitation with startling accuracy. "Know that I would never strive to curb you."

"I know you wouldn't," I say, squeezing his hand, pressing down the sadness that swells up at the flare of hope in his eyes. "It's such a kind offer, Peti. More than I deserve."

He shakes his head, wry now. "'Kind' is not exactly the answer I was hoping for."

"Tell me—is this truly what you want between us?" I peer closely at him, hoping to uncover at least the hint of a doubt that mirrors the legion of my own. "Are you absolutely sure?"

"Of course it's what I want," he replies, vehement. "I've thought of it for years, yearned for us to be even more than we were. Nothing could please me more than to call you my wife."

"Then let me think on it. But before I do, tell me something else. Will you . . ." I pause, uncharacteristically bashful, uncertain how to articulate my fear.

He tilts his head to the side, knuckling a stray lock out of his eyes. "Will I what, bee?"

"Will you still wish to be friends as we are now, even if—if my answer is no?"

Peter sets his jaw, but not before I see the pain skate across his face. It will grieve him sorely to lose me, the prospect of our lives together, I realize. "Of course, always. No matter what you choose to do, you have me, as a fast friend if not a husband. Promise me that you'll never doubt as much."

The relief is tremendous, though I should have known he would stand beside me, stalwart as an oak, keeping me safe in his steady shade. It's not in his fine heart to abandon me only because I cannot give him exactly what he wants. Impulsively, I bring our joined hands to my lips and press a kiss to his knuckles. "I'm the midwife's daughter, aren't I? Privy to women's mysteries. And you know what that means, don't you?"

"I *am* only a man," he teases back. "So why don't you enlighten me?"

I allow myself to smile at him fully, without reservation. "It means that I know better than to doubt you."

Chapter Four

The Web and the Tomb

On the way home, I tread through a spider's web.

One moment, the air is brisk and pleasant over my face. The next I'm gasping with revulsion, my skin alive and crawling as I pick sticky filaments out of my lips and hair. It's all over me, trailing down my arms and bosom, dangling to my ankles. Some of it has even gotten in my mouth, and my gorge rises until I spit by the side of the path, over and over, to clear out the foul tack of it. When I straighten, still lurching with nausea, I survey the branches. But even the closest boughs are far enough above my head that I can't fathom how large the cobweb must have been, to drape all across the path and trap me within it.

Eventually I give up searching and strike down the path again, though my innards still quail. Disturbing a spider's home is another forerunner of evil.

When I reach the cottage, before I even set foot across the

threshold, I know—something is badly wrong. The air itself seems muffled and dense. The crudely hewn stones that form our cottage walls, remnants of a more prosperous time, suddenly seem heavy and foreboding as a tomb. And that is when it hits me; this rampant silence, the utter absence of sound, as if all the birds around our home have choked on their own breath. This silence is wrong, too abundant and unbroken. I don't hear my mother's humming, and my mother always hums when she works if she does not sing aloud. The boys' cries aren't splitting the air, and I don't hear Klara's sweet, warbling tones. Even Zsuzsi's fussy yowl is lacking.

My heart shudders to panicked life. I fling the door open and spill into the front room—where what look like waxen effigies of my family have gathered around my parents' bed.

The sight of their stillness is so uncanny it roots me where I stand, desiccating my throat and bolting me to the packed-earth floor. My mother sits on the straw tick mattress, her hands upturned in her lap like small dead animals, limp and useless, fingers feebly curled. My brothers and sister kneel by her feet, huge-eyed and vacant in expression. Zsuzsi sits curled awkwardly on my sister's knees; she pets the kitten with mindless, spasmodic strokes. For a moment none of them acknowledge me, and it's as if I've stepped through a fairy circle and encountered the changeling versions of my own family, clay-faced mimics with dead eyes.

Gooseflesh erupts all up and down my arms, and I stand like a stone, too afraid to speak.

Then my mother stirs and breaks the spell.

"Anna," she says, vaguely petting the space next to her.

Her voice is hoarse and rasping, as if she hasn't spoken in weeks. "Come sit with me, would you."

The twins shuffle over to make room for me as I pass, so uncharacteristically compliant I gape down at them. Klara reaches up to stroke my calf, letting out a muffled little whimper of distress. Perversely, it comforts me, a welcome contrast to this otherwise suffocating silence.

I lower myself cautiously down next to my mother, taking her hands into my lap.

"What's happened?" I ask when she raises wide eyes to me, glassy with tears like a fancy doll's, the pupils so wide they blacken her vivid irises into nothing. Panic bucks inside me again, and I think of tattered webs and skeletons huddled in nests. When she dips her head, silent, I suppress a wild urge to take her by the shoulders and give her a solid shake. "Mama, what is wrong, tell me!"

"Your father," she says almost dreamily, her eyes flitting over my shoulder as if she sees something in the shadows beyond the dangling strings of peppers and herbs strung from our buckling rafters. "He is dead."

Dead. Father, dead.

The reality, the truth of it, collides into me as though I've run into a tree trunk and knocked the wind straight out of myself. Though he lived only this morning, I abruptly know it's true as I know the lines of my own face, and I feel a terrible sear of relief that we will no longer suffer his rages, the daily squalls of his temper. Then I am overcome by a conviction, like the opposite of foreboding, that precisely this was fated to pass. The entirety of this day has somehow conspired to warn me, from the death nest with its six skeletons to the spider's web, as if I could have forestalled all of this some-how. But it's only in hindsight that I see the signs for what they were—portents strung together by some powerful hand, leading me onward to this very moment.

I cross myself by rote, with trembling fingers. While I do not think God bothers with our pleas, I believe in the devil's work. And right now, it feels dreadfully close at hand.

"H-how?" I ask hoarsely.

"He was shodding a horse for a passing traveler," she says, a corner of her mouth twitching to the side as if yanked. "The horse was skittish, took a fright and kicked him. It—it crushed his skull. Struck him square in the face, burst out his eyes like jellies, it was—"

"But why?" I ask hastily, before she can describe more of the grotesquery in front of my siblings. Klara has already clapped a hand to her mouth, her eyes huge and welling above it. "Father is not—*was* not—a farrier. Why did he not send the man to Antal?"

"I don't know," she replies, just above a whisper. "Maybe the man did not wish to wait, and Istvan thought it easy coin? Andras had come home to fetch their lunch, and when he returned to the smithy . . . it was already done. The traveler stayed only long enough to tell him what had befallen Istvan, he did not even . . ." She heaves a shuddering sigh, her face collapsing like a sinkhole into grief and helpless fury. "He did not even see Andras home, though my boy could barely stand when he rushed back to fetch me!"

I look to my oldest brother, clammy-faced with a tinge of green under his eyes. Normally he would mock me for it, but he does not squirm away when I reach out and sweep his damp hair from his face as I did when he was only a babe. Instead he leans into my touch, his lips trembling. "Was it . . ." A black, terrible suspicion crawls up my throat like a spider, threatening to choke me. "Was it Janos, Andras? The man from this morning? Was it his horse that Father shod?"

Andras shakes his head, his hand rising to hover in front of his mouth. He fidgets with his bottom lip, and for a moment I wonder if he will suck his grubby thumb as he did for so many years, so long that he misaligned his two front teeth. "No," he says, adamant, with a firm shake of his head. "This was a different man. Tall but scrawny, with a strange face." His own screws up with bemusement, a tinge of revulsion. "Almost pretty. Like a lady's, but not."

While I puzzle over this, mother collapses against my side as if her bones have dissolved all at once. "What will we do, Anna?" she keens into my shoulder, reaching for my arms with her gnarled, pitiful hands. "How will we fare when winter comes, without the coin from the smithy?"

"What will we eat?" Balint wails, having retained firm hold of his priorities. It nearly, but not quite, stirs me to smile despite myself. "We will be *hungry!*"

"We will not," I counter firmly. My mind has been whirling, a leaf tossed about by the ferocious winds of fortune, but it settles all at once. Peter's offer of marriage flares up for one last, hopeful moment before I stamp it to cinders under my heel. No matter how well he loves me, I cannot burden my best friend with six more mouths to feed, not without a dowry; such a strain would rupture even the most enduring of friendships. Even if I could bring myself to do it, I find I do not wish to wed him, not even now.

And even if I redouble my efforts, seek the sick beyond our village, I cannot feed all of us by myself.

Not as the midwife's daughter, anyway.

But as a lady's chambermaid, perhaps I could.

"I will go to the countess," I say, unwavering. "I'll leave on the morrow."

Chapter Five

The Journey and the Gauntlet

K lara's plaintive entreaties follow me out onto the road.

"Please don't go, Anna," she'd begged before I set out that morning, her little face wretched with tears. "Please do not leave me, nővér, I *love* you!"

"I'll be back, dandelion," I'd soothed past the lump in my own throat, hugging her tight against my midriff. I love her pet name for "big sister," but today it claws cruelly at my heart. "Before you know it, and with plenty of coin for bread and cheese and roast chickens."

My mother had embraced me, too, sliding her hand over my braid. "Will you be all right catching babies without me, what with your hands?" I'd whispered low into her ear so my sister wouldn't hear my concern. "I wouldn't want you to lose that coin, too."

"I'll take Magdalena's middle daughter as an apprentice, Annacska, don't fret," she'd murmured back. "She won't fill your shoes, but she's done well enough before when we've called on her for help. And *you* take care at the keep, my sweet. If anything is amiss, anything at all, come back to us, do you hear? We'll find some other way."

Except there was no other way, I thought grimly, even as I nodded and made her an empty promise to ease her mind.

There was only me.

Now I walk with my midwife's bag bumping against my hip, a cloth satchel slung over my shoulder, and a small knife tucked into my boot. Fortunately the terrain is flat, as most of Hungary is; a land held in God's own green palm, as people say. It certainly makes it easier to foresee danger coming, without any need for omens. Whenever I hear the rattle of carts and thump of hooves approaching, kicking up dust at the horizon, I melt out of sight like a snake into the roadside undergrowth. I know what may befall a woman traveling alone, and even with my sharp little companion at hand I see no reason to tempt fate. And though the sky threatens rain, a roiling black bank of clouds marching across the blue like an invading army, none falls as I walk.

Without pounding sun, storm, or skulking footpads to stall me, I make good time even with my caution. Still, I do not reach the keep until well after dusk, as the dregs of the day deepen into night. The temperature drops precipitously once the sun has sunk. It leaves the eve brittle-bright with cold, as if a slim pane of ice has been laid across the sky to sharpen the outlines of the stars and moon, bring them into finely cut focus. I feel as if I could crack it open by reaching up and tapping a fingernail against it. Bring it all tumbling to the ground in a shower of glittering shards.

Such silly thoughts, I chide myself as I hasten across the castle bridge that leads to the Nadasdy castle. As if a creature small as me could be big enough to break the sky.

In daylight, the keep is sprawling and lovely, its square, whitewashed towers snowy and roofed with a rich red. I remember its splendor from the one time I came here with my mother, to tend to one of the candlers. At night, I find it much less enticing. I have not dared rest while on the road, and now I am so tired that my exhaustion seems to be playing tricks on my sight. The keep rears up before me like something wicked, a beast lying in wait. Firelight glimmers behind the dark windows, but in my fatigue, I find an infernal tinge to this inner glow. Even the thick copse of trees all around, looming like sentinels, whisper of menace.

Worst of all, there is an unsettling, illusory flatness to the keep. The more I look at it, the more it seems like a mirror image. A reflection rather than something real.

Perhaps if I lifted my hand, I think, I would see myself already in one of the windows.

Already inside the belly of the beast.

"Get a hold of yourself, Anna, for God's sake," I hiss to myself under my breath, reaching up to pinch my cheek. "There is nothing here to fear!"

When I approach the gate tower, heart still rampaging in my chest, I find the great wooden door already bolted for the night. No one answers my knock. I step back, perplexed; it had not even occurred to me that I might not be able to gain entry once I arrived. Visions begin to swarm of a night spent outside in the biting cold. It's much too late to set out for home, and I can't sleep out here, with no shelter. I'll freeze long before morning, and tomorrow they'll find me, blue-lipped and glass-eyed, my lifeless flesh encased with ice, like a child's discarded doll.

There is no need to panic yet, I tell myself, as if I have not already begun to quail. Perhaps the castle is preoccupied with dinner, and I need merely wait.

So I settle in, huddling by the door in the hope of catching a balmy waft through the cracks. I try to warm myself with thoughts of heat; sated honeybees drifting lazily over fat and drooping flowers, the thick, dizzy warmth of a high summer day. But hours pass, and no one comes. I'm so frozen through, my hands and feet numb and my nose dripping salt, that the last measure of decorum deserts me, giving way to a scorching flush of panic almost welcome for its mimicry of heat. Abandoning restraint, I fling myself at the door, battering it with my fists.

"Hello!" I cry, wincing at the high-pitched despair in my voice. I sound like a fretful child, but I'm unable to contain it. Great gusts of my breath billow around me. *So cold, so cold, so cold* beats in my mind like a second, frigid heart. "Is anyone there? Will you let me in? The countess has called for me, and I, I'm so *cold*, I'll catch my death out here, *please* . . ."

Finally, when my hands are bruised to tenderness from pounding, I hear the groan of the bolt being lifted, the scrape of the wood against the iron brackets. I step back, half tripping over my own numb feet, as the door swings outward to reveal a beetle-browed guard with lank scraggles of graying hair. He peers at me churlishly, glowering over a harelip.

"What d'you want at this hour, girl, with your ungodly

racket?" he demands, spitting by my feet. "The castle's sleeping, as are all decent folk."

I'm so weak with relief that my entire body fractures into trembling. My teeth chatter so hard I can barely force the words through them. "I have c-c-come to be the l-lady's chambermaid," I stutter, hugging myself. "Sh-sh-she has summoned me, and I arrived earlier, b-b-b-but no one has come for me. Did you not h-h-h-hear me knocking?"

He surveys me a moment longer with flat, impervious eyes, and I am stricken with the sudden conviction that he will turn me away. If he does, I am dead. I will not survive this night.

"Fine, then," he says grudgingly, without even acknowledging my question. "I'll take you to the stables."

My brow knits in confusion as I follow him into the blissful, fleeting heat of the gate tower and then back outside into the courtyard. "The st-stables?" I ask, willing my ungainly lips to thaw. "But, sh-shouldn't I meet the steward? Or the keeper of house, if not the lady herself?"

"They're all abed," he replies, leading me across the flagstones. "The lady's retired early, and given orders that all others at the keep should hie to their own beds after their meals. None are awake to see to you, so the stables it shall be."

"But why?" I ask, still baffled. "Is the lady ill?"

"'But why?'" he mimics, in a whining tone. "Jesus wept, girl. The hell should I know why the lady does as she does? Because it pleased her, I reckon. Now, here we are. M'lady's quarters for the evening."

He shoves me inside none too gently, then turns on his

heel and marches back across the courtyard. I stand for a moment, squinting in the pervasive darkness; there are no lanterns or candles inside the stable, of course, nothing but the soft whistling of horses' breath, their nickers, and the shift of hooves. But it is infinitely warmer in here than outside, and smells comfortingly of the animals' sweet breath and musky coats. More by touch than by sight, I find my way to the rear, behind the last stall. There I settle myself against a stack of hay bales, wrapped up in my cape with my belongings tucked behind me, where no one can steal them from me in my sleep.

I'm so exhausted that I fall asleep almost as soon as my eyes slide closed. But a final thought follows me under, like a beacon glowing against the clotted dark behind my eyelids.

Could the countess have sent the entire keep to bed for one reason only—to ensure that I would be shut out when I came to beg admittance a day later than summoned? As I succumb to sleep, I can only think that the answer must be yes: She meant for me to suffer for making her wait. And she intended to test my resolve, ascertain if I am fit to serve her.

Tomorrow, I must show her that I am.

The next morning, I wake to hot breath in my face.

In my stupor, I think it must be a horse. Befuddled, I swipe my hand up to push it away—my eyes flying open when my palm encounters warm and unmistakably human flesh.

A freckled face hangs above me, leering. "Morning, little pudding," the lout says, catching me by the wrist. "What a glad surprise, finding a beauty like you among my beasties. Can't say I was expecting you to wake quite so eager to caress me, but—"

In a flash, I draw my leg up and reach into my boot. Before he can so much as stir, he finds the point of my dagger poised beneath the soft flesh of his chin. The knife is a gift from Peter, who also made sure I would not lack the skills to use it. I send a silent thought of gratitude in his direction.

"Get off me," I snap through gritted teeth as the stable-hand's eyes grow wide. "Before I carve out your foul tongue."

He hesitates, muddy dark eyes shifting craftily between mine for a moment longer than is my liking. Clenching my jaw, I press the point up until it pierces the taut surface of his skin. Braying like a donkey, the boy leaps off me, clutching at his underchin.

"You—you stabbed me!" he accuses, breathless with disbelief, when his hand comes away wet and red. "You vicious little *slag!*"

"Oh please, it's no more than a scratch," I scoff, taking care that my voice does not betray the bucking chaos of my heart. I shift my grip on the knife and brandish it at him, tilting my head in challenge. *Be brave,* I urge myself. *Be who you want him to see.* "But I will happily gut you, should you lay so much as another finger on me. My father is a butcher, you see. He taught me how to cut."

The boy's jutting Adam's apple bobs as he swallows, his eyes flicking between me and the bloodied blade. I've always lied well enough, and he is not sure what to believe; the sight of the slight, mostly defenseless girl before his eyes, or the casually murderous intent in my voice. And I see now that he's barely fifteen, even younger than me. Not quite old enough yet to trust in his instincts, nor his own brute force.

"Take me to the keeper of house," I order, swiping at him one more time. "Or I will return in the night with my little blade, and make you sorry that you ever thought to touch me."

Perhaps I mean my threat more than I think I do; perhaps he can tell. In any case, some minutes later I'm standing in the castle's vast kitchens, by the busy hearth. The stable boy vanished as soon as he brought me here, unwilling to linger near my knife. A legion of cooks and scullions bustle around me, paying me no mind as I gaze, transfixed, at the glistening side of lamb roasting on a spit, the crusty rounds of a dozen loaves of bread baking on their stones among the cinders. The castle cannot possibly need so much, but I assume it's the lady's pleasure to enjoy a lavish feast every night. So what if most of it is destined to become pig slop. I'm sure the castle sows appreciate the abundance.

"So you're the girl bloodying stablehands," a gruff voice croaks behind me. "I assume you've come for some purpose beyond such sport?"

I turn and dip into a curtsy. The keeper of house is a mountain of a woman, with steely hair bound up so tight it drags at her temples. A chatelaine encircles her sturdy waist, clinking with keys, scissors, and other little tools suspended on chains. I've seen my father make them, and the toolwork on this one is very fine. The lady must prize her if she compensates her well enough to afford such adornments.

"He got only what he deserved, mistress," I say simply.

"He was forward with me. A bit of a lackwit as well. I would not trust him with the care of noble animals, were I in your place."

The housekeeper's stern expression does not waver, but the amusement deepens in her eyes. I sense that she likes me, perhaps against her better judgment. "Can't say as I disagree with you. Boy's a dreadful dullard, and a ruffian to boot. Unfortunately, the horses' care isn't up to me. The keeping of this castle is, however. What business have you here?"

"The Lady Báthory wants me for her chambermaid," I reply. "She called me here."

The housekeeper's eyes flash with something indecipherable, and her thin lips part, as if she wishes to say something before changing her mind. Then she gives a brisk shake of her head. "No such position is open."

I stare at her, baffled. "She summoned me only two days past! Her manservant Janos came to fetch me. How can it not be open?"

She shrugs, and again there is that odd flicker in her eyes. "If it were, I would know of it—and I do not. Now, be off with you. I've duties to attend to."

I plant my feet and set my jaw. "No, mistress. Beg pardon, but no. There must be some mistake—and I will not be leaving until it is resolved. If you know nothing of it, allow me to speak with the countess herself. Surely . . . surely she will at least grant me an audience."

The housekeeper plants her hands on her hips and rolls her eyes demonstratively, heaving a gusty sigh. "Fine, then, you single-minded nuisance of a child. I'll not bother the lady on your account, but I'll have a word with Master

Aurel, the steward. But mind me . . ." Abruptly, she places a warm hand on my shoulder, drawing me closer. Her palm is so work-coarsened that I can hear it grate against my cape's wool, catching its threads. She pitches her voice low, her mouth close to my ear. "If you know what's good for you, you'll turn tail and run back to where you came from. Do you hear me? This is no place for you, I can already see as much."

My hackles rise, and I shrug off her hand as politely as I can, though my insides surge with defiance. Who is this woman to tell me where my rightful place might be? She may be charged with the running of this castle, but she was born no better than I am. "Thank you for the concern, mistress," I say, struggling to keep my voice even. "I will take your counsel to heart, but still—I'm not leaving until I speak to the steward."

She shrugs her broad shoulders in frustration. "Go, then," she capitulates, mouth pinching. "Wait for him in the great hall. I'll send word, and he'll come find you when he's free."

I sketch another curtsy, deeper this time. "Thank you, ma'am. I'm in your debt."

She shakes her head, almost ruefully, waving away my thanks. "It's that way, down the corridor and then to the left. I hope you've patience to spare, child. I've never known Aurel to hurry."

"I'll be fine, mistress," I assure her, and I will be. It's warm inside, and a night of sleep has revived my fortitude. Once again, I am willing to do whatever it takes. "I have plenty of time."

The castle's great hall is a marvel, paneled with gleaming mahogany and hung with massive chandeliers of such intricately wrought iron that I cannot imagine how something so delicate could have been worked from a material as obstinate as metal. The ironwork comes to viciously speared points, and they creak a little, swaying subtly in the castle's crosswise draft. I make sure not to stand directly beneath one, shuddering at the thought of what would happen should the chains suspending it snap without warning. Above the fireplace hangs a colossal stag's head with an upper lip curled into a half sneer, presiding blindly over the hall. Huge tapestries portraying woodlands, entwined lovers, and warriors in the thick of battle adorn the walls, so vibrant and well-crafted they seem to tremble with barely contained life. Absurd as it sounds, it feels almost as though they can see me just as I see them; when I turn away, my neck prickles with the sensation of being observed by watchful eyes.

Despite the grandeur, the space feels ineffably sinister, as though its trappings only flimsily conceal an altogether different aspect. As though one need only scratch at the room's veneer to expose the teeming rot beneath.

When the steward finally arrives more than three hours later, I'm ready to leap out of my skin. I've resorted to playing cat's cradle to distract myself, adjusting the string with my teeth.

I rise hurriedly while he puckers his mouth, watching me disapprovingly. He has a face like a stewed bone, and threads of hair combed over his liver-spotted scalp. I dislike him instantly. He reminds me of the baby buzzards, clumsily feasting on carrion, that I sometimes stumble upon in the woods.

"Oh," he intones with pronounced displeasure and surprise. "You're still here."

"Of course I am, Master Aurel," I say, taken aback. "I was told to wait here for you. Where would I have gone?"

"Mistress Magda informs me that you've been here some hours." He arches a tufted eyebrow meaningfully. "One might hope you'd have gotten the hint by now."

My heart plunges down, landing in my stomach. It's conceivable, if not likely, that a housekeeper would not know that her lady had set her sights on a new chambermaid. But the steward is the lady's right hand, and if there were still a place here for me, this man would be sure to know.

Unless this too is intended as a test. But how many more hurdles can I leap, if she won't even let me see her?

"The lady does not wish me to be her maidservant, then?" I try, struggling to contain my despair. "Are you absolutely sure?"

"Of course I am sure, you impertinent chit!" he hisses, flappy cheeks mottling. "I am paid to know my lady's wishes! How dare you question me?"

"But she sent for me only a few days ago!" I argue again. "Perhaps there has been some confusion, some mistake! Her man Janos—"

"Is in my direct employ," he finishes, grasping me by the upper arm so hard I'm startled into a gasp. He begins marching me toward the doors, sharp fingernails digging into my flesh. "I know very well that he was sent for you. But her ladyship has changed her mind, and you are no longer wanted here!"

"No," I half shriek, wrenching myself out of his grip. My voice is so shrill that he draws up short, his weak chin withdrawing into his gangly neck. "I—I'm sorry, master, but I will not go. I cannot. Not until I've had an audience with the lady, to be sure she does not want me."

The steward regards me narrowly, still flushed with outrage, his pendulous jowls aquiver. I draw myself up to my full height, slight as it is, bolstered by sudden resolve. My family needs me; I will not fail them when I've come this far, no matter how many obstacles she places in my path. "I will not leave without seeing her," I repeat, quiet but firm. "And if you try to remove me, I will scream bloody murder until I bring the castle down around your ears."

"Wouldn't be the first time," he mutters sourly. "But I've no wish to hear your squealing. Come then, you impudent trull. And may the lady give you exactly what you deserve."

He barges ahead of me, not bothering to see if I will follow. I trot to catch up, hope swelling inside me as we pass through the corridors glowering with darkness, lit by the faintest flicker of candle sconces. I can make her change her mind, I know it. I can make her want me again.

I *have* to make her want me.

The steward leads me up two circular flights of stairs, then draws in front of an ornately carved door with bronze hinges, swinging it open and sardonically ushering me in. I enter what must be the countess's solar, though strangely, the curtains are firmly drawn over the expansive windows.

Perhaps the countess isn't partial to the glare of midday sun. Surrounded instead by a retinue of candles, she reclines in a crimson velvet armchair, needlepoint spread over her lap. Three chambermaids sit on the floor near her feet, perched on large plush cushions like spoiled kittens.

The weight of their regard makes me twitchy, and I wobble a bit as I curtsy, tipping my head. Someone titters at my clumsiness, but not the countess, I think; the sound isn't husky enough. When I rise, the steward is still carping about my stubbornness. "And she refused to leave until you granted her an audience, your grace," he finishes, with a peevish glare flicked in my direction. "Threatened to scream bloody murder."

"Did she," the lady remarks mildly, shifting her indolent gaze to me. "How *very* alarming."

"I told her you did not wish to see her, but—"

She silences him with an elegant sweep of her hand, glittering with rings. "Understood, Aurel. My thanks. You may go."

Once he's gone, the countess beckons me forward. I come reluctantly, struck almost shy by the chambermaids' baleful scrutiny. "My lady," I begin, swallowing against the rasp in my throat. "Thank you for seeing me. I—"

She cuts me off, leaning forward in her seat. "You're filthy," she observes, her lip curling minutely. There isn't a shred of warmth to her, no leftover intimacy from our vigil over her son. I may as well be a stranger to her. "Dirt on your face, straw in your hair. Altogether *slovenly*."

A wave of mortification and ire sweeps over me, reddening

my cheeks. "I'm sorry, my lady. I have not had a chance to wash off the dirt of the road. And I spent last night in the stables."

Her eyes soften a bit, almost admiringly, and I wonder if it's my tenacity that she likes. "I'd almost forgotten what a spectacular blush you have," she remarks, her eyelids dropping to half-mast. It's not my perseverance, then, that's sparked her fancy. "Remarkably florid, as if your skin is transparent! So much blood, and so close to the surface. You look almost like a pomegranate."

I waver, uncertain as to whether this is a compliment. I have no idea what a pomegranate is. "Thank you, my lady?"

The momentary admiration sluices away, replaced by stony resolve. "I fear, however, that your fine skin changes nothing. There is no longer room for you here." She gestures at her pretty ladies-in-waiting, arrayed all about her like baubles, human ornaments. "As you can see, I am well attended."

I steel myself, gritting my teeth. "As you say, my lady. But—you asked for me only two days ago. Can circumstances truly have changed so much already?"

She weaves her head languorously back and forth, as if considering, and I am reminded of corn snakes sliding sinuously through grass. "It was a passing whim," she says airily. "One that you did not seize upon when you had the chance." Her eyes glimmer with subdued malice, and I abruptly understand that behind the cultivated carelessness, she is rankled by my refusal just as I suspected, maybe even wounded by it. And the hurt of it has made her furious, ready to lash out at me. "So now that door is closed to you, I fear."

Out of nowhere, tears prickle in my eyes. I have not cried at all, not when I learned of my father's death nor on the road yesterday, but now I cannot contain my exhaustion, my despair at what will befall my family if I return to them empty-handed.

"It was my father who refused you, my lady, not me. He—he was a greedy man, and wished to wring more money from you. Please understand," I say, allowing myself to sound as abject as I feel. "I would have come at once, had the choice been mine, for whatever you were willing to spare. And now he is dead, and care of my family falls to me." Slowly, like a wilting flower, I come to my knees and bow my head. "My lady, please. Give me another chance to prove my devotion. I will do anything, your grace. Whatever you wish of me."

I wait, head bowed, for so long that my knees begin to ache dully from the cold stone beneath them. Then her low voice comes, on the heels of a long, contemplative sigh. "We shall see about that, I suppose." My head snaps up, giddy with torrential hope. She has her chin rested on her palm, a languid dark curl slipping over her cheek. Her lips are so red, a deep, flushed ruby, as if she has been biting them hard while I waited for her judgment. "You will begin in the scullery. The pay will be nothing like what it would have been as my maid, of course. A few thaler a month, at most."

"Of course!" I rush, dizzy with gratitude. Sculls do the grubbiest, most backbreaking work for a pittance, and I realize that this is to be my punishment for defying her. But no matter, because if I am permitted to stay, it means the door is open again. Just a crack, but enough for me to wedge my foot in, begin squeezing my way through to the light beyond. "That's—that is immensely kind of you, my lady. I swear I will do my best for you."

She flicks her fingers dismissively, then picks up her needlepoint, red lips pursing. "You may go," she says, eyes on her sewing as if I am already gone. "And see that you find no further ways to disappoint me."

PART TWO: Beguiled

Chapter Six

The Rats and the Maidens

The cellars where the scullions sleep are barely fit for rats. Though, from the flurries of movement I glimpse from the corners of my eyes, this does not dissuade vermin of all persuasions from swarming in the shadows.

I sit on my rickety pallet, brushing out my hair, coarse straw piercing my nightgown and poking into my thighs. The low ceiling above my head reeks of mold and mildew, sweating stone that never dries. I keep my feet drawn up so my bare toes don't have to touch the slimy, louse-ridden floor. As I tug at the snarls, I find myself awash in sticky misery, second-guessing the choices that have led me here. This place is so foul that it makes our little cottage seem a palace in comparison. How will I ever sleep here, with the damp cold of the underground seeping into my bones, nothing but a ratty, flea-bitten blanket to cover me, no Klara to warm my back?

It's worse here than in the stables, I think, with a wry twist of amusement. If only I had known how good I had it, with horses for company, I would have enjoyed my last night above ground more.

Amazingly, our accommodations do not seem to faze the other maids. They must be inured already to this ghastly gloom. There are about a dozen of us down here. Around me, everyone else is busy chatting and laughing, trading neck rubs and plaiting each other's hair. I feel a powerful burst of loneliness at the pleasure they're taking in the shared company, in these moments of leisure they manage to steal for themselves before they sleep.

The girl on the pallet beside mine notices my wistfulness. She casts me a smile, earnest and dimpled, lending surprising beauty to her sallow face. She gestures gingerly toward my brush, reaching for it.

"I could help you?" she offers timidly. "Your hair is so long, it must be hard to do for yourself."

"Oh, I would love that," I reply. "Thank you. I'm Anna."

"Ilona," she murmurs back, settling herself behind me on the pallet and taking up my hair. "Goodness, it's so pale and fine. Like raw silk."

"Let me feel," another of the maids demands, overhearing. She tramps over from three pallets down, flopping next to us with such carelessness I'm afraid my pallet might collapse under our weight. I recognize this girl as the ringleader of the room. She's Krisztina, a brash redhead with an impish, freckled face, startling green eyes, and a riot of hair that springs everywhere like encroaching ivy now that it's been released from the confines of her braid. I've heard her name bandied about, and I see the way the others treat her with deference. As if she's the self-appointed lady reigning over this murky, underworld domain.

Without asking, she sinks both hands into my hair. "Ooh," she exclaims. "*Fancy*. And the color, almost white! Have you Austrian blood, maybe?"

"Krisztina," Ilona chides gently, casting her a reproving look. "Maybe Anna does not wish to have her hair pawed without permission."

"*You* were pawing it readily enough, squeak," Krisztina shoots back. "And fawning over it to boot. Had I waited a moment longer, you'd have been rubbing it all over your face like a cat rolling in a patch of nip."

As Ilona blushes so furiously it's visible even in the gloom, I intervene. "I don't mind," I say honestly. It feels so good to be touched, after the past few days I've had, almost decadent. "Usually my mother or sister brush my hair before bed. It's nice to have someone do it here, so far away from home."

Krisztina's face softens at that, and she gives my hair a gentle tug. "We all feel the homesickness sometimes," she says kindly. "Hard not to, in this godforsaken gaol of a cellar. But the smarting will pass, chickadee, I promise. You'll get accustomed." She snorts a little, chuckling through her nose. "And if not, you'll be so bloody tired by day's end that you'll collapse before you can spare home more than a thought."

"I never even got a chance to say goodbye properly," I confess. "I meant to return for a full farewell, once I secured my position here. But the lady did not grant me leave."

"'Course she didn't," Krisztina mutters sourly, her face tightening. "She thinks you're hers now, like as not. Bought and paid for. You're lucky she didn't make you chop off all that pretty hair."

"Chop off my hair?" I exclaim, brow wrinkling with confusion. "Why would she do that?"

"It's one of her ladyship's most favored punishments," old Katalin croaks from the shadows. I'd marked her for her unusual age; most scullery maids advance to higher stations or succumb to illness caused by backbreaking toil long before they reach such years. Her pallet is the farthest from the door, so distant from the spare light that filters in that she may as well be living with the earthworms. The tiny spiders down here are so plentiful and persistent she doesn't even bother to clear the cobwebs that gather in her corner, where the low ceiling slopes right above her nose. I can see them shifting with her breath as she speaks, their strands glimmering in the candlelight. The sight of them so close to her face makes the hair on my neck prickle with revulsion. "Vex her when she's feeling a bit tetchy? Or maybe her breakfast's sitting wrong when you cross her path? Off with your hair, little besom!"

She cackles so wildly I shoot Ilona a disconcerted look. She shrugs at me, rolling her eyes minutely as if to tell me to pay the old woman no mind.

"Sometimes she does it just because she's jealous, I reckon," Krisztina adds, lowering her voice. "It's taken me ages to grow mine back. She had it cut the first day she clapped eyes on me. It'd be distracting for the castle's menfolk, she said." She snorts again, shaking her head. "More like, it pricked her right in her envious eye. Now I keep it braided and wound so tight under my cap that it looks shorn."

"Surely she wouldn't do such a thing for no good reason," I say cautiously, taken aback by how scathingly they speak of the lady that puts a roof over their heads. And I consider the stable boy's advances; maybe the countess has all our best interests at heart, and they are simply fortunate enough not to know it. "I've seen her be very kind."

"Kind?!" Krisztina hisses, eyes widening with disbelief as she leans closer to me. "You must be mad, or jesting. That snake wouldn't know the milk of kindness if it bit her on her narrow arse. I had a friend that worked here, as the lady's seamstress. The nimblest fingers on her that you ever did see. But she didn't sew fast enough for the ladyship's liking—so the bloody bitch made her stitch her own fingers together as punishment. Can you imagine?"

My eyes dart to Ilona's, wide with disbelief. "Surely not. That's—that is mad."

"We could hear her pitiful caterwauling all the way down here, pet," Katalin drones. "You couldn't mistake the clamor for aught but agony."

"Was Lord Nadasdy here when it happened, by any chance?" I ask, another vile possibility occurring to me. I still remember the force with which he grabbed the countess's wrist in the carriage on their wedding day, the look of implacable command in his eyes, barely restrained ferocity. What these women think to be the lady's cruelty may very well be her husband's doing, masquerading as her own.

Krisztina squinches up her freckled face in thought. "Far as I know, the lord's away at war more often than not, but he comes home for visits, so he may have been? Why?"

"He doesn't seem like a . . . kindhearted man," I offer

warily, reluctant to antagonize her. "I'm only wondering if these punishments might be at his bidding."

"It's possible, sure," she concedes with a spindly shrug, pulling a dubious face. "Makes little enough difference, if you ask me. If she's the one carrying them out."

"And what if the lady has no choice in the matter?" I forge ahead, suddenly vehement, heedless of what Krisztina might think of me. "My father—he's dead now, but he wasn't a good man. My mother, sister, and I, we did everything we could to dodge his ire, and still we rarely managed to avoid his blows. It can turn you hateful, living like that. I wonder if such is the lady's lot as well."

Krisztina appraises me quietly, her shrewd green gaze shifting between my eyes. "You've a tender heart, chickadee," she concludes, squeezing my shoulder. "You don't look it, not with those cold eyes, but I see you do. Mayhap it makes you more willing to trust than you should be. But I'll say this much—you weren't there when she made Marta stitch her own skin."

"And were you there?" I demand. "I mean, did you see it for yourself?"

She pauses, chewing on the inside of her lip. "Marta was gone before the morning," she admits finally. "But I heard it from Judit, one of the lady's own chambermaids. She's a cousin—the reason I found work here in the first place."

"And is Judit so honest?" I drill down, thinking of the countess's smug triptych of maids, their poncey little faces. I remember the lady calling her chambermaids baby vipers when we first met. "Is *she* kind?"

"No," Ilona chimes in softly, looking so tormented that

I wonder what those uppity prigs have done to her. "Not always."

"Well, then." I lean back a little, vindicated, crossing my legs under my nightgown to warm them beneath my behind. "We have no idea what really happens behind her doors, do we?"

"I suppose we don't," Krisztina concedes shortly, with a jittery little shudder. "But I know what I've heard. And I've no wish to witness her ghoulish work firsthand."

She rises from my pallet, flicking me a small smile to let me know there's no ill will between us, then rejoins her chattering flock. Ilona resumes brushing my hair, then plaits it loosely for me. "There," she says, her little voice so low it's barely more than a whisper. "This way it won't tug on you while you sleep, give you nightmares. You need proper rest."

Her kindness draws tears to my eyes for the second time today. I need to watch myself, lest I become a fretful ninny weeping at every passing breeze, but I can't help but be moved. Something in her sweet, self-effacing manner puts me in mind of Klara, though they look nothing alike and Ilona is much closer to my age.

"Thank you," I say, impulsively brushing a light kiss over her cheek. "You've made me feel at home. I won't soon forget it."

"Oh, it was no trouble!" she responds, looking so starstruck I finally understand—she's beguiled by my face, as if it somehow elevates me to a much higher station than the one to which I was born. "I was—I was glad to do it. May your dreams be sweet, Anna."

I doubt they will be, I think as I settle onto my creaking pallet. I can still hear the others gossiping about the countess, spinning tall tales of her depravities. It seems she slapped one girl so hard her cheekbone cracked, forced another to play the lute until her fingers bled, had a third mercilessly lashed for breaking a plate. I listen because I cannot help but hear, but I do not believe a word. From the sound of it, our mistress simply does not countenance sloth or clumsiness, and I can find no fault with that.

They don't understand her as I do, I think, shifting uncomfortably on the narrow bed. That is the trouble. How can they, when they know nothing of Gabor? When they haven't seen Lord Nadasdy peel her smile from her face with his vicious grasp?

I lay there for hours, awake in the dark with my mind spinning. Burning like a stray ember in my bed.

Thinking of how I can show her that I understand.

Chapter Seven

The Toil and the Brace

I've worked hard all my life, by my mother's side. Since I was little, I helped her tend to our hearth, grind her medicines, pull babies and dress wounds and do whatever else was needed to help the sick. At home, I wrangled my roughhousing brothers, cleaned and swept and baked, butchered animals when we had the luxury of meat.

None of it could have prepared me for the accursed drudgery that is a scull's daily lot.

My main job is to scrub, which comes as no surprise. I clean mostly the floors, hunched over on my knees to scour the castle's cold, begrimed stones. But I am also responsible for scrubbing the cavernous cauldrons that steam in the kitchens and the laundry, and the soiled serving platters that ferry delicacies to the lady's table three to five times a day, depending on how often she and her retinue are feeling peckish.

As Krisztina promised, the end of my first day finds me

dog-tired, swaying on my feet. I barely remember eating a tasteless dinner with the rest of the servants before collapsing fully clothed into my miserable bed, comforting myself with thoughts of the coin I will send home to my family before the month is done. Much less than I would have made as the lady's chambermaid, but still more than they would have had otherwise. When I wake before dawn, I'm so sore that it seems unbelievably cruel that I should be expected to do it all again. In that respect, the second day is even more demanding. My knees are already tender from kneeling, my hands beginning to crack from the harshness of the lye we use to wash everything. My back feels like it must be a column made of the red-hot metals my father pounded with his blacksmith's hammer. Even my scalp aches from how tightly Mistress Magda demands we keep our hair braided beneath our caps.

It all puts me hugely out of sorts.

"It gets better, Anna, you'll see," Ilona soothes, noting my grim-faced look as we half wrestle, half drag a cauldron that must weigh more than both of us combined outside for a thorough scrubbing. "I was plagued by aches and pains the first few weeks, myself, but you do get used to it. And you get stronger."

"And will I sprout hands like hooves, too, do you think?" I grouse, unable to help myself. "To help withstand all this stinking lye?"

When her sweet face sinks and she bites the inside of her cheek just as Klara does, I feel so pained for snapping at her that I bend over backward like a contortionist to apologize. Ilona's dauntless cheer puts me to shame. She hums under her breath as she works, a tuneless but endearing drone, and her smile is always ready, no matter how dreary and taxing our work. She is too good for this life, I often find myself thinking—especially when I see the lady's overindulged maidservants swanning by, groomed and cossetted and more like ladies themselves than help. It makes me seethe over the unfairness of our respective lots.

And yet, I find it isn't the arduous labor that grinds on me the most, but the sheer, dragging boredom of the days. None of the menial tasks set before me even begin to challenge my mind. I'm used to full and unpredictable workdays, being called upon to treat ailments that even my mother sometimes doesn't recognize. Now the most challenge that I come across is a pot so stubbornly encrusted that I'm forced to scrape at it with my fingernails, cursing poisonously under my breath. Nothing relieves the crushing tedium, not even the nightly chitchat in our cellar quarters. I could not care less about the other sculls' dim-witted sweethearts back home, and while their talk of family stirs my heart, it's my own kin's plight that looms large in my mind. I find that I've precious little sympathy to spare.

Even if I had any to go around, it isn't commiseration that my fellow drudges need, it's more coin and less work. I can do nothing about that, either.

But what I can do, I find, is tend to their bodily wear and tear.

"Would you let me look at that for you?" I ask Krisztina one day, noticing the way she favors her left hand. We've been sent outside to pound the dust and dirt out of one of the castle's splendid bearskin rugs. It's much more pleasant to tread on, I think sourly as I batter the thick fur, than it is to maintain. "I might be able to ease the strain."

She grimaces, rolling the offending wrist back and forth. "I doubt the good lord himself could do anything about it, short of cleaving it off for me and have done with it. It's been keeping me up at night, aching fit to fall off—so maybe all I need do is wait to be free of it." She snorts, then peers at me curiously. "Why, what is it you think *you* could do?"

I twitch one shoulder in a shrug. "My mother is the village midwife," I say. "I know a bit about medicine."

She grins mischievously, waggling her patchy ginger eyebrows. "Is that so? Shouldn't a midwife's daughter know that a sore wrist is no sign of being with child?"

I chuckle at that, shaking my head. "She sees to folks' other ailments when she can, too," I clarify. "I learned at her knee. Nothing too complicated, just the odd ache and twinge," I hasten to downplay, remembering the trepidation on Zorka's face when the lady called me a witch in front of her. No need to sow rumors here, where they might grow into nasty weeds to trip me.

Krisztina considers the offer a moment, the rug whip gripped in her good hand. "All right, then, might as well. Surely your tinkering can't make it any worse," she decides.

She allows me to examine her hand over our midday respite. I turn it over, marveling as I always do at the intricate truss of tendon and bone, the modest miracle hidden under a roughened layer of her pale, freckled skin. I run my fingertips searchingly over the splay of her hand, pressing at tender spots and pulling her fingers tight, until her muffled hiss assures me that I understand.

"Does your hand go numb, or tingle here?" I ask, sweeping my fingertips over the base of her thumb and then up toward the first three fingers. When I close my eyes, I almost imagine I see the pulsing flare of the inflamed filament throbbing beneath her skin, where it spirals around the central spoke of bone.

"Yes!" she exclaims, cocking her head with surprise. She's gone pale under her cinnamon spatter of freckles, clearly pained by my examination, but she hasn't uttered a word of complaint. "How did you know? Sometimes I beat it against my thigh to get the blood flowing again, but on the worst days, it turns so dead I can scarcely feel it." She casts me a searingly hopeful look. "Can you fix it, do you think?"

I squeeze the fleshy pad under her thumb, working out the strain, and her eyelids flutter with relief. "Some things are soothed by a simple tonic or poultice, but I'm afraid this isn't such an easy fix. I can rub it for you in the evenings, if you like," I offer. "Sometimes massaging the shoulder, arm, and wrist will grant relief. But what it really needs is rest."

"Oh, well then," she jokes, but I can sense the tremor of fear beneath. If it progresses enough to incapacitate her, how will she work? Like me, she has a gawping legion of mouths to feed back home. "I'll just ask for a fortnight of leave, shall I? Tell Mistress Magda I need to put my feet up, physician's orders."

"I can make a brace for you," I say. "Immobilize the hand and let the wrist heal as it should. Your other hand will have to pick up the slack, but it'll give you reprieve."

Weaving the brace out of leather cords consumes my free hours for three nights after that, but I yearn for such constructive labor, and I don't mind a single stitch of it. I instruct Krisztina to wear it all the time, even to bed, and I sit with her each night and rub her shoulder until my own fingers go numb. Her hand improves in a fortnight, and her gratitude is like a salve to my flagging spirits.

It takes me back to who I was before. No grubby scull, but a midwife's clever daughter, with a leaping mind and nimble, healing fingers.

It reminds me that even amid all this clinging, inescapable muck, I'm still who I've always been.

After that, the requests come in droves. Acid stomachs, swollen hands, and itchy rashes abound. Ilona often suffers from headaches that she compares to a mallet splitting walnuts; old Katalin cannot shed the chesty cough that rattles the rafters above her bed. Though I feel for them, I'm also selfishly glad for these complaints—qualms like these, I can address. Tending to them begins to lend substance to my dull days. I slip outside the keep's confines whenever I can steal a moment to myself, to gather fresh herbs. Fortunately, I also still have the contents of my midwife's bag, full of ready remedies.

You'd think I was some saint dispensing miracles, so disproportionate is the gratitude I receive for the relief I can give them. But I also understand it. This life is desperately hard, so constantly crushing, that even a brief absence of discomfort seems a remarkable gift.

And just like that, I find these strangers, who toil by my side and sleep around me, growing into friends. I've never been so surrounded by women not of my blood; my village peers never took to me this way. But here, everywhere I turn I encounter friendship. An arm flung carelessly over my shoulder; an amiable squeeze of the hand; a shared, silly joke. Krisztina has them calling me Anna the Cunning, but there's no malice in it—only heartfelt admiration for my talents.

I might be halfway content, had I managed to shed that sense of eerie sentience I'd felt the first night I came to the keep. But if anything, the feeling has intensified with time; the castle now seems to coil around me like something feral and serpentine, as if it's more dragon than stone. Perhaps it's the incessant darkness that preys on my mind and whips up such senseless fears, but I've come to hate any task that separates me from the safety of our little herd.

As though with one wrong step I might stumble into one of the many pitch-black recesses and lose myself forever.

Consumed by the keep, swallowed by its malign stones.

My constant unease translates into my dreams. Most nights I'm plagued by nightmares of a ravening beetle horde, a glistening flood that skitters over me and gnaws me down to the bone. I know what the dream portends—fear, starvation, death—but understanding does nothing to hold it at bay, not when I know the coin I make will barely scrape my family by when winter comes.

And beyond that, I cannot shake the feeling that this was never meant to be my life.

I know the lady knows it, too, that she saw the potential that teems in me, begging to be released. I need only find a way to remind her of it. But my path never intersects with hers. Why would the lady of the castle ever soil her slippered feet by stepping in the kitchens or the scullery? It leaves me aquiver with tension, ever searching for openings, paths that will lead me to the solar or her chambers. My eyes must always be wide open so I can leap as soon as I spot my chance. With every cauldron I clean, I can feel my teeth gritting, grinding together with resolve.

Because if I cannot see an opportunity, then I must learn to craft one for myself.

Chapter Eight

The Flux and the Tisane

I have been at the keep for three weeks when I learn, from one of the maids tasked with cleaning the countess's chambers, that the lady herself has taken ill. My heart flutters hopefully at the news, like a moth brushing against a lighted window. Perhaps this is it, my coveted opening.

"What ails her?" I ask the maidservant as I prepare a settling tisane of peppermint, chamomile, and burdock for her. Rumors of my skill have spread beyond the scullery, creeping like fast-growing vines, and now even the higher-ranking servants seek me out for their complaints. This woman has a nervous stomach, aggravated by the spicy foods she favors but staunchly refuses to give up, and I often see her thrice a week. "Do you know?"

"I'm not sure," Agata says, wariness stealing over her weathered features. "It isn't my place to know. I only make the lady's bed, stir her coals, and fill her washbasin—she does not confide in me as she does in the chambermaids."

"Still," I push. "You're there every day. Surely you've heard *something*."

Her thin lips press together, forehead furrowing with discomfort. "Like I said. It isn't my place to speak of what passes behind her doors."

"But perhaps I could help the lady!" I argue, keeping my voice low. The maidservants' quarters are not so crammed as the cellars, but I don't know these women, nor do I trust them as I do the sculls. "As I help you. And if I ease her pain because you have told me of it, it would only do you credit, don't you see?" Of course, this would only be true if I weren't out of the countess's favor, but that much I keep to myself.

Agata's eyes cloud over as she considers it, grappling mightily with the opposing sides. Bless the woman's good intentions and devotion, but a sharp mind does not count among her talents.

The thought of ingratiating herself finally seems to sway her. She leans toward me, dropping her own voice. "It's her flux, I think," she reveals, hushed. "It pains her something awful, worse than I've ever seen. Sometimes she writhes in her bed like a worm on a hook, for a week or more. It's as if the devil himself has sunk his claws into her womb."

Realizing what she's said—or rather, how she's said it—her eyes flare wide and she claps her chapped hand over her mouth, staring at me with mute horror.

"Don't fret," I soothe, patting her other hand. "You did right by your lady, telling me. And unless I find that I can help her, what you've told me shall remain between us. You have my word."

She slumps with relief, so overcome that I wonder what the punishment would have been for her loose lips. Krisztina would surely know, I think irritably, and would only be too happy to be asked. Detailing our lady's alleged misdeeds is her favorite topic of conversation. The latest outlandish tale is that one of the lady's chambermaids has been dismissed, for having laced the lady's stays a touch too tightly, enough to leave an unsightly bruise. Apparently the countess had her manservant and the other two chambermaids lace the woman into her own corset so tightly that they broke her ribs. Some even whisper that her lungs were punctured, that she almost died before being sent home to recuperate.

I wouldn't be inclined to believe this for a moment, were it not for the fact that I haven't seen the girl about myself. Something clearly befell her, though I doubt it's what they say—who would mete out a punishment so severe for mere incompetence? But her absence means that the countess is short one chambermaid.

And now she's in need of healing hands.

With this new information, I seethe with urgency, aflame with the fervor to show the countess that I can be of use. But she has still not summoned me, and I can hardly stroll into her chambers without any invitation; impatient as I am to court her favor, I know the dangers of being too bold. As much as I struggle with it, besieged by doubt and the prickling of my conscience, I can devise only one thing to do.

The next time I see Agata in the morning, before she begins her day's work, I slip some bearberry into her tisane.

She stays with me while she drinks the tea, regaling me with the details of her intestinal distress, as if she expects me to be goggle-eyed with fascination over every stray fart. It never ceases to amaze me how some folk revel in their own ailments. For once, I egg her on until I see beads of sweat begin to pearl on her forehead. Bearberry is not a kind herb; I would never have resorted to it were my own need not so great. But at the very least, it will do no lasting damage beyond a day's severe distress.

"Anna," she struggles, fisting a hand against her churning gut. "I think—"

I have a basin ready for her when she abruptly purges the contents of her stomach. My own shoulders hunch with sympathy, my stomach clenching like a fist with guilt, as the poor woman heaves helplessly with convulsions. She looks up at me, teary-eyed, haggard with pain. "But, it's making me worse, what—" Another violent retch cuts her off.

"Sometimes chamomile can cause purging," I lie. "Especially if the belly is already upset. Did you indulge in anything overspiced last night?"

I know the answer is yes, because it always is. Pressing her trembling lips together, she shoots me a guilty look. "Aye, I did," she admits. "But only a bite, two at most! How could it have—" I look away, my skin crawling with guilt, as another grievous bout overtakes her. When it passes, she glances up at me desperately, panting with exertion. "How will I tend to the lady's room in this state?" she gasps. "What if I should befoul her things? She would whip me, she . . ." She dissolves into tears, weeping over the slop basin.

"What if I were to go in your place?" I offer. "Would that help?"

She shakes her head hard, swiping her hand over her mouth. "You aren't a maidservant, not fit to attend to the lady's quarters." Contrite as I am, it raises my hackles that this foolish, undisciplined woman would think herself above me. "Maybe one of the others could . . ." She trails off, realizing that the other maidservants have already flocked to their duties.

"The others have gone, and you're in no fit state to serve," I counter. "Give me your work dress, and I shall take your place for the day. The lady hardly bothers with who tends to her hearth and washing water, I'm sure." This is a lie of course. The countess will surely take exception to my sudden presence, but I plan to cross that bridge when I come to it. "I'll do just as well as you—and you will lie here, quiet, and recover your strength."

She casts me another doubtful look, heavy with misgivings—*What have you done to this poor woman, Anna,* I think, *for your own miserable gain?*—then nods reluctantly, reaching for the basin. "Just remember," she says hoarsely, her throat spasming as the bearberry torques her innards again. "Should she order you to do something, do it, at once, exactly as she tells you. And if her husband is about, you'd be wise to make yourself scarce."

I nod grimly, my suspicions confirmed once again. "Thank you, Agata. I'll do as you say."

In my borrowed work dress, I hurry through the keep's oppressive corridors. The innermost hallways always feel like midnight, even at the very break of dawn. They have no windows, and the meager light shed by the candle sconces barely pierces all that dark. And their frail flicker throws such ghastly shadows, skittering like spiders up the walls, that sometimes I think it would almost be better to simply succumb to the darkness. Creep blindly through it like a mole rather than resisting in vain.

The countess is still sleeping when I let myself in, slipping on mouse-quiet feet to stoke her hearth. Her chambermaids have not yet risen, either, so we are left alone. It smells like a different world up here compared to the rat shit and mildew of the cellars, an airy, floral haven shot through with the bright peal of citron. I steal thieving little looks at the lady as I clean, compelled by the way the shadow of her canopy competes with the dawn's pale light to play upon her cheeks. She is paler than normal, I note, her skin a touch sallow, high points of fire burning on her cheekbones. Her sleep is uneasy, restless; she whimpers a little in her dreams, like a pained pup. It twists my heart to hear it.

By the time I've filled her basin, one of the other chambermaids has come in. I keep to the corners, dusting the windowsill as she helps the countess rise, draping a velvet housecoat over her shoulders and leading her to the vanity to dress her hair.

"Nothing too complicated, Judit," the countess says, her low voice a rusty rasp. She peers closely at her reflection in the mirror, meeting her own dark eyes as she prods at their corners, tutting dispiritedly at the blue half-moons of fatigue beneath. "What a weary wretch I look, so blanched and sluggish and damnably old. Not a single rose in my cheeks or lips. I've a mind to retire again after I break my fast. If I can keep anything down, that is," she adds ruefully.

"Aye, my lady," the chambermaid agrees. She does look a bit like Krisztina, I note, though her hair is a pale copper like apricots rather than my friend's fiery red, and tastefully restrained. She picks up a silver-backed brush and begins to drag it gingerly over the lady's curls. But her hair is snarled into stubborn knots, likely from a night of tossing and turning, and the chambermaid has unsteady hands. I can hear the bristles catching as they yank on the lady's hair—and her ensuing, furious yelp.

"Leave *off*, you ham-fisted twit," she hisses abruptly, snatching the brush out of Judit's hand. In the mirror, I see her face contort with pique. "You shall have me stripped bald as a newborn babe if you continue with this ineptitude!"

"I'm sorry, my lady!" The chambermaid gulps, her blue eyes huge with panic. "I did not mean—"

"Did I *ask* what you meant? Did such a question pass my lips, you ninny?" In a flash, the lady whirls around and cracks Judit across the cheek with the hairbrush. I stifle a gasp, and the chambermaid flinches with her entire body, releasing a shrill whimper. The lady glares at her, her cheeks splotched with heat, and I think of my brothers in the throes of a wicked tantrum. She is clearly in pain, at the very end of her tether, else she would not have lashed out like this—like a wounded animal.

Judit stands frozen, trembling like a leaf, eyes wide with terror. She has clearly never withstood the ire of wild, overindulged brothers, and she does not know what to do to defuse her lady's rancor. So I step into the silence, my heart thrashing like a caged bird. This may very well be the worst mistake I will ever have a chance to make. But I have no choice; I cannot let this opportunity pass me by.

"My lady," I say quietly, dipping into a deep curtsy despite my protesting knees. "May I try my hand at dressing your hair? I've a light touch—I promise not to cause you pain."

The countess's infuriated gaze flies to me for the first time, her eyes widening. "Anna Darvulia," she says, low, dangerous, like something hidden rustling through tall grass. "Do my eyes deceive me with a phantom, or do I truly see you standing here before me, though I haven't asked for you?"

I dip into another curtsy, flicking a cool but deferential glance up at her. I sense that I cannot allow a jot of my fear to seep through, to goad her with vulnerability when she's so irascible. "Beg pardon, my lady," I say smoothly, betraying no semblance of my clamoring heart. "Your maidservant has fallen ill this morning, and I was sent in her place."

It's not exactly a lie; after all, I did send myself here. Though my choice of words *would* suggest that Mistress Magda sent me. I can only pray that the lady never thinks to ask her.

The countess beholds me narrowly, torn between rampant displeasure, the urge to punish me for my insolence, and the yearning for the comfort she knows I can give. She worries her full lower lip between her teeth until it reddens. Even in her pain, she's unaccountably lovely, her tangled hair falling over the milky lace of her nightgown like some black, storm-tossed river. The kind of beauty that strikes up a help-less aching in the gut.

"Fine," she bites off, turning back to the mirror. "Judit, remove yourself from my sight this instant."

"Yes, my lady," the chambermaid whispers, hand clapped to her cheek as she scurries gratefully out of the room. She certainly flees more adeptly than she dresses hair.

Relief and trepidation sluicing through my veins, I take her place behind the lady's shoulder, gently picking up her tangled locks. I twist them against her nape as I brush so that the hair bunched in my fisted grip takes the brunt of each stroke, not the lady's scalp.

"Is that all right, my lady?" I ask, angling my hand so I can massage the knobs of her skull with my knuckles as I brush. I know how good that feels, from the head rubs my mother used to give me before her hands failed.

"It is," she murmurs back, her eyelids fluttering with relief, nibble-reddened lips parting slightly. I suddenly think, with an unexpected flush, that her mouth must look just this way after her husband kisses her. "If you would continue . . ."

"Of course." I let the silky mass of her hair fall through my fingers as I bury my fingers into her scalp, searching for tender spots. If her flux is so painful as to keep her abed, the tension will likely have given her a headache, too. When the tightness ebbs from her cramped shoulders, I see that I am right. She tilts her head back with a faint, grateful sigh, resting it in the cups of my hands, and I feel a tremendous satisfaction at having eased her pain.

"Forgive my forwardness, my lady," I venture. "But you seem aggrieved. Does something torment you?"

She takes a deep breath, then exhales it through her nose, the smooth space between her eyebrows cinching. "My blood is upon me," she says, morose. "Again and again and again, such monthly agony. It seems that I do not take easily to my husband's seed. As if both my soul and body are dead set against producing the heir he so desires."

Her eyes flutter open, impossibly black and lustrous, like polished jet, and she watches me in the mirror to see what I will say.

"Is it because you already have a son, my lady?" I ask evenly, holding her eyes fast with my own placid gaze. "Do you not want another child?"

"I do not." She gives a shuddering sigh, as if relieved to admit it. "Gabor—well, you have seen him. He is singular, so thoroughly mine that it is as if I see myself when I look upon him. Beautiful as the day is long, clever, so aflush with youth. So like I was, when I was young."

I make a sympathetic moue. "But my lady, you are not yet twenty. Still so young."

She rolls her eyes ruefully, her fingers floating up to palpate the delicate skin at the corners of her eyes. "And yet I wrinkle like neglected crepe already. How much worse will it be after another child suckles at my blood from within, draining me dry?" Her delicate features twist with distaste, the hand in her lap clenching into a fist. "Especially a child of Ferenc's, riddled with the taint of him, sure to grow just as fulsome as its sire. Sometimes I think I could not bear to host such a creature in my loins, much less withstand the agony of giving birth to it. And yet, it seems I will have no choice."

"I'm sorry, my lady," I reply, pressing my thumbs into the hollow above her nape. "A woman's lot can be so cruel that way."

"In *every* way, you mean," she says with a bitter huff of a laugh. "When Ferenc is away fending off the Ottoman horde, I feel as if I am hefting the whole world on my shoulders, all on my own. Like some bedamned pack mule. I look after not just Sarvar, you know, but all our estates. Keresztúr, Varanno, Léka, and Csejthe, too." She flits an inquiring gaze up to me. "That last was meant to be my wedding gift, did you know that?"

"I did not, my lady," I murmur. "It seems a splendid gift."

She scoffs, pressing her lips together. "And it should be, resplendent estate that it is. But how am I meant to preside over it effectively from so far away? As it is, it feels more like a millstone around my neck." She pitches her head forward wearily, pinching the bridge of her nose.

"And is the work of keeping it very great?" I ask her, partly to keep her talking to me, partly because I'm genuinely curious. I suppose I never considered that the rich have their own burdens beleaguering them, just as we poor do. I find that I wish to know what hers are, even if they're likely to be far beyond my grasp.

"Oh, it's just *horrid*," she mumbles, with such a petulant pout that I almost laugh before I master myself. She holds up a hand and begins ticking off her duties. "I must oversee the stewards, to see that they manage servants properly and maintain the estate. And not a steward has ever lived who was not an officious prick."

This time, I cannot stifle my laugh. Her eyes dart up to mine, mischievous, and her lips twitch with a restrained grin. "I see you know what I mean," she adds dryly. "I tolerate Aurel only because he is so effective in tending to Sarvar's needs himself, odious though he is. So much must be done, always. Livestock must be bred, crops sowed, furniture repaired, the ledgers balanced. And the tenants, well—they are forever unable to pay their tithes. I could live for a year off the oats, sheep, and wine that the Keresztúr vassals owe us alone."

It is an impossible situation for most, given the unforgiving winters we've been having, but I do not say so aloud. "That sounds terribly aggravating," I reply instead. "I'm not sure how you withstand such effrontery."

"Nor am I," she agrees vehemently. "And yet, I must also see to their health, for no one else will do it. And to top it all off, there is always some greedy scoundrel duke scratching at the door, harrying our estates where they seem weakest. Attempting to steal our lands."

I start a little, surprised. "Other nobles try to take *your* lands?" I had no idea the blue-blooded assailed each other just as ruthlessly as they do those below them.

She gives me a vindicated nod, pleased that I sympathize with her plight. "Indeed. You'd think such conduct unbecoming of nobility, and yet." Her lip curls slightly. "They know that Ferenc is away so often, that a mere woman holds those lands in his stead. And so they test me whenever it amuses them to do so."

"That seems like a great deal to contend with, my lady," I murmur.

"It is," she replies, chin dipping again. "Were I a man, I do not think I would mind it at all. But as it is . . . Well. Though I work twice as hard as Ferenc to keep what is ours, as soon as my husband returns, my effort no longer counts for aught. And whatever I did in his absence, he claims he could have done better himself. It is as if . . ."

"As if you accomplished nothing, though you know full well you did," I finish for her, as I realize what chafes her. The same thing that galls me whenever I think of being wed. "As if being his wife makes you merely a convenient extension of him. Another limb, rather than a full person in your own right."

"That is it *exactly*, Anna," she says in a breathless rush, her eyes gleaming with something like jubilation—elation, perhaps, at being understood. Then she casts the wedding ring on her hand a scathing look. "As if I am nothing without him, less than nothing! I cannot bear it, being so diminished. And if I do not conceive soon, I fear that Ferenc might—"

The doors to her chambers bang open, revealing the lord's lanky silhouette—as if he has been summoned like the devil by hearing his own name spoken.

"My lady Beth," he drawls with that sardonic twist I remember from years ago. His colorless eyes slide over me, assessing. There is something disquietingly predatory in them, though his face is otherwise weak-chinned and bland. Only his hair is remarkable, as black and riotous as the lady's own. And he reeks of some overpowering cologne, like amber, honey, and tobacco, so sharp and sweet it cloys the room only moments after he has appeared. I would have thought such a fragrance unbecoming of a soldier, a military man, but he clearly fancies himself a dandy, too. "A new pet, is it? I trust I'm not interrupting."

I see her twist her hands together in her lap. "Of course not," she says quietly, but I don't miss the furious flash in her eyes before she drops them demurely, dark lashes fanning over her cheeks. "Please, Ferenc. Come in."

He takes only a half step inside, slumping against the jamb. "She's certainly comely," he remarks, his gaze raking over me, lighting with a gleam I know well in a man's wandering eye. My skin crawls beneath his regard like a living thing. This lord is no better than the stable boy who accosted me; he only thinks he is. "My, my, such hair, such skin. All extremely fine. Where did you procure this one, Beth? Rather a cut above the rest."

"I'll thank you to keep a civil tongue, Ferenc," she says lightly, but again I sense that flame racing just beneath the surface. "Anna is a distant cousin, a penniless relation. From a branch of the family fallen on difficult times. I've seen fit to take her under my wing."

I stand bolted in place, both brittle and reeling, as if I've been turned into a pillar of salt. Why would she say such an outlandish thing, claim me as her cousin?

"But family nonetheless," she adds, delicate face hardening, a clear note of warning in her voice. "Do you take my meaning, husband?"

"Oh, I won't interfere with her, Beth, she isn't to my taste, regardless. Nowhere near plump enough. No need to stake your claim so crudely," he says, rolling his eyes. "It is unbecoming in a lady. In any case, I did not come to chastise . . ."

"For once," she mutters under her breath, allowing herself a hint of defiance.

". . . but to inquire after you," he finishes in an acid-laced tone, feigning that he has not heard her rejoinder. "I heard you were poorly, and I wondered if, perhaps . . ."

I catch a distant glimmer of hope in the way his gaze drifts over the lady's abdomen, and I steel myself for his disappointment and the violence that may come with it.

She shakes her head dully and averts her eyes. "No. Still no."

His long face contorts, fists clenching by his sides. "You are straining the limits of my patience, wife," he forces through gritted teeth. "Be warned that I am almost finished tolerating your antics. We have discussed this ad nauseam, your disappointing—no, *maddening*, unacceptable—behavior. Do not forget that I am this country's Black Knight, the king's greatest champion. And with all the latitude I allow you with your games . . ." His hooded eyes glitter so dangerously as they fix on her that I cannot imagine how she does not wilt under the acrimony of his regard. I almost do, and it is not even intended for me. *"I should have had my promised heir by now."*

"And you shall have one, Ferenc, I swear it," she entreats him, still with downcast eyes. My heart shudders with sympathy for her, wed to this boorish, overbearing man. "Please, just . . . grant me the courtesy of a little more time."

He surveys her for a moment longer, silent, his nostrils flaring. "I leave today; you shall have your reprieve. But come

Christmas, Beth, I will return for the duration," he warns. "See to it that, by then, you have remembered whose wife you are—and all the things I do for you."

With that, he whirls on his booted heel and strides out the door, slamming it viciously behind him.

Chapter Nine

The Tonic and the Bath

The next day, the countess calls for me.

I am not entirely surprised when Mistress Magda materializes in the cellar quarters before dawn, to drape a finer work dress over my pallet and instruct me to report to the lady's chambers with my midwife's bag in tow. Yesterday, the lady was so loath to let me go that I suspected I would be returning to her soon. "Your presence is remarkably soothing, Anna," she'd said pensively while I finished braiding her hair and leading her back to bed. She'd had me brush her curls for nearly an hour, as long as it took her to calm after the lord's riling visit. "Like a salve of sorts. And perhaps you could craft me something for this damnable pain?"

"Of course, my lady," I'd said, struggling to maintain my composure while my heart leaped inside me like a rising dove. "It would be my pleasure."

Now, as I dress, reveling in the softness of this fresh linen,

Krisztina watches me with a sister's apprehensive gaze. "Whatever would she want a scull for?" she frets, tugging nervously on a fiery coil of her hair and letting it spring straight. "I can't see how this bodes well for you, Anna. The closer you are to her, the more peril you're in."

She cannot possibly understand the fledgling kinship the lady and I shared yesterday, and even if she could, I know better than to share the lady's vulnerabilities with her. Though I do appreciate her genuine concern for me. "Her health is suffering, that is all," I reassure her. "I'd wager she wants to make use of my herbs before she resorts to calling for a physician."

Krisztina nods reluctantly, looking unconvinced. "Mayhap it is. But take care, Anna, will you? Not even your cunning will save you, should you vex her in some unpredictable way."

I grit my teeth, narrowly restraining myself from rolling my eyes. "I doubt she'll even want to speak to me," I lie. "I'll attend to her needs and be back before you know it."

She grins, stretching her arms over her head. "Oh, let's not go *that* far. Were I given a chance to be rid of the blasted cauldrons for a day, I wouldn't hurry back myself."

"Too right," Ilona confirms wryly, before favoring me with one of her sweet smiles. "Enjoy your rest, Anna. I'm sure you'll know exactly what to say to keep the lady happy with you."

Of course I will know, I think to myself as I ascend the spiraling stairs toward the countess's chambers, my mind bursting with images of the two of us sharing confidences by her crackling fire. My silver tongue is what the lady wants from me, even more than my clever fingers. I am so rapt with these imaginings that even wending through the gloom of the corridors feels less like straying into some gaping maw than it normally does. My step is light for once, despite the keep's toothy darkness.

But my spirits sink abruptly, like skipping stones plunging when their flight can no longer sustain them, when I find the countess white-faced and ailing, curled up wretched in her bed. Judit and Margareta cower in the corners, wringing their hands, as if afraid to approach their mistress. The kittenish insolence I remember from the day I arrived is entirely vanished, leaving a pair of slinking cowards in its wake.

"A tonic, Anna, quickly," the countess orders as soon as her eyes fall on me, sinking her teeth into her lower lip to stifle a moan as she huddles with her knees drawn up to her chest. "I fear I may expel my own womb if these cramps do not cease soon."

"At once, my lady," I reassure her, already rummaging in my bag. "And may I suggest that your maids draw you a bath? As near blistering as they can make it, without burning you."

"A bath?" she demands, lifting her bleary head. Despite her fretting over age, she looks tousled and exhausted as a querulous child, much younger than her nineteen years. "Is my womb not inflamed already, with an excess of sanguine humor? Would hot water not make it worse?"

I'm loath to bother her about it now, but I resolve to have her explain these bedamned humors to me as soon as she is well. "The womb is a muscle, my lady," I explain. "And like any muscle, it pains you when contracted for too long. The tea I will brew for you will help with that, too, but there is nothing like hot water to coax those tight tissues toward coming loose."

She scrutinizes me with a touch of skepticism, black eyes narrowed, then nods. "As you say, then," she says, flicking an imperious hand at the chambermaids. "Judit, Margareta—you heard what Anna needs. And make sure to fetch her anything else she asks."

They dip into twin curtsies, and even incline their heads to me, before scuttling off to do her bidding. *My* bidding, I think wonderingly with a giddy rush. For the first time in my life, someone else is carrying out my orders, doing as I please. What an intoxicating sentiment it is. No wonder the nobility and their ilk never remove their feet from common necks.

Half an hour later, after Judit and Margareta have hauled in a massive copper tub and filled it with bucket after bucket of steaming water, I help the countess shrug off her robe and hold her hand while she steps in, hissing through her teeth. I try to avert my eyes from her body as the silk slides off her shoulders, but she is captivating, so unmarred by injury or illness that her smooth silhouette seems like it cannot be real. She looks like dessert, I think absurdly, like something fashioned from swoops of heavy cream. Her hair is startling, decadently dark against all that pale skin.

"You aren't trying to boil and eat me, are you, Anna?" she jokes, as if she's somehow privy to my thoughts. Fortunately, I'm already so pink from the billowing heat that she doesn't notice when I redden further. "I would not take kindly to being the centerpiece of a feast, with an apple in my mouth."

I laugh lightly as she sinks to her knees, steam wafting around her face and curling tight the stray tendrils of hair at her temples. "If it's too hot, my lady, I can see to that for you."

"No," she exhales, resting her head against the rim. Water laps up over her collarbones, pearling the bow of her neck. "No, it feels divine. Just as you said."

I hand her a goblet of red wine stirred with chaste berry, black cohosh, fennel, cinnamon, and cramp bark, with just a touch of valerian to relax her. I had intended to brew it into a tea, but apparently her ladyship prefers wine to mask the taste of medicine—and in this case, the alcohol will only ease her further, so I complied.

She takes a sip, making a little moue of distaste at the flavor. "It tastes like skunks," she complains. "It had better do wonders."

I laugh again, more freely this time. "And have you eaten many skunks in your time, my lady?"

"No, but the woods behind the keep are rife with them, and the stench is unmistakable. And *very* like this, besides the cinnamon." Still, she takes another sip, and I can see the strain seep away from her features. "Oh, this is so much better, what a blessing. You have my eternal thanks."

"And I did not even have to consult a handbook to the humors," I respond before I can stop myself. As soon as the words are out, an icy flurry of panic suffuses my skin. What if she takes exception to this disrespect?

Instead, she lifts her head and releases a bright, delighted laugh. "Such quiet scorn!" she exclaims almost gleefully. "I take it you're not a fan of Galen's?"

"I know nothing of Galen, my lady," I admit. "Save that his advice has steered you wrong at least twice now. But I would learn, if you abide by his . . . wisdom."

She surveys me appraisingly, her lips still pressed together with mirth. "I would prefer to abide by yours, given the results," she says, swallowing more wine. I can see it take effect in the heavy-lidded glassiness of her eyes, the indolent way she rests her head against the rim. "But I'll gladly tell you of them, while you wash my hair."

I take the bar of soap from where Judit left it on a silver platter, and dip it in the water. I've never touched soap before, at least not a fine-grained bar like this; it coats my hands with silky suds, and releases a fragrance of exotic flowers and some beguiling musk I don't recognize. It reminds me of the oil she uses for perfume.

"What is the smell, my lady?" I ask, too curious to refrain. "I'm not familiar with it."

"Plumeria, sometimes also called frangipani. I love its scent. And ambergris as well. I'm told it comes from the entrails of whales, the leviathan creatures that roam the seas."

"I see," I murmur noncommittally, keeping my own counsel. The sea is so distant that it's always seemed more a tale than a truth, but I've seen Lake Balaton and the Raba river with nary a leviathan between them. Whales sound like a child's fancy, a fireside yarn.

"You don't know of whales, then?" she asks, amused, reading my mind again.

"About as much as I do of Galen and his humors."

"It was actually Hippocrates, another Greek physician, who discovered the humors," she tells me as I pour a ewerful of water over her hair, careful that it not sluice into her eyes. "They're the four bodily fluids that determine one's character, and cause illness when in imbalance. Blood, phlegm, black bile, and yellow bile. An excess of each yields the sanguine, phlegmatic, melancholic, and choleric temperaments."

"How would that be?" I ask doubtfully. "As far as I know, we're all of us brimming with blood and phlegm. And yellow bile is common when an empty belly purges. Though I've yet to see this black bile for myself, unless your Greek sage refers to tarry stools."

"You know, I've often thought the same," she muses. "What could this 'khole' mean, if not excrement? Perhaps I'll return to the Hippocratic Collection and see if I can find a clearer reference to it."

I pause in my soaping of her hair, taken aback. "You—you speak Greek, my lady?"

"Certainly," she replies, nudging my hands with her sopping head to indicate that I should continue. "German and Latin as well. It was part of my studies as a child." She snorts a little, almost daintily. "Along with less agreeable subjects, such as the teachings of Thomas Aquinas, for which I had very little patience. I was never much given to the study of religion."

"How wonderful," I breathe, thinking of the vast multitude of doors that must be open to her, that will forever be closed to me. "I can barely write my name."

She tilts her head so far back that she's looking at me upside down, with knitted brow. "And yet you keep such an immaculate store of herbal knowledge," she marvels. "How is that possible, without record?"

I shrug, failing to see why this would be perplexing. "I simply remember it, my lady. It's not such a demanding task."

"So *you* think," she remarks a trifle tartly. "Because it's easy for you, with such a sparking, agile mind that it leaps about like flames. And yet you are unmistakably phlegmatic, with your healer's heart of stone. So calm, collected, never a misstep or flare of temper. Perhaps even too cool for some tastes."

"Or maybe, my lady," I suggest, upending another ewerful of water over her head, "it's that I've never had the luxury of indulging myself with sparks."

She reaches behind her head and catches my hand, drawing it forward and threading her fingers through mine. A sharp, aching thrill like nothing I have ever felt races through me at her touch. "And would you like to?" she asks, her voice husky with wine. She plays with our tangled fingers, bringing them so close to her lips I can feel the heat of her breath skip over my wet skin. "Have an opportunity for fire? I am decidedly choleric myself, you know. Strong-willed, decisive, vengeful. And always very prone to flames."

"I should love it, my lady," I answer, my voice low. "If it will please you."

Again, she angles her head back so she can look at me, inverted, those red, red lips curving into a languorous smile. "Oh, it does already, Anna," she says. "I could not be more pleased that you've made your way back to me."

The following day, she summons me again.

This time, she is pert and refreshed when I arrive. Margareta and Judit are nowhere to be seen.

"Good morning, Anna," she says in response to my curtsy.

"I woke feeling quite myself again, thanks to your ministrations. I've dismissed the others, so we can pass some time together. Talk more as we did yesterday, perhaps. I thought you might help me get ready in Judit's stead—and then we could break fast and occupy ourselves with some pleasurable pursuit."

She wishes my help to get ready, I think, my heart soaring at the thought. *To pass time with me, even!* What a miracle, a marvel, an answer to a prayer I never would have thought to utter.

I can scarcely believe my good fortune as I help her dress, gently tucking silk stockings over her finely turned calves, drawing a shift and underdress over her head, slowly—and very carefully, just in case—lacing her into her stays. Finally, I dress her in a gown of plummy brocade, my fingers racing up the row of tiny pearl buttons, like drops of milk, that stitch up the back.

As I finish buttoning the lacy cuffs at her wrists, I notice a bright splotch of blood along the inside hem, which is slightly crooked. How would it have gotten there, I wonder with a pang of misgiving, if there is no stain anywhere else on the garment? Krisztina's hushed words float to the forefront of my mind, whispering of the seamstress whose fingers were sewn together as a price for clumsy work. Could the poor woman have been forced to correct these inner stitches with her fumbling hands once the dread punishment was done?

I dismiss the macabre fancy with an effort, thrusting it from my mind. The lady embroiders in her spare time, I have seen it. Surely she merely pricked herself and failed to notice a stray drop of blood as it rolled beneath her sleeve.

She watches me in the full-length mirror as I fuss about her, making sure that nothing is out of place. Her scrutiny is so candid and admiring that I struggle not to let it make me clumsy. "How exceptionally beautiful you are," she comments, "for one with ignoble blood. One would never think, to look at you, that you were born so common. Your jaw, your chin, the way your cheekbones underpin your flesh like tidy little wings. Your bones look noble, just like mine."

"Oh, surely not, my lady," I demur. "I'm nothing like you, how could I be?"

"Don't be silly, just look!" She draws me to her side, brooking no refusal, linking her arm through mine. "Imagine if you were in a gown like this, with your hair dressed to suit you. Where I am dark, you are unwontedly fair, but our skin, see? Almost the same hue."

I see what she means. Though different, our coloring is equally dramatic, and our features seem to snag and hold the eye. There is nothing unprepossessing about either of us, nothing plain or sturdy to hide behind.

"You are beautiful, my lady, which is as it should be. But sometimes I wish I wasn't," I mutter, averting my eyes from where she holds them in the mirror. "It has not been any great boon to me."

She cocks her head, taken aback. "What do you mean? What greater power could a woman wield than a face and figure that command awe and inspire desire?"

"For one in my position, desire can be . . ." I chuckle a little, wry. "Well. Decidedly undesirable."

She watches me, silent, jutting her chin to indicate that I should go on.

"It is not just that," I continue, hesitant. "The other girls in my village . . . they did not find my company pleasing. Not so much because I'm comely—many of them were, as well—but because of the shape my beauty takes. As you said yourself, my coloring is unusual for Magyar blood. They thought me strange, aloof."

The lady shrugs, pursing her lips dismissively. "Small minds. The fault lies with them, not you."

"Perhaps, but the end result is the same," I forge on, gaining in boldness. "And then the first night I came here, I slept in the stables, as I told you. When I woke, the stable boy was atop me. Had I not had a knife to fend him off, he might have forced himself on me. That's— That is desire, isn't it?" I shudder convulsively, like a horse twitching flies off its withers. "And I want no part of it."

She nods slowly, pensively, sinking down into her vanity chair. Without her asking, I come to my knees by her feet. She doesn't seem perturbed to learn of the stable boy's advances, I note, nor my possession of a knife. Like me, she knows such things happen far, far more often than they should.

"I see your meaning," she says thoughtfully. "And I can understand how, given your circumstances, you failed to find that coin's other side. But I disagree with your gist, which, if I understand aright, is that the liability of your beauty outweighs its worth as an asset."

She arches an eyebrow at me, seeking confirmation. I nod, because that is exactly what I meant.

"Everything I know, I learned at my mother's knee, much the same as you," she says. "Your face, she always told me, is your greatest asset, a weapon that you wield. And what she taught me of herbs was not to heal—but rather how to exert and magnify the little force a woman is granted in this world."

"My lady?" I ask, not understanding. What could be a greater asset, I think, than knowing how to stitch a wound together, or which herbs can be used to staunch the flow of blood?

"Cosmetics," she supplies after a pause. "How to redden lips and darken eyes subtly, without looking like a common trull. Which oils clear your skin when it blemishes, which remedies keep it supple when it threatens to sag. For instance, goat's blood mingled with milk has an especially potent effect when applied to the face."

She laughs a little at my disconcerted expression, a silvery chime. "What a lot of useless bunk, you're thinking. Such vain, silly nonsense. I can see why you would think so—and yet, how do you think I keep my lands, Anna, when my husband is away? What weapon have I against those avaricious dukes I told you of, when I cannot heft a sword or lance, or even sit a horse properly when hampered with skirts?" Her face hardens like sap snapping into amber, and she leans close enough that her breath sweeps across my face, smelling of caraway seeds and mint. "My charm, my wit, my beauty—they are what I have. *All* I have, to secure my place. Without them I am nothing. Already a ghost."

I lean back, digesting what she has told me, marveling again at how oddly similar we are despite the gulf of birth that lies between us. Just like I do for me and my family, she does what she must, for herself and the vassals in her estates.

"I understand, my lady," I say slowly. "At least, I think I do. Unlike me, you cannot rely on your hands—it would be too lowly, not befitting of your rank. So you make other things into your tools."

"Yes!" she crows triumphantly, clasping her hands with pleasure. "What a quick study you are, so swift to understand. You are like a gift—my own little sage, delivered to me by the wings of fate. How have I even done without you for so long?"

I can feel my cheeks bloom with pleasure, even before she trails appreciative knuckles down the left side of my face. "Thank you, my lady."

"Oh, no, no," she tuts, gathering my hands in hers. "If we are to be as close as I wish us to be—you must call me Elizabeth."

Chapter Ten

The Spheres and the Shards

For the next week, the countess—Elizabeth, as she insists that I call her, claiming that her name has never sounded so sweet on another's tongue—summons me each day to help her dress. I do so in darkness, relieved only by the pools of light shed by the candelabra that crouch around the room; Elizabeth prefers to keep her curtains drawn late into the day, allowing barely any sunlight to penetrate her chambers. Too much exposure will only mar her skin, she says, wrinkling her before her time. As much as I detest the cellars' murky depths, I find that, up here with her, I hardly mind the absence of light. With the dark drawn close around us, she shares her breakfast with me, an impossibly indulgent array of sweet porridge, candied cherries, and eggs poached so gently they burst into a golden flood of yolk as soon as they're prodded with a fork. My wonder is tempered by guilt at each new delicacy I try; how Klara would love the unabashed richness of the yolk, I think each time, or the tart sweetness of the cherry cakes.

But I find solace in the coin I send back home, and Elizabeth's assurance that my salary will only grow. And though I almost do not dare extend my hopes so far, I cannot help but think that perhaps, if I please the lady, she might even allow my sister to visit us.

Each day, she reads to me by the fire, sometimes for hours. I love to hear her speak in other languages, and she indulges me by reading selections from the Hippocratic Collection in the original Greek before translating it for me. I don't believe a word of these teachings—hot and dry temperaments, what utter rot, almost as worthless as bloodletting and leeches—but I love that I am learning what she knows, beginning to understand her thoughts. And I haven't seen a trace of the cruelty that Krisztina accuses her of. Merely kindness and a curious, attentive nature; a tart, ready wit; and an insatiable mind. I particularly enjoy hearing her read Aristotle and his treatise on the heavens, her avid interest in what rules the skies. I lean back on my elbows and close my eyes as she reads of celestial bodies made of imperishable aether, impervious and flawless as they transcribe circles around our earth.

Whether Aristotle believed that the stars hold sway over our human hearts, I am still not sure, but Elizabeth seems to think they do.

"Do they not sound so wondrous, his crystal spheres and wandering stars?" she muses as we sprawl together over the bearskin in front of her fireplace. "Charting the courses that our own souls strive to follow. Stitching us together from above, determining our destinies." She casts a half smile at me, faint and dreamy. "Do we not feel somehow fated, you and I?"

"Is that why you called me your cousin, to your lord husband?" I ask her, my cheeks burning with the presumption of saying so aloud. "Because you feel that we are—destined to be close?"

"It's because I don't want him touching you, should he have a mind to do so," she replies sharply, reaching out to trace the curve of my fire-flushed cheek. Nothing pleases her more than the thinness of my skin, how readily it reveals the activity beneath. "He thinks all our servants belong to him, to do with as he pleases. And yes—also because it feels true, does it not? You feel like my blood already, perhaps like a sister. My newfound kin, as if our hearts have yearned for each other long before we met."

"I have a sister as well," I tell her. "But what I feel for her is not the same."

"No?" she asks indulgently. "And what *do* you feel for her?"

I think on it for a moment, resting my chin on my fist. "We are so similar that sometimes looking at her feels like peering into a mirror. Just as it is with you and Gabor, perhaps. She feels like my own younger self. More tender, sweeter, mostly untouched by the world's cruelties. And when I look at her . . . the urge to protect her trumps all else."

"Is she truly so like you, then?" Elizabeth marvels. "It seems improbable for two of you to grace this world."

"She is her own person, of course. Quieter than me, and more biddable, always eager to please. I call her my dandelion." A smile skates across my lips as I consider Klara, all her hidden facets. "But she's more mischievous as well. She plays such clever tricks on our three brothers, confounding them absolutely, and they are never any the wiser for it. They do not even think to look to her when searching for the culprit, instead feuding among themselves."

"I'm sure you could pull a trick or two yourself," Elizabeth teases, dimpling at me. "Had you a mind."

"A mind, and a need," I add. "I'm not given to such mischief for the sheer fun of it, as she is."

"Well, she sounds glorious," my companion pronounces, reaching out to trace the slope of my nose with a light fingertip. "And if you prize her so highly, I hope to meet her one day."

When she instructs me to return the next morning with all my belongings, so that I may sleep on a pallet by the foot of her bed as her chambermaid, I can scarcely believe my own good fortune. I will be receiving two forints each month, just as she originally promised.

Finally, my family will have nothing to fear from the encroaching winter.

I barely sleep that last night in the scullery, feeling like I have swallowed stars, brimming with their fiery aether. When I wake the next day and begin gathering my things from the wooden chest beneath my pallet, I already know my departure won't be met kindly. The mutterings have grown in volume each day that I am called upstairs, though none have challenged me to my face. But they call me a witch when they think I can't hear them, whispering behind their hands. They think I've compelled the countess, caught her in my thrall. Somehow forced her to dredge me up from the muck of the scullery and stitch me to her side.

If there is a thrall, I wasn't the one who cast it.

I can feel all their eyes on me, but I don't care, not with my heart swelling inside me like the sun vaulting over dawn's horizon. Me, the Countess Báthory's new chambermaid. Me, Anna Darvulia, born in a village so small it wasn't even worth a name. Me, whose only lot would have been to catch babies like my mother, and eventually grow fat with them myself.

Instead, I'm here; I'm *hers*. And now that I've steeped in the fragrant darkness of Elizabeth's chambers, I'll never let myself sink back to these rancid depths.

Krisztina watches me fold my smocks, her green eyes baleful. "Won't you tell us all about it, Anna the Cunning, your new milk-and-honey life?" Krisztina finally spits when she can no longer restrain herself. Her thorny tongue is now bent toward me, as if I've somehow betrayed her, despite all I've done for her health. The thoughtless expanse of her ingratitude astonishes me. "How does our lady's newest lap cat spend her days? Tell us, does she have you purr for her while she reads to you from her wicked books? Do you lick cream from her cupped palms?"

"Krisztina," Ilona chides, darting a glance at me. "Let her be. Anna has no choice in it, and you know you'd be up there in a whit yourself if the lady had wanted *you*."

"I wouldn't," Krisztina retorts coldly. "That snake doesn't even know my name, and I pray she never learns it. Besides, I don't look the part, not like our Anna, with her corn-silk hair and twilight eyes. Half a lady herself already. And I'm no—"

I cut her off before she says it out loud. They can think what they want of me, but I won't let them speak brashly, breathe words like "witch" out into the wind, where the devil himself can snatch them. "Then I suppose you have nothing to fear," I snap, though I'd promised myself I'd be gracious with them.

"All of us have something to fear, from her," old Katalin intones from her spot in the shadows. "You'd do well to remember it, Anna. Whatever it is she truly wants from you."

I can't listen to them any longer. They seethe with envy, boil with it. Perhaps I would, too, if I were them. If she hadn't chosen me.

But she has. I don't belong down here, not anymore, and I'm not bound to listen to their welling poison.

Silent, I gather up the rest of my smocks and ball them carelessly into my cloth satchel. Then I leave this dank pit behind me, and step out onto the stairs that lead only up.

ΛΛΛΛΛΛΛΛΛΛΛΛΛΛΛΛΛΛΛΛΛΛΛΛΛΛΛΛΛΛΛΛΛΛΛΛΛΛΛΛΛΛΛ

It's early yet, hours before Elizabeth likes to rise. So I head outside into the crisp November morning, my breath rising above me like fog as I gather milk thistle and motherwort to replenish my supply. I think of Elizabeth as I cut them with my little sickle knife, and feel the tugging of the still-invisible waxing moon in the velvety sky.

The midwife's sight has been stirring in me of late, uncurling and stretching like a waking cat.

I never saw that shadowy opposite of glow in a person, not before I met Elizabeth. But now, when I close my eyes and look at her, I can almost see it, writhing like smoke all around her silhouette. I feel that same dark pull that the moon exerts, and I surge toward her helpless, like the tide.

Maybe they're right, when they call me a witch. After all, it's only a fearful name devised by the rabbit-hearted for what truly I am—Elizabeth's little sage, delivered unto her by the stars.

Thinking of her makes me eager, and I rush back inside, fairly trotting up the tower steps that lead to her chambers. Outside her door, the faintest sound draws me up short. It's both muffled and high-pitched like a mewl, a still-blind kitten crying for its mother.

Her door is heavy but well oiled, and it doesn't so much as squeak when I crack it open, just enough to see. Her bed is empty; so is her plush settee, and her vanity. But there are flowers strewn across the floor, crushed into the bearskin rug and scattered over the stones. A vase lies shattered among them, in a winking spill of shards.

"What did you think, hmmm? Tell me again. That because I have so many, it would not matter? That maybe I would not even notice?"

At the sound of Elizabeth's voice, my mouth goes dry. It's the same as always on the surface, rich and low and creamy-sweet. But beneath, there's a vicious, cutting rasp, a chill that slithers like shifting scales. I've never heard her like this before, but it's so familiar all the same. As if this is the voice that lives within her voice, the one that always lurks beneath.

My skin bursts into gooseflesh, from my nape to my soles, and for the first time I know why Krisztina calls her a snake.

"No," someone whimpers back. "I swear, my lady, it was an accident. I was putting a shine on it, and it—it slipped through my fingers—"

I crane my neck to glimpse farther, past the door—and then I see them both. Ilona, sweet-faced, cheery Ilona—so like my dandelion sister—kneels on the floor, her dun skirts hiked up so that her legs are bare. Why is she even here, I wonder desperately, when sculls have no business in the lady's chambers? And then I know. She must have come under the pretense of some invented task, in search of me, to let me know there was no ill blood between us. Just as my own sister would have done.

Her face is pale and tear-streaked, and every time she shifts she lets out that awful mewling sound, biting down on her bloodied lip. Because she's kneeling on the shattered remains of the vase; I can see where they've bitten into her skin, thin scarlet rivulets dripping onto the polished stones. Behind her, Elizabeth stands with one slim hand on Ilona's shoulder. Pressing, pushing, bearing down, grinding Ilona's bare knees harder into the shards.

Her face is avid, almost gleeful with delight. More rapt than I've ever seen, even when she reads her beloved books to me.

"It sounds as if your fingers are more trouble than they're worth, doesn't it, you clumsy little sow?" Elizabeth is smiling now, dimpled and wide, so sweet I can't understand how these barbed words fit with her face. "But don't fret, for it will be a very simple fix. I'll fetch my pruning scissors, the heavy ones—then you'll give me your hands, and *snip snip snip!*"

Ilona's face turns ashen with terror, and I can't help it. A gasp hitches in my throat.

Elizabeth's head snaps up. Her eyes fly to mine, slitting narrow and dangerous. I should turn and run, but it's far too late; I can't pretend that I haven't seen. That I haven't heard.

The change that rushes over her is so sudden, it's like I can see her molting. Her face sheds that vicious elation as if it had never existed, and she becomes who she always is. The Elizabeth I've come to know.

"Anna!" she calls merrily, holding out a hand to me. "Ilona did the silliest thing, come see. She broke Ferenc's vase—his *best* one, the one his mother gave us as our wedding gift."

Biting on the inside of my cheek, I step warily in, terrified that I will tread on broken porcelain, or show my fear, or do anything to make this worse. I stand like a statue, trying to quell my trembling as Elizabeth sweeps over to me, ignoring the crunch beneath her slippered feet. She takes my icy hand and clasps it tight between both of hers, dry and very warm, like embers.

"Oh, why that face?" she exclaims, peering into my eyes. Hers are so black and deep, so shiningly inviting, that I fear I may inadvertently tumble into them and be somehow lost. "You did not— You do not *actually* think I was going to cut this silly little slattern's fingers off, did you?"

"I . . ." I can't finish, my heart is so slick in my throat. It cuts at me to hear her call Ilona such names, but I don't know what to say in her defense. I can't even think properly, not with such dread crouching inside me like a poisonous toad. Do I believe her? Dare I risk her displeasure, maybe even her wrath, by protecting my friend?

"Oh, *Anna* . . ." Elizabeth bursts into ringing peals of laughter, lifting a hand to graze her knuckles down my cheek. "What nonsense. She broke a vase, a precious one; she needed to be taught a sharp lesson, that is all. And fear teaches caution like nothing else."

She drops my hands and comes closer, running pale strands of my hair through her fingers, like she might with a pet. I can hear Krisztina's mocking "lap cat" echoing in the hollow caverns of my head. "You believe me, don't you, my Anna?" she says glibly, so near I can feel the soft brush of her breath fan over my lips. "That I only meant to teach her to be better?"

I nod, not trusting my own pounding heart. I can't believe she would have done it. And yet, I also can't forget her face, that all-consuming rapture. Then there's the caution in her eyes, a serpentine wariness I've never seen before.

I have a sudden, lurching feeling that if I don't lie—and don't lie well—I will find fangs buried in my throat.

So I force a smile, gentle my face into the admiration she's accustomed to from me. "Of course," I appease her. "She broke a precious thing. She must—she must be taught." I almost crumble at the short sound of Ilona's betrayed gasp, but I must hold fast. For both our sakes.

Elizabeth examines me a moment longer, her gaze flicking shrewdly between my eyes. Barely breathing, I keep my face rigorously placid until her own relaxes. "Good," she says, her eyes softening. "I knew you would understand."

Then she lets me go and heaves Ilona up, clucking at her like a mother over a foolish, awkward child, rolling her eyes almost indulgently when the girl's legs buckle. "Go fetch a broom, and wrap up your knees before you ruin my rugs, you silly girl," she says, giving Ilona a little push toward the door. "And try not to bring the rest of the castle crashing down around our ears if you can help it."

To her credit, Ilona does not need to be told twice. Flicking me a wounded dart of a look, she stumbles by me and pelts out the door, dropping her skirts to conceal her cuts.

Suddenly there's a commotion from the courtyard below: the bellows of men, the creak of carriage wheels, the high-pitched whinny and stamp of stallions. Elizabeth's delicate face hardens, grows taut. "It's Ferenc," she says darkly, stepping away from me. "Damn the stars. My husband has come home early."

While I help her get ready to greet her husband, trying to hide the residual trembling in my hands, she talks to me in a desperate stream, words tumbling over each other like rocks swept by a river. We've avoided speaking of Ferenc until now, but something has slipped loose inside her; I hear her loathing for him laid bare, splayed out and dissected like a butchered beast. How cruel he is, how pedestrian, how far beneath her. How her flesh recoils from his grasping, icy touch.

"I shudder to think what he would do, if he ever learned of Gabor. And he thinks I am too lenient with servants," she adds, fidgeting nervously in her lap as I plait her hair. "That I do not punish them properly in his absence. That is why I scolded Ilona as harshly as I did, you understand. I . . ." She falters. "I cannot afford to incur his displeasure in that, too."

"Of course, my lady," I murmur soothingly, my heart turning over with such sympathy and relief that it quashes the sour tang of my lingering misgivings. I knew such naked bloodlust over a minor misdemeanor could not have come naturally to her. "You did only what you had to do."

"Elizabeth, please," she corrects with a dismayed pout. "Else it will make me feel as though this has driven a wedge between us. And I could not bear such a distance from you."

I smile at her, taking the liberty of stroking the thick fish tail of her braid before I coil it up around her head. "No such wedge exists, or ever could," I comfort. "My lady Elizabeth."

"You will dine with us, then," she declares, flinging me an entreating look in the mirror. "I need you there, my sage."

"But he's been gone for so long," I protest, uncertain. "Would it not rile him to have me there, if he wishes to be alone with you?"

"Hang what he wishes," she says mutinously, setting her jaw. "And I have already claimed you as my cousin. He cannot keep you from your rightful place by my side."

So I take a seat beside her in the great hall, drowning dry mouthfuls with rich, red wine. We're eating the finest food, tender dumplings stuffed with braised pheasant and simmered with paprika and leeks, but every time I think of Ilona's bloody knees it all turns to sawdust in my mouth. At least Ferenc doesn't seem any more comfortable than I am. He hasn't washed, or even changed out of his commander's regalia; his boots are still dull with the dust of the road. I catch him sneaking slantwise looks at me, his colorless eyes shrewd with thought.

I shift uneasily beneath his deceptively placid gaze; I can

see it for the lie it is. He's furious under that frosty veneer, all the muscles in his jaw drawn tight, notched like a ready bow. When he finally speaks, we'd been eating in dead silence for the best part of an hour, and both Elizabeth and I startle at the sound of his voice.

"My lady wife," he says, wiping roughly at his mouth. "Why are the fields not freshly tilled?"

Elizabeth sets her fork down, very deliberately. She's chosen a low-cut burgundy bodice for the evening, and candle-light gilds the creamy swell of her breasts above its rim. Her face is composed, but I'm close enough to see the frantic tick-ing of her heart in the hollow of her throat, like an insect trapped under her skin. "Excuse me, husband. Did you say 'tilled'?"

"Yes, *tilled*." He throws down his fork with a clatter, sway-ing his jaw from side to side. "The thing that must happen to the soil after harvest, before the land is planted in spring. Our land, Beth, which you've been stewarding in my absence. Or should have been, at least."

I see her swallow, the convulsion of her slender throat. "I have been otherwise occupied," she forces through clenched teeth. "With the four other estates that I manage, all on my own, while you are gone. Perhaps you recollect them? Or shall I list their names for you?"

He slams his fist on the table, once, a single controlled thump that still slops wine from our goblets. "Do not dare speak to me of our holdings," he grates out, his voice rising. "I made the rounds today, spoke to the headmen of the Sarvar villages. We have seventeen of those, if you've bothered to count. You've not shown your face in a single one for the past month. Those are *our* people, our vassals. And as my wife, you're meant to tend to them in my stead." He flashes an enraged look at me. "Not play house with your new pet."

"You forget yourself, Ferenc, if you think you can speak to me this way," Elizabeth says softly, but I can hear the steel beneath that spun-silk tone. "I was a lady and a Báthory long before I became your wife."

"That you wouldn't take the Nadasdy name means nothing anymore, do you not understand that? I allowed it then only out of respect for your family's greater standing."

Ferenc's face roils with subdued rage, growing thunderous, and his clouded, suspicious gaze flicks to me again. He pushes back from the table, mouth working, his words tolling in my head. The room seems to swell and throb with menace, pulsing around us like the chambers of a malevolent heart.

"But if you insist on carrying on like this—on abdicating your responsibilities—I will have no choice," he goes on. "I have family, too, Beth. Unmarried uncles and cousins I could call upon, who would only be too pleased to watch over my holdings while I am gone. To watch over *you*."

I can imagine how she must hate this, the thought of Nadasdy men roaming her domain. She bows her head, shining curls trembling in the candlelight, and when she looks up her lips quiver with anger. Her eyes are huge and glistening, but she does not trust herself to speak—not even when he stalks over to me.

I freeze where I sit, all my muscles turning taut. It takes everything I have not to tremble when he slides a cold hand over my shoulder and up my neck, twines my braid around his wrist. But when he yanks my head back, arching my neck, I cannot suppress a gasp. The smell of him, sweat and horse musk and the drench of the noisome cologne I remember, nearly makes me gag.

"Is this your doing?" he croons into my ear. "I have ears in this keep, you know. And I've heard tell of you, my lady wife's snow-skinned sorceress, her favored dove. Have you been whispering sweet nothings to Beth, distracting her from her work? Helping her play her games?"

Elizabeth scrapes back from the table so abruptly the chair tips over, clattering against the stones. "Unhand her, you black-hearted bastard," she hisses, eyes blazing, hands curling into claws by her side. I have never seen her so riled, so furious—and a warm vein of pleasure threads through my encasing terror, fissuring its surface. That she would attack him in my defense without a thought spared for her own safety. No one has ever done such a thing for me before. "It is not her fault that I prefer her company to yours, you wretched whoreson, you—"

Ferenc releases me in one fell swoop, so abruptly that I slither to the ground before I can catch myself. He storms over to Elizabeth and backhands her casually across the face. Though she doesn't make a sound, I can see her lip split like ripe fruit from the force of the blow, a glistening spatter of blood raining across the pale skin of her chest.

"I see you've quite forgotten yourself in my absence, you feral little bitch," he remarks, so composed he may as well be discussing the onset of winter. While I gape at them, disbelieving, he grasps her viciously by the upper arm and hauls her toward the doors. "It will be my very great pleasure to remind you whom you belong to, before I take my leave again tomorrow."

She has the chance to fling one last, desperate look over her shoulder at me as he drags her through the doors.

Chapter Eleven

The Salve and the Kiss

The next morning, I dare slip into Elizabeth's dark chambers only once Ferenc is gone, his company thundering out of the courtyard in a cloud of dust and churning hooves.

"Elizabeth?" I whisper warily, padding over to her bed. The velvet curtains are drawn; there is barely a chink of light, though I come with a candle to pierce the gloom. "Are you awake?"

She doesn't respond beyond a low, anguished whimper. I creep up onto the bed on my knees, bending over her. She's cocooned in covers, only the unruly mop of her hair peeking out at the top. Gently, I peel its corner off her so I can see her face.

"Shhh, it's all right," I soothe when she bites back a sob. "I just want to help . . ."

The words wither in my mouth, shrivel like dead petals, when she shifts out of the shadows enough to show her face.

Besides her crusted lip, half of her face is such a mottled mess that it seems grafted onto her from some feckless survivor of a barroom brawl. Her left cheek is a doughy mass of black and blue, and there's an angry cut along her cheekbone, where that demon clad in human flesh must have struck her with one of his rings. Above it, her left eye is so swollen it nearly disappears, slitted closed so that her lashes mesh together.

"My God," I manage, my heart pounding at the very base of my throat, as if it has lifted itself up with rage. "What has that monster done to you?"

She huffs a dry wisp of a laugh. "Nothing he hasn't done before, Anna," she croaks, a single tear sliding down her battered cheek.

"But the pain must be terrible!"

"It is not the pain that concerns me," she says, stifling a groan when I graze the most glancing touch over her skin. She scrambles clumsily up to sitting, eyes flaring wide with panic as she turns toward me, offering her face for my inspection. "Tell me, does it look very dreadful? Do you—do you think I might scar? Do not lie to me, Anna! Oh, if that bastard has ruined my *face*—"

"He has done nothing that cannot be undone, do not fret," I assure her with blithe confidence though I am far from certain this is the case, sensing that she has too much worry of her own to wrestle with my doubt. What she needs is my fortitude, my so-called healer's heart of stone. "I'll make you a tonic for the pain, and a poultice for the swelling. The worst of it will pass in a blink, you'll see. And you will be yourself again, just as lovely as you were."

She nods fretfully, worrying delicately at her burst lip with the tip of her tongue. "Is he . . . Has he gone?" she whispers. "As long as he is not here, I can bear anything."

"He is, my lady," I reply grimly, wishing he were truly gone, dead and buried like my own beast of a father. "We are alone, and I will take care of you."

As I grind witch hazel, comfrey, arnica, mullein flower, and honey into a paste, I find myself seething, so engulfed in great gouts of anger that it feels as though I may drown every time a fresh wave of wrath breaks over my head. I know well what it is to fear for your life, cowering impotent while a man towers over you with his battering-ram fists, so much stronger that escape is but a dream and rebellion inconceivable. My mother and I made this very paste for each other so many times that my hands do the work of their own accord, leaving me to think. By the time I am done with the balm, I know what I need to do to heal Elizabeth. Not just her body, but her bruised and fragile soul.

I must show her what it is to be gently loved. To be treated with tenderness and care as she deserves.

I must be soft with her even when she acts out, when she channels the echo of her husband's brute violence through the conduit of her own misdeeds. It is like my brothers, who learned their wildness at my father's knee—only worse, because while they merely watched his blows rain down on me, Klara, and our mother, Elizabeth suffers Ferenc's assaults herself. His cruelty seeps below her skin and festers there until the only way she knows to rid herself of it is to lance it open—by slicing into someone else.

But there is another way out, through gentleness. And I will guide her to it.

The strength of my assurance calms me, and I hum my mother's favorite folk songs to her as I dab her crusted lip with water, apply the healing salve to her cheek. I've asked Margareta to fetch me ice from the cool house, and when she brings it I crush it with a mallet and wrap it in linen, then press it to Elizabeth's face.

"Oh, that's lovely," she sighs, slumping against me. "So much better already. What a miracle you are, my little sage. Such a comfort in the bleakest times."

Once I've cleaned and poulticed her, I tip lukewarm broth between her lips, followed by a citron tonic designed to heal her from within. She does everything I tell her, pliable as a child. "Will you hold me?" she whispers, curling onto her side. "I am so damnably cold, Anna."

"Of course," I whisper back through trembling lips as I slide under the covers and clasp my body around hers, cupping her in my warmth as Klara used to do to me.

"Could you stay while I sleep?" she murmurs faintly, nestling closer against me. I rest my chin on her shoulder and tip my forehead into her hair, which still smells faintly of her fine soap, plumeria and musk. "No one has ever taken such good care of me as you."

"You know that I will," I murmur back, tightening my arm around her waist. She reaches down to thread her icy hand through mine. Though the circumstances are dire, I cannot deny the searing thrill of being chosen to be so close to her, to give her what comfort I am able. "As long as you need me."

"How fortunate am I," she whispers, even as she begins slipping into sleep. "To have you by my side."

It takes over a fortnight to bring Elizabeth back to her feet. But I persevere, keeping up her strength with a steady stream of porridge and broth, tending to her face every few hours. Nursing her, at what feels a creeping pace, steadily back to health.

And holding her as she sleeps. By the time she is ready to rise, I feel that my body has been turned to clay and bonded to hers, remolded to fit the contours of her silhouette.

"Let us have air!" Elizabeth demands as she dashes to the window in her nightgown and flings it open, though I see she will still not risk her skin by drawing the heavy damask curtains. They hang before the window like limp tongues, thwarting most of the breeze. Desperate as I am for fresh air and sunshine after two weeks of dismal torpor, I am so grateful to find her face unscarred by her ordeal that I do not have the heart to press her. "And merriment, and play! I feel as though I have been disinterred from an early grave—rescued by your own fair hand, Anna." She turns to cast an elated smile at me over her shoulder. "And I intend to make the very most of my freedom!"

"Perhaps we start with a bath," I interrupt mildly. "You should not overtax yourself, Elizabeth. Your body is still on the mend."

"Hang my body, and any leftover weakness it may yet harbor!" she says cheerfully. "I feel quite myself again, all thanks to you. And I wish to celebrate!"

Still, I have Judit draw her a bath to wash off the sweat from her confinement. True to her word, she fairly frolics in it, splashing around and dipping beneath the surface like an otter. Giddily exuberant now that she is hale again.

"I wish you could join me." She pouts, settling down into the steaming heat. The water in the tub grows so still it offers wavering replicas of the candelabras I've lit for her, down to the flickering points of their flames. I can even see the rippling path her breath takes when it skates across the surface. "It seems I've become accustomed to having you always with me."

She dips lower, until her mouth is submerged, then her nose. Finally only her eyes remain above the surface, candlelight reflecting like diffuse pearls within them.

"I doubt there would be room for the both of us," I demur, though my skin tingles at the thought of our legs entwined, the soapy length of her limbs silken against mine. It unsettles me, tips me off balance, how easily I can imagine the sensation. The thought of it brings an unfamiliar pulse to life at my very center, a sweetly aching throb. "Maybe once we procure you a larger tub."

Both sets of her gleaming eyes, the true and the reflected, watch me unblinking. "Fine," she grouses playfully, breaching the water. "But fetch my book, then, the Balassi. And come sit behind me."

I drop the book into her damp hands, and she reads her favorite poems to me aloud while I reach around her, between stanzas, to tip a goblet of herbed white wine to her lips.

" 'Precious fortress, fastness dearest,' " she recites, a smile spreading like a sunrise in her voice. "Listen, Anna—it is as if

Balassi's Julia was to him just as you are to me. 'Crimson rose of perfume rarest, violet daintiest and fairest, long be the life thou, Julia, bearest!'"

I tip my temple against hers. "You flatter me, Elizabeth. I am no dainty flower."

"If anything, it doesn't do you justice. Perhaps I will take up a quill and write one of my own. An ode to my steadfast sage, loyal above all others." She tips her head back and forth, considering. "Though you are neither violet nor rose. Both are entirely too common, when you are something far more elegant and rare."

"Marigold, maybe, or snakeroot," I suggest, my cheeks simmering with heat. "Something meant to heal rather than please the eye."

"But why not both?" she asks breathlessly. The water sloshes as she squirms around in the tub, coming face-to-face with me. The lighthearted humor between us dissipates, and something smokier, more dangerous, wreathes up to take its place. "You certainly do heal as though your touch were magic. But you know full well that you are also very pleasing to the eye."

Before I can utter a word she reaches out, trails wet fingers over my cheek with agonizing languor. When I do not shy back, her fingertips sink lower, down my chin, over the curve of my throat and the sharp jut of my collarbones, creeping beneath my work dress's neckline. Scoring me lightly with her long nails. Everywhere she touches bursts into stippled goose bumps until my skin feels as though it surges from within, lit by the heat of my own blood.

While I kneel as if hypnotized, barely able to spur my

lungs into breath, she curls her fingers around the hem and tugs me forward—until I'm so close her dark eyes blur into one, her breath rushing sweet over my lips.

"Elizabeth," I manage to half gasp. My heart gallops as though it might buck straight through my chest, pulverize my ribs. "What . . . This isn't . . ."

"Be quiet, Anna," she murmurs in a throaty whisper, forbidden and enticing as a crossroads promise. Her other hand rises from the water, dripping, and snakes through my hair to cup my nape. She grips me so tightly it nearly hurts, yet I would have happily died before I ever thought to pull away.

In the space of a breath she extinguishes the distance between us, her plush lips sliding over mine. Even before she parts them with a silken sweep of her tongue, I am aflame. All my cool transmuted to fire, set furiously ablaze. She tastes like white wine and lemons and she kisses me with fierce and deft abandon, her sharp teeth sinking delicately into my lower lip.

"Elizabeth," I attempt when she pulls back to trace her lips down my neck. I have never been kissed before and it has left me dumbstruck and reeling, clutching her shoulders as though to keep from drowning, my fingertips sinking into her soap-slick flesh. I wonder for the barest moment if it might have been this way, had I ever let Peter kiss me. But I know, just as instantly and surely, that it would have been nothing close to this. Not even the pale ghost of a reflection. "What of your husband? And this is, I don't know, a transgression, a sin maybe . . ."

She exhales a laugh against my throat, soft as velvet, and I nearly shudder in response. "To hell with my husband, for all I care. And surely you don't believe this is wrong, clever as you are," she chides, setting her teeth into my skin until I gasp. "For who could know a woman's deepest heart, her sacred secrets, better than another woman?" She draws back properly to look at me, water sloshing around her. Her eyes heavy-lidded and lustrously black, palms cupped to my cheeks. "And who else could know *your* desire better than I could? I, who knew what was between us from the moment we first met each other's eyes?"

"No one," I whisper raggedly as she moves to unlace my stays, slides my work dress off my shoulders. So this, then, is desire. Implacable and all-consuming, a ravenous maelstrom that obliterates even the memory of modesty and restraint. I've never felt even an inkling of this for Peter, could not have fathomed that it would feel like such a delicious, honeyed madness. No wonder it makes fools of men. "No one, my lady. Elizabeth."

"Then abandon shame and come, Anna," she commands, rising from the water in a single fluid movement like some raven-haired sello.

A siren offering me her hands.

�※〜〜〜※

Much later, she turns to me and smiles.

"Well, while I did not intend to find myself drawn back into my bed so soon after I left it," she jests, her eyes sparkling with humor and the aftermath of passion, "I cannot think of anyplace else that I would wish to be."

"Nor I," I admit, reaching up, almost shyly, to tuck a lock of her mink hair behind her ear. "Did you truly know when you first saw me, as you said? That we belonged together?"

"Oh, you are so easy to read, Anna, for all your deliberate ice," she murmurs back, her eyes slitting with pleasure as I stroke her hair. "Of course I knew. It is no difficult feat to recognize a desire that mirrors one's own so well."

"Now that I know how it is meant to feel . . ." I lick my lips, considering. I understand much better now why I could not return Peter's affections. I was simply not capable, and I know that I will never be; such is not the pattern of my grain. Had I known as much before Elizabeth, I might have felt guilt, perhaps even revulsion for the uncommon shape of my desire. But I cannot, not when she has divested me so easily of shame before I ever truly felt it. "I do not think that I . . . I have ever wanted anything like this from a man. Is it the same for you?"

"Not quite the same, my dove," she replies. "Though Ferenc is loathsome to me, I do not find all men as repulsive. The farrier's son, you already know about, and there have been others since. Women as well from time to time, when I have a mind. It is easier, in a way; I need not trouble myself to hide them from my husband. My female lovers do not bother Ferenc, since they cannot make a cuckold of him." Her lips curve a touch wickedly, her eyes lighting like little torches. "It is the choler that lives in me, I suppose, the coiled passion at my core. It has never seen fit to discriminate. Not when it could have everything instead."

"Well, I am not that way," I say, more boldly than I feel;

so that is what Ferenc meant, when he spoke of her pets. The thought of Elizabeth with others turns my stomach. "I have only ever wanted you," I realize aloud.

"And rest assured you have me," she whispers, reaching for my hand and wreathing our fingers together, trailing our joint knuckles over her lips. "And while Ferenc is away, we are free to indulge, to enjoy ourselves together. You've worked too hard, Anna, taking care of me. I wish to spoil you in return."

"Being with you like this is more than enough indulgence," I say honestly. "I wish for nothing more."

She nuzzles her nose against mine, wrinkling hers adorably. "Hardly. This was just for starters. I mean for us to have *much* more fun. I know what we shall do—we shall have a ball, just for the two of us, after dinner! We must find you a dress first, of course, one to complement your face. I may be taller, but otherwise we're of a size. I'm sure we shall find something perfect among my gowns. And then I shall be *your* chambermaid!"

"My—have you lost your wits, Elizabeth?" I gape at her as she leaps out of bed, blissfully unconcerned by her nakedness. "What would the other servants *think*? They hate me enough already for how well you treat me. Flaunting your favor this way, it wouldn't be fitting—"

"Oh, please, what is *fitting*, after the morning we've just had?" she demands, arching a brow. "Who's to decide but us? It's fitting if we say it is, and we do. Here, help me into my dressing gown, and we shall look together!"

Half an hour later, we've sifted through her vast wardrobe and drawn out two gowns, one for me and one for her. She's chosen gem hues that complement each other, a deep sapphire brocade for me—"To bring out the jewels in your eyes!"—and a resplendent amethyst trimmed with Venetian lace for her. Rather than allowing me to lace her into her stays, she remains in her dressing gown and coaxes a corset over my head, directing me to cling to the bedpost so she may lace me up instead.

"My ribs," I gasp as all the breath flees out of me in the crush. I've never been squeezed into a corset in my whole life. "God's truth, Elizabeth, is it always thus? How do you manage to draw breath?"

"Sparingly," she supplies, giddy with laughter. "Breath is not vital to a lady, as you will learn. Not at the expense of bosom and posture, at any rate."

Though I doubt she has ever had cause to dress herself, her fingers are nimble as she attends to me while I stand with blazing cheeks, torn between heady elation and a burning sense of impropriety. Somehow this feels much more sacrilegious than anything we've already done in her bed. Once she's finished, the blue gown falls over my head in a heavy, perfumed spill, and then she guides me to her vanity, draping a towel over the mirror to hide me from myself until she's done.

"Something understated, but exquisite," she tuts, considering, as she weaves her fingers through my hair. "You need to be framed like the artwork that you are. Not overwhelmed with tasteless curls and frips."

I sip my wine while she works on me, basking in pleasure as she dabs me with camellia oil, adorns me with her own jewels, and dresses my hair. Never have I been so cosseted, with such a light and loving touch. I can feel myself unfurling in response, expanding to fit the space she seems to believe I should rightfully occupy. Becoming who she envisions me to be—even as guilt gnaws at my outer edges, that I should be lavished with such largesse when my mother and sister have never even touched the luxuriance of brocade.

But even this is for them, I tell myself. Depriving myself does them no good, not when pleasing Elizabeth, allowing her to spoil me as she wishes, will ultimately secure them an easier life.

"Et voilà!" she exclaims, tugging me up toward the full-length mirror. "May I present my Lady Sage!"

The breath seems to die in my throat, extinguished by the rising swell of my wonder. The gown is too long, but its pooling length seems almost artful, intentional as a queen's sweeping train. The pointed bodice hugs the slim arrow of my torso, nipped tight at the waist and flaring to reveal the modest swell of my breasts. My hair has been braided away from my temples, coiled up and around my head in a pale corn-silk crown. An impossibly fat ruby, like a pigeon's egg suspended from a satin ribbon, sits in the hollow of my throat, its facets winking with light. My cheeks are still flushed, and the heat of it lends fire to my glacial eyes.

For once, I am not even dismayed to see myself shine so brightly. I wish my mother and sister could see how far I've come, for all of us.

"What was it that my beastly husband called you," Elizabeth murmurs, almost reverent, hands set lightly on my shoulders. "A snow-skinned sorceress? My favored dove? I am loath to admit it, but he was right on both accounts. Look at yourself, my love. How tremendous and splendid you are."

"Thank you," I whisper, my voice faltering, thready with emotion. Though I'm sure she did not mean it more seriously than a superficial endearment, "my love" echoes inside my head like the tolling of some majestic bell. *My love, my love, my love.* "You have made me so . . . so grand. So lovely."

"Nonsense," she says briskly, dropping a kiss on the curve of my neck. "I have only made you yourself—what you already are, or should be. Now if you would do me the honor of helping *me* dress, my lady. Our ball awaits us."

Chapter Twelve

The Harp and the Switch

In Elizabeth's company, and without Ferenc's glowering presence, the great hall sheds the heavy pall of menace that I remember. Instead, the massive fire roars cheerfully, and the clusters of candles cast a mellow glow over the room. Even the great stag head mounted above the mantel seems to have lost its hollow-eyed, leering aspect.

Elizabeth has me take her seat at the table's head with the hearth roasting my back, while she alights at my right hand. "And will Lady Sage enjoy some capon, fed on nectar and ambrosia until it expired of happiness, then brined in brandy for a thousand days to spice its flesh?" she japes, preparing to spear slices of golden-roasted meat onto my plate.

"Indeed," I say haughtily, lifting my chin. "I feast only on ancient, drunk capon that has met its death by contentment."

"Of course you do. It's a mark of peerless taste. And what of boar goulash, braised in our humble homegrown peppers and fruit ferried from the Orient, so rare and exquisite it has yet to be named?" she continues, gesturing with a copper ladle.

I pretend to consider, then turn up my nose. "Perhaps later," I decide. "When it's aged to match the capon."

She bows extravagantly over her arm like a dandy courtier. "As my lady pleases."

I eat and drink until my head spins, indulging in a compote of spiced pears, crumbled apple cake, root vegetables glazed with honey and citron, and so much wine that the room seems to drip around me like tallow, softening at the edges.

"Do you think," I muse between sumptuous bites, "that we could have some of this sent to the scullery, once we're done?"

"The scullery?" she exclaims. "Why ever would we do that?"

"I lived with the sculls, is all," I mumble, my cheeks heating. "I know they've never had better than plain bread and gruel, rarely anything fresh. And all this will . . . It will go to waste anyway . . ."

I falter, fearing I have overstepped. But she surveys me warmly, resting her chin in a cupped hand. "Of course we may, if it would please you. Though I admit I am a bit taken aback to find that my icy sage has such a generous heart for her inferiors. Tell me, what else would you have of me tonight?"

Elizabeth goads me into voicing my desires, and indulges my every whim. She shares mouthfuls of wine with me through kisses and feeds me pomegranate seeds by hand, holding out a plate for me to spit the husks when I've sucked off the dainty flesh.

"See?" she says, showing me the fruit's glossy crimson rind. Something about it, its gleam and fleshy size, puts me in mind of poison apples from the tales my mother used to tell me as a child. "It is just as I once told you. The very same color as your cheeks when something stirs you to passion."

"*You* stir me to passion," I murmur, leaning toward her as if drawn by a compulsion, my face pounding with heat.

"Later, my dove," she whispers back, tracing a fingertip down my cheek. "Now, I think it must be time for us to dance."

I glance over to the far corner where Margareta and Judit sit, playing the lute and harp. Neither of them were invited to dine with us, and Margareta meets my eyes with a look so venomous it could be distilled into poison, like a viper milked against a glass. I wonder, with a scalding swell of jealousy, if it is her that I have ousted from Elizabeth's bed. And if the two of them know what passes between me and their mistress, surely it is only a matter of time before the rest of the keep does as well. I almost cannot bear to consider what kind of grasping harlot my friends in the scullery will think me, so hell-bent on currying favor that I am willing to go so far as warming the lady's bed. Of course, that is only the shallowest, most vulgar perversion of what Elizabeth and I share, miles from the truth. But I know it is what they will believe, through the distorting lens of their envy.

Since I cannot do anything about it now, I push it firmly from my mind. Why allow such ugly thoughts to ruin a jewel of an evening like this?

"I'm afraid I have not danced a day in my life," I admit,

swallowing the last of the fruit. "I would not know where to put my feet."

She leans closer, twinkling at me with a close-lipped smile. "Then I shall have to teach you," she mock-whispers, rising and offering me her hand. "Judit, Margareta—an allemande!"

Her former chambermaids alter the tune, and Elizabeth leads me through a series of exaggerated movements that resemble nothing so much as a bird's mating dance.

"Would you cease pulling such *faces*," she cackles, falling against me. "Oh, I am fit to wet myself."

"I'm sorry!" I cry helplessly, dissolving into giggles myself. "It is just— It is so ridiculous, Elizabeth, how can you restrain yourself?"

"Perhaps we shall try something else. A galliard might suit better."

The music picks up its pace, and soon I'm whirling in mad circles around Elizabeth, my hands clasped tightly in hers. I doubt a true galliard consists of such manic twirling, but I am so giddy with her closeness, her grinning face a breath away, that the last thing I wish is to question any part of this. My lady looks so beautiful tonight, her skin like milk against the vivid amethyst of her dress. She has healed so well that she seems almost lovelier than before, impossible though that should be. And all I can think is that I have never been so happy, rushing around her like one of Aristotle's stars.

We're still leaping about like savages when one of Judit's harp strings snaps.

The crack of it echoes through the hall, so loud that both of us start at the sound. Our interrupted momentum carries us, stumbling, right into the wall by the hearth. I recover my balance, but Elizabeth trips over her voluminous skirts. In the sudden absence of music I can hear the grate of Margareta's harsh gasp, even as I grab Elizabeth by the elbow and catch her right before she lands on her knees.

"Thank you, Anna," she says, so quietly that for a moment I think she's shaken by her near fall, maybe even embarrassed by it. But when she lifts her face, I almost recoil. She looks murderous, tight-lipped and huge-eyed, so abruptly and ghoulishly unlike herself that I nearly do not recognize her.

I know what is about to happen even before she rounds on Judit—and I have no idea how to stop it, to derail her from this path.

"Tell me, Judit," she begins, and there it is—that serpentine note of danger I've heard in her voice only once before. There is something so insidious to it, as though it might slither deep inside you, insinuate itself into your hiddenmost fissures. "Is your service to me a very great burden to you?"

Judit's mouth works feebly, but no words emerge. Tendons stand out stark in her long, thin neck, and glossy tears bead in her eyes. "N-no, my lady," she finally manages through trembling lips. "Never."

Elizabeth nods with a theatrical pensiveness. "So I do not ask very much of you, then, you would agree?"

"No, my lady."

She wrinkles her nose delicately, as if in thought. "I see. Forgive me, sometimes I cannot be sure what is real and what is my own fancy, so tell me this as well—was it you tending to me this past week, waiting on me hand and foot? Are you so very weary from these exertions?"

Judit cowers like someone stranded in the path of a rock-fall, hounded by a danger so inexorable it cannot be averted. "It was not me, my lady. It was— That was Anna."

One of Elizabeth's pale hands darts out like a flitting bird and grips Judit by the hair—exactly as Ferenc caught me by the braid. I can see the echoes of him now in every taut line of Elizabeth's face, the way she has learned to reenact his cruelty. As though she knows no other way to make herself be heard.

"Then why, you stupid, *useless* simp," she hisses through gritted teeth, her lovely face contorted beyond recognition, "can you not manage so much as a simple tune?"

Overcome, the chambermaid dissolves into sobs. "I'm sorry," she wails, at such a volume that Elizabeth winces. Why can Judit not see, I think wildly, that she is only making this worse for herself? "My lady, I am so sorry, sometimes the strings snap of their own accord, it cannot be helped—"

"Oh, can it not?" Elizabeth grates back, releasing the girl and slapping her smartly across the face. Once, twice, and thrice, the last in a ruthless backhand that wrests a shrill, helpless cry from Judit. "And could you not have found the time to check on it, before you brought it to play for me tonight? Do I pay you to laze about with your equally indolent accomplice"—here she slices a vicious look at Margareta, who whimpers and stares at the ground, blinking in spastic twitches—"while someone else tends tirelessly to my needs? Does that sound familiar, you wretched little leech?"

"I will fix it, my lady, please," the girl begs, hand clasped to her blotched cheek. "Just, just grant me another chance to show—"

"Oh, I intend to," Elizabeth snaps, her chin lifting imperiously. "Margareta, fetch me my switch."

When Margareta scuttles off, I turn warily to Elizabeth, my thoughts spinning like a spider's web, fast and intricate. "Elizabeth," I say casually, making as though to suppress a yawn. As if I am not quaking on the inside, fault lines webbing through my composure. "Why tire yourself over such a worthless ninny? Instead, maybe we could play a game of chess, did you not wish to teach me how to—"

I cut myself off when she darts me a quelling look, dark and implacable and a touch incredulous that I would think to test her now. "Later," she says shortly. "Do you not see that I am occupied with discipline?"

"Of course, beg pardon," I correct myself smoothly, though my heart is lodged in my throat like a peach pit. "I only meant that maybe you should not overexert yourself, as you're only just risen from the sickbed."

She nods, appeased. "You are sweet to worry over me, Anna. Do you see, Judit? That is what proper care looks like. Take heed and learn from your betters."

"Yes, my lady," Judit whispers miserably.

Margareta slinks back in like a whipped cur, offering Elizabeth a slender little switch. Though it looks innocuous, almost delicate, I know the kind of bite its slim girth can inflict.

"Undo her stays, Margareta," Elizabeth orders, her eyes ablaze. "Bare her back."

When the chambermaid is naked to the waist, Elizabeth orders her to play.

Shuddering all over, the girl complies. The song is faltering and weak, and each time the strings twang sour, Elizabeth brings the switch hissing down onto her back. The first few times, Judit swallows back any sounds—*Good girl*, I find myself rooting silently for her, *stay strong*—but when the third lash coaxes a stippled trail of blood from her skin, she can't bite back her shriek.

"The more you weep, the worse it will be," Elizabeth warns, struggling to restrain the wide, rapturous grin splitting her face. After the first blow, the mask of restraint had begun to slip, until it hung dreadfully askew. Now that blood has been drawn, her aspect has shifted fully, from fury into something almost transcendently inhuman. As if she's become an instrument of an unholy thing, a bloodthirsty deity working through her hands—perhaps even the thing she calls her choler. And for the first time I find myself aghast, truly terrified of her. "Remember, your fate is in your own hands. Play well, and it will stop."

"But it's *broken*, my lady," the poor wretch cries, her fingers plucking feebly at the instrument. "I, I cannot make it sing sweetly, not when I'm missing a string, please . . ."

"Then *you* will break!" Elizabeth roars, unleashing a volley of merciless blows. Eventually, though she tries, Judit can no longer keep her seat. She thrashes herself to the floor, writhing and screeching. As Elizabeth rages on, I almost marvel at the expanse of Judit's fear, so vast that no matter what agony she suffers she does not even consider an escape. It's almost a kind of twisted courage, that she finds it in herself to endure this interminable punishment.

Or perhaps it is not bravery, but merely that she is trapped just as I am. By the shackles of a family who can abide only so long as she provides them with coin.

And is it truly Ferenc's abuse, I begin to wonder, watching the corded muscles in Elizabeth's neck, the wild elation flooding her face with every fall of the switch, that casts her to these abject depths? Or might there be some black vein of malice riving through her, too, nothing at all to do with him?

But that cannot be, it *cannot*. I could not love someone evil, and yet I love her so dearly, shudder with yearning for her touch.

By the time Elizabeth tires, what feels like hours later, Judit is slumped unmoving on the stones. The room reeks of her acrid sweat and the cooling, copper tang of blood.

"Come, my lady Elizabeth," I say softly, taking her by the arm. She sags against me, wrung out by the force of her own wrath. "I'll take you to bed."

"Thank you, Anna," she murmurs into the curve of my neck, head lolling. I glance back over my shoulder at Margareta, who is patting at Judit's slack cheeks, trying to rouse her. When she meets my eyes, I mouth, "I'll come see to her later." The girl's face shutters, grows frigid—I can see she holds me complicit for Judit's plight—but she nods curtly before looking away.

"You were right," Elizabeth continues, yawning hugely. "I should not have pushed myself so hard. I am fearsomely weary."

You are certainly fearsome, my love, I think to myself, my heart sinking like lead. And how am I to contain you?

"But now the discipline is done," I soothe her. "And you may rest."

⋀⋀

Though she barely managed to stumble into bed, Elizabeth wakes not long after me, hearty and refreshed, as if the blood spilled last night has rejuvenated her.

"Good morning, Lady Sage," she murmurs languorously to me, stretching her arms high above her head and arching her back like a cat. "Did you sleep well? And enjoy our night?"

"The feast was lovely," I say, allowing her the opportunity to repent for the grotesquely outsized ire that followed it, to make even an attempt to explain herself. But she merely beams at me, making no mention of Judit—though I spent an hour cleaning and tending to the welts on her striped back.

It is like a nightmare dissolving in the dawn, dispelled as if it never even happened. In a way, I am relieved, for the longer the memory of Judit's anguish is allowed to draw breath between us, the more abjectly guilt-ridden I would feel for having merely stood aside, a silent, useless witness to her suffering.

When it's clear that she does not intend to bring it up, I continue. "We have our first snow," I remark placidly, gesturing at the window as I drip almond oil into her washbasin. I've taken the liberty of drawing the curtains for once, as the day is so densely overcast that no sun will dare threaten Elizabeth's precious skin. A frosty flurry wheels beyond the glass, flakes so fat and perfect they seem almost unreal. Like a child's first dream of snow. "Winter is truly here."

She gasps, delighted as a little girl, tumbling out of bed. "Oh, it's beautiful," she exclaims, crossing her arms over the sill, her cheeks flushing with excitement. "I do love snow. We must go outside, Anna, and catch it on our tongues as I used to do when I was small. Perhaps we will even take a winter ride!"

Snow is usually no cause for rejoicing in the village, as the harbinger of even emptier bellies and ruthlessly cold nights, but her enthusiasm seems to be catching as brushfire. "I would love that. It's been a long time since I sat a horse by myself."

She turns, cocking her head at me in question. "Have you ever had one of your own?"

I chuckle at the thought of such luxury. "Not even close," I say ruefully. "But my best friend used to let me borrow his. A lovely dappled mare."

"His?" She raises an eyebrow. "Your best friend was a man?"

"Yes." I tilt my head, considering. "Though I suppose I often still think of Peti as a boy, not the man he is."

"How funny," she ponders. "I've never even considered befriending a man. I would not know how to trust one."

"Usually I would feel the same. But Peter is a rare person," I say fondly. "Clever, well-mannered, so gentle. I've never heard him so much as utter an unkind word."

Her lips twitch, and I am run through by a sudden spike of fear—what if she takes these compliments as backhanded criticisms, for her own distinctly ungentle behavior last night? "You sound as though you are half in love with him," she retorts, almost accusingly, and I relax a fraction. Jealousy

I am equipped to handle. "Despite what you told me yesterday. Is he so very handsome, then? Enough to sway even one such as you?"

"He *is* handsome, but it has never made me want him, not even for an instant," I assure her, purposely leaving out his proposal. It would only irk her further. "We were raised together. He is more like a brother than anything else."

She nods, satisfied that he poses no threat to her. "And I'd venture that for all his admirable qualities, he has never given you a horse," she offers coyly, widening her eyes in delight. "As I am about to do."

"Elizabeth!" I gasp. "That is far too generous, I cannot accept, I—"

"Nonsense," she counters. "Let us get dressed, and then we will visit the stables and pick one out for you."

"I . . ." I falter, wrapping my hands in my apron. "I don't know what to say."

"Say nothing, then." She reaches over and presses a soft kiss to my mouth, drawing back to wink at me when my breath hitches in response. "And let me spoil you as you deserve."

After a breakfast of hot milk porridge and mulled wine, we cross the courtyard and traipse to the stables, swathed in Elizabeth's luxuriant furs. A fluffy dusting soon gathers on my borrowed ermine hood. Elizabeth has dispensed with hers altogether, letting a sugared sprinkle gather in her hair and sparkle in her lashes.

"How lovely everything looks," she gushes, parting her lips to shape the billow of her breath into neat little puffs. "So clean and new. All the dirt and ugliness concealed, hidden away until the spring."

"You think Nadasdy Castle ugly?" I ask, surprised that she might unwittingly mirror my own feelings on the keep.

"There is ugliness everywhere, when you peel back the skin," she responds darkly. "But let us not ruin this day by speaking of it."

"Certainly, not when everything is so . . ."

The words sour in my mouth as we step over the stables' threshold and into the musky animal heat—to find the stable boy who had accosted me pressing a girl against one of the stall doors. They're tangled in an impassioned embrace, the girl's smock pushed down to reveal the sharp jut of her collarbones, the pert bob of her breasts. Unlike me, at least she seems more than willing.

"What is the meaning of this?" Though Elizabeth's voice is soft, it slices like a scythe. "Have my stables become a bordello for my servants to rut in at their leisure? How extraordinary. Here I thought they were for the keeping of horses."

The two spill apart, the girl frantically arranging herself back into her dress. I recognize her now, though I don't know her name; she's one of the scullery maids, a particular friend of Krisztina's. By the flash of revulsion that gallops across her face before panic chases out everything else, she recognizes me as well. My stomach hollows out at the look, at having my worst suspicions confirmed. The rumors of my doings must already have reached the cellars.

"Beg pardon, mistress," the boy croaks desperately. "I was—we was just stealing a kiss and a fumble to warm up in this blasted cold, not—not rutting—"

"Silence," Elizabeth orders, sparing barely a glance for

him. "You, girl. What is your name? Beyond shameless harlot, I mean. I assume your mother saw fit to give you one."

"Orsolya, mistress," the scull whispers, flushing beetroot as she drops a frantic curtsy.

"Orsolya," Elizabeth repeats, articulating the name so delicately she might be tasting some delectable dessert. "What a fine, unlikely name for such a filthy strumpet. My husband's mother is called the same. Your parents must have had lamentably high aspirations for you."

The poor girl trembles like cornered prey, her eyes darting this way and that, unsure what she should say or do to save herself. *Don't bother*, I wish I could tell her. *There is no way out, save to endure.*

"Come, Orsolya," Elizabeth commands with another mocking emphasis on the name, turning on her heel and sweeping out of the stables. "And you, too, boy. I have a mind to teach your trull a lesson while you watch."

"Why spare *him* the punishment, Elizabeth?" I hiss under my breath as I fall into step with her, ahead of the other two. I find myself desperate to protect this hapless girl, shield her from Elizabeth's wrath. "He is the ruffian I told you of, the scoundrel who accosted me! Perhaps she had no choice!"

"Come, Anna, you saw that the trollop was acting of her own volition just as I did," she responds, casting me an acerbic glance. "Sullying *my* stables with her wantonness."

"Of course I saw it," I agree hastily, though in honesty I cannot see the harm at all—not when she and I were lustily *sullying* her own bed only the day before, and certainly not when she herself has a son out of wedlock. "But he—"

She lifts a hand, silencing me. "As to why I will not discipline him as he deserves, that is simple. Punishing men is simply not worth the trouble. A family will take even a broken shambles of a daughter back without raising a ruckus, but harming so much as the hair of a boy, a precious carrier of the bloodline . . ." Her voice curdles with disgust, her lip lifting into a half snarl. "Men are assigned a great deal more worth than women, be they common or noble. And I would rather not bring a slavering mob down on my head."

The unfairness of it, and the undeniable truth, rankles me as we tramp through the courtyard and beyond the castle's western wing like some solemn congregation, forging through the gathered snowdrifts until we reach the little pond just behind the keep. When I first arrived it was a lovely spot, shaded by aspens and firs and ideal for gathering water-loving herbs. Now the trees extend eager, naked limbs above it like pilfering fingers, and cloudy slabs of ice float on the surface like blind eyes. Elizabeth draws up short at its edge, turning to rake Orsolya with her contemptuous gaze.

"When you were little," she begins. "Did your mother ever scour your mouth clean of foul language, using soap and water?"

"O-once, my lady," the scull stutters, so terrified I can almost see her bones clatter with her shaking.

"Then you'll know I do this for your own good. To purge your filthy body." She gestures toward the water. "In you go. And do not make me ask you twice."

The scull flings a desperate, disbelieving look at the icy water. Her lips part in question, but before she can entreat Elizabeth and secure an even worse fate for herself, I break in. "Did you not hear the lady, trollop?" I demand harshly. "She said get in. And if you disrespect our mistress further by tarrying, I shall flog you myself until you've no blood left."

The girl's eyes fly open wide—she is as afraid of me as she is of Elizabeth, I realize with a wash of horror—and she takes a shaky step toward the pond, then another. Her halting progress proves too slow for Elizabeth's liking; she reaches out and calmly shoves Orsolya into the water.

The girl's shriek as she pitches into the icy depths pierces me directly through the heart.

When she surfaces, she is dangerously purple-lipped and pale, trembling so hard she can barely master her mouth enough to form words. "P-please, m-m-mistress," she begs piteously through chattering teeth, wrapping mottled arms around herself. "It—it—it is freezing! I, I will *die!*"

I think of how desperately cold I was the night I arrived at the keep, and that was months ago, and dry besides. How much worse must this be for her?

"Perhaps," Elizabeth allows airily, and I realize with a dread knell of shock that she is perfectly willing to let Orsolya die. "Or you will abide and be the wiser for it."

The girl begs for mercy a while longer, but her energy ebbs quickly as the cold pervades. I can see her become woozy and witless, her lids drooping over foggy eyes. If she does not emerge soon, she *will* die; even the dullard stable boy, the cause of all this trouble, can see as much. He weeps silently, clear snot gushing from his nose, but even he knows better than to plead for her life.

There is no one left to help her but me. And if I do nothing, her death is on my soul.

"Elizabeth," I murmur low into her ear. Careful, so agonizingly careful not to overstep. I must dilute her ire by offering what seems like a more complex punishment—more interesting than this, but one that will spare the girl's life as well. In the moment, I can devise only one. "The slut is at death's door already. And what have you accomplished, if you merely let her freeze?"

She whips her dark gaze to me, canny and shrewd. "What do you mean? What would you have me do instead?"

"Take her out and strip her," I suggest. "Since she is so proud of her nudity, have her walk naked to the castle and through the corridors until she repents."

Elizabeth weaves her head back and forth in the same considering motion I remember from when she was deciding how to deal with me, the first day I came to her. "I like it," she finally decides. "It is fitting, and just. Presents a certain pleasing symmetry. Orsolya! You may come out, you slattern!"

The girl is so weak and frozen through that she can only wade clumsily to the edge before collapsing onto it. The stable boy and I drag her out, but he leaves me to peel the clothes off her alone, struck by shame rather belatedly. The garments are frozen fast to her, and in some places I yank painfully at her chilblained skin despite my ginger touch. "I'm sorry," I whisper to her under my breath. "But you'll be warm soon, I promise."

By the time we march her back to the keep, Elizabeth has lost interest in her predicament, much as I suspected she would. Her malice seems to spark easily and then burn bright but fast, leaving her dull and bored once sated. She instructs me to supervise the girl's procession of shame in her stead, retiring to the library to read while I hasten Orsolya through the halls, nudging her as close as I can to every open flame. I only relax once I have her safely bundled in her pallet, with bottles of hot water tucked at her hands and feet. She won't be dying; at least, not today.

Though I am only helping her, the scullery echoes like a cavern with whispers of "Witch, witch, witch" every way I turn, the word snapping like the crack of frozen branches in the wind. But whenever I whirl to confront someone, I'm met with a bland, impassive face. Even Ilona will not look at me, averting her gaze from my eyes. She remembers how I failed to defend her and her knees.

It all makes me long terribly for Peter, my mother, and my sister, and even my mutton-headed brothers. What I wouldn't give to see them smile at me, speak to me with warmth.

Only Krisztina has the temerity to address me directly, and only to my back.

"You may be her favored witch now, Anna the Cunning, even her dearest plaything." Her voice follows me, so corrosive I can nearly feel it burning through my skin. "But as surely as she is a snake, the worm will turn—and then *you* will find yourself twisting, impaled upon the hook."

I turn back to her, slow and deliberate, unflinching when I meet her gaze. "You had better hope that's not the case, if you know what is good for you," I say grimly, keeping my face composed, though my heart batters furiously at my chest. Now that they have turned against me, I cannot let them see how deeply the loss of their regard wounds me. And I don't know what else to do but cling to my precarious ground. "For if I lose her favor, who do you think will stand between her wrath and you? And who else would send you food from her table?"

Her freckled face flickers with a rage to match Elizabeth's own, though hers is pure and somehow clean, almost wholesome in its earnest fury. "We don't need your protection, witch," she snaps, spitting at my feet. "Nor your filthy scraps!"

"Then you may well die painfully, and hungry, to boot," I snap back, bile welling up my throat. "I hope that suits your *scruples* better."

When I whirl back to the door and stalk out, the room resounds with a deafening silence behind me.

Chapter Thirteen

The Pennyroyal and the Fléchette

Sometimes I think Elizabeth must have two faces.

There is the one I see each morning when she wakes, cheerful and eager to meet the day and all it offers. That Elizabeth is indulgent and kind, quick to offer praise and shower me with affection, teach me letters and ciphers and the mind-bending stratagems of chess. She is also quick to learn: insatiably curious as to the properties of plants, how they might be applied not just for sickness but to augment health and bolster beauty. She makes me consider familiar herbs in entirely unexpected ways, as if a wholly different world exists nested within the one I know so well. And all I must do is tilt my head to see it.

I find it impossible not to love that Elizabeth, the one who is beguiling in a thousand different ways. I *want* to hate her, now that I know what she is capable of, but how can I, when everything I have—my fine new garments, the rich food that leaves me fully sated for the first time in my life, and most important, the coin that keeps my family hale—I owe to her generosity? And the pleasure she wrests from me is beyond anything I could have imagined, second only to the closeness between us. She speaks of such enticing things under the cover of the dark, the secrets and hopes she concocts for us.

Her favorite is imagining what we might do if there were no Ferenc.

"Can you imagine, if he simply never came back," she likes to muse while nestled in my arms some nights, blinking dreamily up at the canopy. Her eyes glitter like black water in the darkness, to match the wet glint of her teeth when she smiles wide at the thought. "If the war would only be so kind to us. We could be the mistresses of the keep, ruling side by side. We could even bring your family here, imagine! Your sweet sister and boisterous brothers, running wild in these halls. Your mother would never have to strain her poor hands again."

"They are already so grateful for the coin I send them," I always assure her, and it's true. She has increased my salary to three forint a month, more money than I could have imagined earning. I send almost all of it to them—what use have I for it, when she showers me with such plenty? The letters that I receive in return, written on my mother's behalf in Peti's clumsy but careful hand, are joyful and exuberant with gratitude. My mother reports that Klara is even packing some meat onto her bones for the first time.

I have so much to be grateful for. And even more to fear.

Because there is the other Elizabeth, consumed by the raging choler, like a dark twin that writhes close beneath the surface. Sometimes I fear she will tear my beloved's skin to shreds. I can see that thrashing shadow in her eyes even when she is at peace, as if that part of her never quite subsides or rests. Even when she is placid, there is the distant flicker of a rage just beyond the horizon. Like the threat of lightning playing across a cloudless sky.

That other Elizabeth breathes fire more readily than the dragons on her family's banner, rises to rage like hot summer air whipping into wind. That Elizabeth thrust the head cook's hand into the hearth for burning her favorite poppy-seed rolls; the smell was hideously like roasting venison. I still can't eat meat for remembering it. That Elizabeth caught one of the maidservants pilfering sweets from the kitchens, and made her eat so many figs the girl was violently sick onto herself.

That Elizabeth haunts the halls like a lovely reaper. Only ever a breath away from wreaking torment and death.

And yet, every week that Ferenc is away, I count our blessings. As bad as it is, how much worse would it be if we had him to contend with, too? He is not the sole cause of her malice, I can see that now. Whether she was born with the ember of her choler already blazing within her, or developed it as she grew, it is undeniably her own. But his presence surely stokes her flames, fans them to ever greater heights. While he is gone, I can work at diluting the venom even if I do not understand it, gently quell her when she bursts into rage like a phoenix, ashes raining everywhere. Because of me, the clumsy cook retains use of her hand, and the gluttonous maidservant was able to expel the sticky mass of unchewed figs that would have choked her otherwise. Because of me, unsightly chilblains are the worst of lusty Orsolya's fate.

You'd never know it from the foul looks they fling me, but I do what I can to watch over them, cleaving to the corners of every violent spectacle. Subverting the worst of Elizabeth's will whenever I am able, bringing her to some uneasy balance.

I take some comfort in the fact that she has never raised a hand to me. Her affection and regard for me seem unshakable, entirely at odds with how easily she inflicts violence on others; it makes me believe there must be some hope for her yet.

And then Ferenc returns home for Christmas, and dashes all my efforts to hell.

WWWWWWWWWWWWWWWWWWWWWWWWWWWWWWWWWWWWWW

"I. Will. *Not*."

Elizabeth paces wildly across the confines of her chambers, storming back and forth, spinning on her heel like a whirling dervish every time she encounters a wall. More mobile obstacles, she kicks or pitches over, until the two of us are standing in a jagged sea of shrapnel. Were anyone else responsible for such destruction in her vicinity, I think darkly, they'd be lucky to escape with their life. Her hair tumbles in snarled curls around her stark-white face, and her lower lip blazes scarlet from being dragged viciously through her teeth. I hate to see her chew on herself so heedlessly in her distress, as if she has no care for her own flesh.

But I can't blame her, not for this particular frenzy. Last night, Ferenc demanded that they dine alone, and she did not retire to her chambers to meet me after. I tossed and turned all night, alone in her vast bed, wondering how she fared.

Morning saw my worst fears confirmed; she came tumbling in with another livid black eye, her fingernails splintered where she had tried to fend him off.

But this time, she does not take to her bed.

"I will not bear his foul, wretched get," she hisses again, beating her fists against her hips to punctuate each word. "Even if he kills me for my barrenness."

"But, Elizabeth," I argue, "how can he blame you for what isn't your fault? You can't help it that you haven't conceived."

She casts me such a blisteringly scornful look that I lift a hand to shield my heart, as if she has nocked an actual arrow at me. "Don't be such a naïf, Anna," she spits scathingly, pacing away from me. "It doesn't suit you. Surely you, of all people, know how pennyroyal, rue, and angelica may be used by a woman in need."

"Pennyroyal . . ." I trail off, blinking stupidly. All the herbs she has named are emmenagogues, used to purge the womb of unwanted get. As the realization descends upon me, I roll my shoulders like a twitching cat, wondering how I could have missed the signs. It had not even occurred to me that the excruciating pain of her flux might have been artificially induced—and yet she was so familiar with the abortifacient's smell that she sniffed it on me the first time that we met. Which means I should have seen her desperation, understood what she was doing to herself. "Is—is *that* why he is so furious at you, Elizabeth? Does he know what you have been doing?"

She looks away from me, gritting her teeth so hard her chin juts like a blade. "Ferenc is many things, but not a fool," she murmurs. "He does not know for sure, but he suspects. *Strongly* suspects."

"But why did you not tell me?" I whisper, my stomach clenching with pain. I think of that first conversation I witnessed between them, Ferenc railing at her for failing to provide him with an heir. I had thought it his boorishness and cruelty—not the additional fury of a scorned husband whose wife was intent on scouring her womb clean of him.

She rounds on me again, nostrils flaring. "Because I am no fool," she snaps. "We barely knew each other then. How could I have known for sure you would not find me monstrous for it? Besides, my reason remains the same. I will not be sucked dry by his foul spawn, nor imperil my son's future inheritance. *My* child is perfection; *his* would be the devil's own get."

It is as if she believes she made Gabor wholly of herself, as though he budded off like some replica of her flesh and blood and bone. As far as she is concerned, his father may as well have not existed.

"But—every *month*, Elizabeth? Since you were married three years ago?" I cannot keep the dismay from my voice. "Such powerful, scourging herbs are not meant to be used thus! You could have killed yourself that way!"

"And I would have, happily," she retorts. "If it would have spared me this. I cannot suffer myself to live as the mother of his get, and I will do anything it takes to prevent it! Anything, do you hear me?"

I surprise both of us by bursting into tears.

Elizabeth is so taken aback she draws up short, as if bolted in place. I myself am so shocked I press my palms to my cheeks, as if I could ward the weeping off. But it will not be thwarted, boiling up through my fingers, mortifying and irrepressible. The opposite of my usual, painstaking control.

"Anna, are you—are you crying?" She says it so tentatively, with such incredulity—as if my tears are an unheard-of wonder—that a hysterical hiccough of laughter burbles in my throat. "I have never seen you cry before. I—I think I may have believed you could not."

"Well, I obviously can," I blubber through tears so thick they slide like a hot wash down my face. "And if you die, Elizabeth, if you kill yourself because of him, I will cry for months, I swear it. Perhaps I will never stop. I *love* you, Elizabeth. If you, if you die . . . I do not know what I would do with myself."

Her face softens, melts with concern. "Oh, Anna . . ."

She sweeps over to me, enfolding me in an embrace so tight my head tucks into the perfumed curve of her throat, so close that I can feel her swallow hard. I forget sometimes how much taller she is than I am, but now she rocks me back and forth like a swaddled babe, swaying us in place.

"My little sage," she croons into my hair. "My sweet, loving dove. You would help me, wouldn't you?"

"Of course!" I gasp against her skin. "Of course I would!"

"Well, there is one way out for us," she muses thoughtfully, resting her chin against my head. "Only one way that I can think of, at any rate."

"What?" I gasp, hope flaring so painfully inside me that my chest burns with its force. "Anything, anything I can do—"

"If he were to die, instead of me . . . I would be set free. Liberated by my widow's weeds."

"Die?" I twist in her embrace, brow wrinkling as I look up at her. "But Ferenc is hale and healthy, isn't he? I don't think I've ever heard him so much as clear his throat. Why would he oblige us by dropping dead?"

Her grip loosens, and she steps away from me—but her eyes, so dark and bottomless, with all the star-pricked dimension of the night sky, maintain their hold. "As I have often said, so many things can befall a man," she says with studied lightness, twitching one shoulder in a careless shrug. "Disease, malfeasance, accident. A fall down the stairs, a tumble from a balking horse, a slim knife speared through an eye under cover of the night."

Or poison, I can almost hear her saying. The unspoken word echoes in my mind, expanding in volume, like a whisper growing into a shout.

Poison him, Anna, that is what she is truly saying. *Poison him for me.*

"Are you—" My heart seems to have grown and hardened in my chest, ossified into a rough-skinned stone that bangs against my lungs. "Are you truly asking me to kill him?"

"Anna, mind your words!" she chides, her eyes growing wide with shock—but I can see a hint of an approving smile tugging a corner of her lip. "Who speaks of murder? Have I said any such thing? I am merely saying what might happen, should the world be kind to me. To us."

"But . . ." My mind races, whirling end over end, as if tumbling pell-mell down a hill. I would give so much, almost anything, to spare her pain. But I am a healer above all else, above even my love for her. As much as I loathed my father and do not mourn his death, I never envisioned killing him. The thought of such violence runs against my grain, hitches up hard against the solid, unyielding, impermeable core of who I am. Against my own inner star.

As I think, Elizabeth watches me avidly, unblinking. She

is barely breathing, though the delicate hollow at her throat thrums with the frantic force of her pulse. I can see the glinting ember of her hope catching cautious flame in her eyes.

It pains me sorely to huff it out.

"I cannot," I whisper finally, my own heart cleaving when her face falls. "I'm sorry."

"For what?" she says dully, turning away from me as her face caves into itself. Curling into her misery alone. "I did not ask anything of you."

WWWWWWWWWWWWWWWWWWWWWWWWWWWWWWWWWWWWW

That night, I accompany Elizabeth to the great hall for dinner, despite my misgivings.

"Apparently my demon of a husband has something special planned for me tonight," Elizabeth tells me smoothly, having recovered her composure. Though the lurid bruise around her eye cannot be concealed even with my best efforts, the rest of her is impeccably groomed, shiningly coiffed and perfect. Her arm is hooked through mine as we walk the keep's corridors, and I am so grateful to be forgiven for my lapse in devotion that my feet may as well be feathers, so light is my step. "To atone for his uncouth behavior last night."

"And he wants me there, too?" I balk as she draws me along. "Are you sure?"

"You saw his note for yourself, did you not? It called for both of us."

It did. My reading has progressed enough to allow me to decipher most writing for myself, though it is still a strange, disorienting thing to see my own name written, made indelible. *Bring Anna, please*, Ferenc's note had read, written in a smooth, assertive hand that sprawled across the foolscap. As if to claim even the paper as his own. *All has been arranged for you. Both of you shall be my honored guests.*

"'All has been arranged' . . ." I quote nervously. "What do you think that means?"

"I haven't the slightest." She cocks her head pertly, considering. "But Ferenc does have a marvelous sense of occasion; it is one of his few redeeming qualities. Whatever it is, I'm sure it will be acceptably diverting."

I do not know why I allow this reassurance to allay my foreboding when I know full well what Elizabeth considers sport, and what kind of wolf peers through her husband's eyes. And yet, when we step into the great hall to behold what Ferenc has arranged, I find that I have allowed myself to be lulled—and I am miles away from prepared for the sight that greets us.

"What—" I croak through a throat gone so dry my voice rattles in it like seeds in a gourd. "What is this?"

Ferenc lounges at the head of the table, its surface buckling with food. But at each of the four corners, there now stands a whipping post secured to the floor. Orsolya and the daydreaming cook who burned Elizabeth's pudding are lashed to the two posts on either side of Ferenc. At the opposite end of the table are the sweet-toothed maidservant and my own poor, dear Ilona.

I can see Janos and another manservant I do not recognize, likely Ferenc's own valet, prowling the room's shadowy corners, their faces studiously blank. They must have been the ones to drag the poor women here, I think, awash in loathing, as if I have a leg to stand on.

As if they and I are so very different in our service.

"A gift," Ferenc proclaims, reclining in his chair with his hands clasped behind his head. He is smiling lazily, a sardonic curl that twists my insides with its heedless self-assurance. As if he does not have four helpless women strung up like carcasses on posts. "I have heard rumors that these ill-mannered wenches have displeased my lady wife in my absence—imagine my astonishment when I found them surprisingly hale. So I thought, what better gift than a reprise? A proper punishment, unencumbered by the mercy of the fairer sex."

Unbelievably, he has the gall to tip Elizabeth a wink.

Something unfathomable passes between them then, an electric current that leaves me out. Whatever it is, it brings a gratified, almost feline smile to Elizabeth's lips. She dips into a deep curtsy, inclining her head. "It is a lovely gift, husband," she murmurs. "Very apt. I appreciate the thoughtful gesture, and offer you my thanks."

"Good," he says silkily, interlacing his fingers on the table. "I am pleased to hear we've ventured back to common ground. Come, sit with me. Some wine for you both? You're looking especially peaked, Anna. A draught might serve to relax you."

I find that my hand has drifted to my mouth, that I've sunk my teeth into my knuckle without noticing. "Thank you, my lord," I manage, eking out a clumsy curtsy before following Elizabeth to our end of the table.

"Are you all right?" I whisper to Ilona as I pass by her, keeping my gaze from straying toward her. She whimpers against the post, but I hear the soft exhale of her "Yes" trailing behind me.

A maidservant fills both our goblets as soon as we sit. I drain mine in one fell swoop, nodding at her to refill it. I will need to be fortified for tonight, I think grimly. I sense already that it will test me worse than anything I've borne thus far.

"Look, Anna!" Elizabeth exclaims, gesturing at our plates. "What a cunning addition to the place settings!"

I glance down, my breath rasping in my throat as my gaze wanders over the switch laid to my right, beyond the knives; the paddle and bullwhip to the left, beside the forks; and the wicked little fléchette knife above the dessert spoon over my plate. An instrument of torture set for each course planned.

My vision sparkles at the edges, swimming with flecks like tiny, swarming moths. If I weren't already sitting down, I would have fallen to my knees, lost my tenuous hold on myself.

"I thought you could join us, Anna," Ferenc drawls, his eyes glittering maliciously. "In this more piquant feast. I am told you rarely take the pleasure of indulging in such . . . rarified pursuits yourself. I mean tonight to be a gift to you as well, for the *unparalleled* service you provide my lady wife."

I glare at him, sucking shallow breaths through parted lips. The bastard clearly knows what has passed between me and his wife—though as she surmised, he does not seem to care beyond taunting me with it. He must know, too, that I have no stomach for these torments. Whoever feeds him information would also have relayed my role in tending to the victims of Elizabeth's ire.

"Thank you for thinking of me, my lord," I say quietly, not bothering to conceal the arch undercurrent in my tone. "It was most considerate of you."

Ferenc gives me an appreciative nod, as if acknowledging a surprisingly worthy opponent, before transferring his gaze to Elizabeth. "Well, my lady? Shall we begin, before our entertainment falls asleep?"

Scant chance of that, I think darkly, catching Orsolya's terrified gaze as she twitches to attention on her post.

"We shall," Elizabeth confirms, picking up the switch, giving it an experimental slap across her palm. "They do say activity whets the appetite!"

The rest of the night unfolds like some jittering, gruesome vision of hell, a mirage beheld through the wavering smoke of an inferno.

I keep my seat when they rise, and drink glass after glass of wine in an attempt to obliterate myself, while Elizabeth and Ferenc caper like Lucifer's own fiends, laughing and toasting each other. "To my lady wife, Beth," Ferenc proposes first, with a wry twist to his lips. "A singular woman, truly like no other."

"And to you, Ferenc," she responds, tilting her shining head demurely. "The Black Knight of Magyarország—and as fearsomely spectacular a husband as he is a champion. When he is so inclined, that is."

I can barely force a single morsel down my throat, but the two of them feast ravenously, as if the acrid reek of fear pervading the room is the finest aroma. They hold a strange, courtly conversation, him regaling her with tales of victories wrested from the Ottoman emperor's invading troops, all while he rises to lash Orsolya's back.

"And then the janissaries strove to harry us at our flank, can you fathom it, Beth—as if I had not executed such a stratagem myself with our own troops, only the week before!" he exclaims, bringing down the bullwhip to draw out a keening moan from Orsolya.

"What sublime arrogance," Elizabeth breathes, watching him beat the poor woman with avid, glittering eyes. "They do not know whom they think to bedevil, do they?"

Even the steady stream of wine I swallow cannot block out her anguished cries, yet the two of them barely seem to bend an ear. They compete as if to outdo each other, playing out some struggle I cannot comprehend. For every blow he strikes, she matches him with two, until the ill-fated cook sags unseeing against the post.

It is as if Elizabeth strives to prove herself more than his equal at exacting punishment. Maybe she thinks, if he finds her to be his match, he will leave her be and stop forcing the matter of a child. I can almost believe it, witnessing her feverish ardor, the furious yet ebullient way she applies herself to causing harm. This is far beyond even her own cruel appetite—so depraved I think she must truly believe she can buy her own freedom with someone else's flesh.

But when they graduate to the fléchettes right before dessert, I finally push back from the table. Anything else, I can endure. But I won't let them cut Ilona.

"May I?" I slur when Elizabeth takes a step toward her, struggling to unknot my drink-sodden tongue. "She—she used to be my friend, when I lived below the scullery. But now she only looks at me askance, as if she begrudges my every joy. I would punish her myself for her insolence."

"Of course, Anna," Elizabeth purrs in a languid, indulgent tone. Though her face is flecked bright with blood, her hair curling sweaty at her temples from her exertions, she looks heavy-lidded and indolent. "Who is she to hold you in such contempt?" She takes up the fléchette by my plate, pressing it into my hand. My fingers curl reluctantly around it, and I am abruptly and wholly stone-sober, as if icy water has been upended over my head. "Do me proud, my little sage. Show my husband how it is done, when a woman wields a blade."

The fléchette grows sweaty in my hand as I approach Ilona, inwardly cursing Ferenc with every step for driving us both to this. The way Ilona is restrained prevents her from turning her head, but she can see me from the frantic corner of her eye, and she squirms madly against her bindings. As if she is truly terrified of me, just as she would be of our lady. Like mistress, like pet, I'm sure she thinks.

In her mind, I'm now cut from the same cloth as Elizabeth.

"Please, Anna," she whines desperately, tossing her head like a panicked filly. "Please, don't hurt me!"

I grip her by the hair, bring my mouth close to her ear under Elizabeth's rapt gaze. "Don't be afraid," I whisper, my heart quailing at her ragged breathing. "I will try not to hurt you very badly, though it *will* hurt, I won't lie. But if I do not cut you, one of them will—and they will not take care that you live through this. Do you understand?"

She hesitates, panting against the wood, then jerks out a nod. At least she still trusts me this far.

"One more thing," I whisper, bringing the knife up to her bared back, pressing it to her skin so she can feel the cold blade and prepare herself. My gorge rises in my throat at the thought of bearing down. But I tell myself that I have done as much before, to heal. My intent is the same, only the execution different. "Scream, Ilona, if you value your life. As loudly as you can. Now is not the hour for holding back."

Chapter Fourteen

The Angel and the Gripe

I will never forget the sound of Ilona's pain.

Though I have scrubbed myself over and over, my hands still feel hot and sticky with my crime, the rollicking echoes of her shrieks resounding in my ears. Perhaps they will plague me to my dying day, hound me into hell. For that is surely where I now belong, regardless of my intentions.

The only thing I can do to atone is ensure that Ferenc arrives there first.

Elizabeth would not let me clean her when we staggered back to her chambers, rubbing the blood over her cheeks like some savage goddess reveling in sacrifice.

"No, Anna, leave me be—it will do such wonders for my skin! Goat's blood and milk could not compare to such freshness and heat; you will see it gleam like silk in the morning," she raved, rubbing it into her face as though it were some vile unguent.

Now she sleeps, leaving scarlet smears across her pillow, while I rouse myself and venture out into the woods by the keep. As I slog through the soggy, mud-choked ground, softened by an unexpected thaw, I cannot thrust Ilona from my mind. True to my word, I cut her shallowly and only where I deemed safest. It ensured that she would bleed profusely enough to slake Ferenc's bloodlust, while protecting more crucial tissues from harm. Preserving the soundness of tendon and ligament.

At the end of the evening, she was the only one of the four left alive.

All my work to save them from Elizabeth's wrath, undone in one debased night. Just as he intended, I'm sure. A precisely crafted punishment for my claim to Elizabeth's love.

I left Ilona slumped senseless on the post, but breathing still. I can only hope whoever tends to her in my stead has the sense to send her home once she is bandaged up, her scull's salary be damned.

"We showed him, didn't we, my little sage?" Elizabeth kept repeating as we stumbled back upstairs, so drunk off wine and torment that she fairly bounced along the walls. "Now he knows, now he *finally* understands, who it is that he took to wife!"

"Yes, Elizabeth," I'd said woodenly, my face feeling numb, throat stripped and sore from the tears I'd swallowed while working on Ilona. "I have no doubt that he does."

And I have no doubt that if he lives, many, many more will die as he continues to fan Elizabeth's flames, coaxing her to ever more infernal depths—including myself, eventually. His indulgence of me is bound to sour, once he sees for himself how Elizabeth dotes and relies on me. Then he will see fit to cull me, too.

Unless I cull him first.

I understand now that it must fall to me. I owe it to Elizabeth, who has given me so much, to guide her back to her humanity as best I can. Without Ferenc's fangs at her throat, I can try to purge her of the choler, or avert it into less deadly channels. If I do not at least make the attempt, the deaths within these walls will surely multiply at his hands. And I cannot simply stand by and watch, not any longer. Not now that I am tainted, too.

At the very least, perhaps I can save Elizabeth's blackened soul from him.

When I step into the woods, fragrant with pine needles and bark and squelching mud, I know exactly where to look. In my first weeks here, I came across several squirrels dead right near this spot, having dropped out of the trees during their madcap rush to fill their winter caches. They would have eaten something, I reasoned, that disagreed badly with them. It behooved me to know exactly what. The search led me to a cluster of amanita mushrooms, of the destroying angel type, nested within a rotten log. Their cloistered home should have sheltered them from the snow, and the recent thaw encouraged even more to burgeon up.

There are other methods, of course, different poisons I could procure or brew. But all of those are rare or otherwise difficult to obtain, and the appearance of the amanitas now seems an omen, a fortuitous gift. As if they were left here for me, meant for this very moment.

Holding my breath, I kneel before the log and bend to

peer in. In the darkness I can spot the destroying angels'
ghostly gleam, the clammy, bulbous shape that has tricked
countless foragers to death. They look fleshy, appealing,
mimicking many other mushrooms that are safe and good to
eat. It allows them to hide in plain sight, flourish while small
and pale.

The destroying angel mushroom is not so unlike me.

As soon as I return, I slip the amanitas into Ferenc's breakfast.

The new head cook blanches when I appear in the kitchens, as if I am a floating shade, a specter presaging her own
death. I tell her that Elizabeth has requested that, from now
on, I will see to both her and Ferenc's meals to avoid any more
unfortunate mistakes. The woman is so terrified of what
befell her predecessor—surely no one in the keep could have
avoided hearing of the lord and lady's diabolical diversions,
even if they weren't tasked with scouring the great hall—that
she bobs a nervous curtsy and scampers off without a word.
Only too happy to cede me her place.

I slice the mushrooms up and dredge them generously
through butter, then fry them with eggs, spiced sausages, and
plum-stuffed dumplings rolled in cinnamon and sugar. I know
that amanitas taste deceptively mild and pleasant, so I foresee no trouble there. To further deflect suspicion, I cook the
other batch of the mushrooms I gathered—harmless, edible
parasols—into an identical meal for Elizabeth.

I carry it up to her myself, instructing one of the maidservants to bring Ferenc his breakfast, just to be safe. I doubt he

would think to question who cooked it for him, not here in the sanctity of his own keep, where he cannot imagine himself threatened. But I won't risk alarming him.

Elizabeth is awake and washed when I slip in with her tray, though she looks limply hungover. But she accepts the tray gratefully, smiling at me when I instruct Margareta to draw her a bath. "Thank you, my dove," she sighs, prodding at the food. "This will do me good, I'm sure. I feel dreadfully wrung out from last night. Though my skin feels quite taut today, just as I told you it would! And perhaps, now that my husband has seen my strength, he will no longer strive to bend me to his will." Her face brightens, glows almost incandescent with hope—almost as if the blood has truly worked the wonders she ascribes to it. "Perhaps everything will be different now, don't you think?"

You have no notion, my beloved, how different things will be.

"Perhaps it will," I say instead, as mildly as I can, though my heart rages like storm-racked waters. "We can only hope."

∿∿∿

The destroying angel is an insidious, languid sort of poison. Though it takes effect quickly, its first symptoms are quite mild. It can take weeks for it to fully debilitate the liver and kidneys, to churn the hapless victim's innards into an agonizing slurry. And once it has begun there is no antidote, nothing at all that can forestall its course.

Once admitted, the angel will not be denied.

The death it brings about is so excruciating and prolonged that it almost hints of the eternal torments that await some beyond the veil—hence the name. It's the sort of death that Ferenc deserves, has more than earned for himself.

By the time night falls like an unraveling curtain, he is already well within its thrall.

I attend to him readily when he calls on me, unwitting, to make him a tonic that will soothe his griping guts. He complains of a turbulent stomach and loose stools, which I know precede the bloody flux to come. I make a great show of examining him with care, brewing him tisanes of chamomile, licorice, and peppermint, graciously accepting his grudging thanks when they provide temporary reprieve. I don't mind tending to him; the act only casts suspicion away from me. I treat him as I would any other patient, tending to him night and day—seemingly as devoted to my lady's husband as I am to her.

By the fifth day, Ferenc is beset by such pain that he can barely speak sense. He thrashes like an eel and soils himself, incapable of stomaching more than a drop of water. In his delirium he rails against us all, from his manservant and Elizabeth to King Ferdinand, his patron, blackening his name. By the time he finally fixates on me, ranting of malfeasance and poison, he is such a reeking wreck that only I can stand to see to him. There is no one to hear him condemn me, not when even his valet deserted him days ago, unable to bear the ungodly miasma of his stench.

Elizabeth has not been to see him once since he fell ill.

"Witch," he rasps at me in a rare moment of lucidity, glaring at me with one rheumy, bloodshot eye. *"Murderess."*

"At your service, my lord," I say, not pausing my wiping of his brow. "I've done quite a fine job of it, wouldn't you say?"

"You . . ." He struggles, panting, his head falling back to the sweat-soiled pillow. "You will burn in hell for this, you wicked bitch, you vile abomination. You are even worse than her."

"If I do," I reply equably, shifting my weight on his bed, "I trust you will be there afore me, ready to show me all the sights."

When he finally dies three days later, I believe it comes as a relief to the both of us.

Chapter Fifteen

The Confession and the Malady

The weeks following Ferenc's death streak by in a blur. There are funeral arrangements to be made, the winding shroud to be woven, the Nadasdy and Báthory families and their friends to host as they trickle in, gathering for the ceremony.

Elizabeth manages it all with grim, white-faced efficiency. I keep to the shadows of the overcrowded castle, not wanting to draw attention to myself by interfering unless I am called upon. Small scraps of guilt have begun to hatch inside me, squirming like maggots, and I cannot bring myself to so much as meet his grieving family's eyes. And Elizabeth and I barely have a moment to exchange more than a few words until after he is delivered into the ground, his family dispersed.

It is only then that I finally feel as though I can draw a full breath again.

"It must be a relief to you to have them gone," I say to her that morning as I dress her hair. She has been uncharacteristically terse with me since he died, quiet and withdrawn. I have been so eager for this moment, counting down until we had the time and room to rekindle the warmth between us. "His mother, in particular, all that ceaseless wailing and carrying on. I thought it would burst my eardrums."

Her eyes, sharply rimed with frost, flit up to mine in the mirror. "How unkind of you to say, Anna. He was her son," she snaps, tight-lipped. "And a healthy man, in the prime of his life. Of course she was aggrieved. How could she not have been? In some ways, she lost even more than I did—and I had my husband stripped from me."

"But . . ." The words wilt on my tongue, and my hands still in her hair. "Do you mean to say that you—that you *miss* him? That you are sorry for his passing?"

"What a foolish thing to ask," she retorts, still in that caustic tone. "He was my husband, and now he is gone. We did not always get on, and he had a heavy hand. But I would never have wished such an ill death on him."

"But you *hated* him!" I blurt, unable to restrain myself. "You used to fantasize for hours about what it would be like if he were gone, do you not remember? You—you asked me to kill him for you!"

"Asked you to kill him . . ." she repeats, incredulous, her eyes growing so wide in the mirror I can see a ring of white around them. "Anna, are you unwell? Fevered, perhaps? What could cause you to utter such a thing, such unspeakable, morbid nonsense?"

"I—I am fine," I reply weakly, stepping back and winding

my suddenly cold hands in my skirts. My mind mills with a thousand biting little thoughts. The sober widow sitting before me seems so far removed from the half-crazed, desperate woman I remember storming about this very room, railing against her brutish husband, plying herself ruthlessly with emmenagogues to rid her womb of his get. And yet, she blinks at me now with such disbelieving eyes that I almost question what I recall. "But you, you *did* wish him dead. You told me so, after he beat you the last time, for not wishing to bear his child. You asked me to—"

I cut myself off when she rises, pushing away from the vanity and turning slowly, warily, to face me.

"Anna," she says, so somber it is almost sepulchral. "Are you saying that my husband's death was no sudden illness? That Ferenc, may the good lord rest his soul, died by your hand?"

"Of course that's what happened!" I say, my voice shrill and tremulous. "I—I poisoned his food. I did it to free you, Elizabeth! At *your own* behest!"

Elizabeth turns away from me, clapping a hand to her mouth. Silence ensues, stagnating around us like a swamp. When she wheels to face me again, her face is taut, aghast, colorless save for the blazing red of her worried lower lip. "Listen to me, Anna," she manages between clenched teeth. "I would never have asked you to do such a thing. I was angry, certainly, but it is often thus between husband and wife. And he *was* my husband. Sometimes I even loved him, especially in the early days."

"So, what, now you claim to mourn his death?" I ask, disbelieving. This admission of this past love for him, even if distant, tears at me like talons. *What about me?* I want to shriek at her. *Do you still love me?* "If you were so distressed, why did you not visit him once while he lay dying?"

"Because I could not bear to see it!" she lashes out, eyes snapping with ferocity. "For all his faults, he was always so robust. How could I have withstood it, seeing him weak and diminished?"

"But you *said*!" I counter frantically, my heart stamping like hooves against my ribs. This cannot be happening, it cannot. And yet it is. "You talked of what could befall a man, malfeasance and accident and assault, you spoke of poison . . ."

"I admit to having dark thoughts, yes, in the extremity of my distress," she concedes, inclining her head. Her grave mien is terrifying, though not as much as the strange, roiling furor in her eyes. "Those are on my soul to bear. But I never spoke of poison, Anna, and I certainly never directed you to kill him. Go on, cast your mind back. Do you truly remember me saying any such thing?"

I reel my recollection back to that day, rifling through the memories. And it is true, dreadfully, fearfully true; I cannot remember her outright asking for his death, or even mentioning poison aloud.

I had surmised that it was what she wanted, but the words themselves were never spoken.

"No," I falter, feeling the blood sluice from my face in a flood. It leaves my body weak and shaking, my head swimming upon my shoulders. "But I could have sworn that it was what you wanted. That I heard it between us quite clearly, though unspoken."

She bites her lower lip, and something subtle and

unnerving creeps across her face. "When you say you hear it, though it was not spoken, what do you mean?" she asks in a low tone. "Do you mean that you heard it inside your own head, perhaps as though it were whispered in your ear?"

My breath grows short as I struggle to pin the fluttering memory down, spear needles through its wings. I simply *knew* that she meant poison, that she wished for me to do it. But how could I have known, if she did not say as much herself?

"Something like that," I admit feebly. "It was as if I heard what you were not saying. As if I felt, understood in my heart, what you wanted of me."

Out of instinct I lift my hands, reaching toward her for comfort. When she shies back a step, away from me, the pain is fit to break my heart. I clutch both fists against my stomach, fearing that I might double over, collapse to the floor and spew out my own shattered innards.

Because I finally recognize that unfamiliar expression on her face. Elizabeth is afraid. Of *me*.

What dread reversal of fortune is this? That I have driven her away by attempting to secure her freedom? What if she is thinking back to all the times she accepted medicine for my hand, considering how close she might have come to death herself?

What if she stops loving me, casts me away? Not only will my heart break, dash itself to bitter smithereens, but my family will starve to death.

If I lose her, everything is lost.

"Is it possible, Anna," she begins hoarsely, in an overly cautious voice I have never heard from her before, "that it was not *my* voice you heard inside your head?"

"What do you mean?" My voice scales up to a needling shrill. "Whose voice would it have been?"

"Not who," she replies, shifting her jaw. "But what. After all your talk of omens and portents, and the midwife's sight you have told me of—perhaps this is of the same otherworldly ilk. Whatever spirits or demons granted you such sight . . . maybe they now grow bolder. Whispering directly in your ear."

I shake my head a little, so dumbstruck and appalled I think at first that I must have heard her wrong. Yet how could I have, when the horrid accusation echoes in my ears, spooling around itself like a worm curling inside my brain.

"They do call you a witch," she says gently, sensing my agitation. "I heard it said even before we met."

"But . . . But the sight is merely intuition." I flail, pressing my hands harder against my stomach in an effort to thwart the building panic. "I know it isn't real, so much as a tool. My own instincts leading me toward what I already know to be true."

She closes the distance between us, her hands alighting on my shoulders with such caution, such restraint, that my lips tremble with all that she is holding back. As if I am both a hissing viper and a frail, shattered shell. As if I might either bite her or crumble beneath her touch.

"I believe that you believe that," she says softly, leaning forward to tilt her forehead against mine. "You are a good person, Anna, I would never doubt as much. But whatever this is, this loathsome taint, it has clearly crept inside you. Made itself at home. And if that is not the case . . ."

"What?" I ask fearfully, my insides contracting at her billowing sigh. "What else might it be?"

"A malady of the mind," she replies after a weighty pause. "They do say the deranged hear things that others do not. And is that not exactly what you complain of? Hearing things that aren't there? Things that drive you to fiendish acts—to murder?"

"I don't know, Elizabeth," I whisper, and suddenly I cannot restrain myself. Scalding tears come seeping down my face, and a guttural sob wrenches itself from my throat. "I do not feel deranged, but if I were—would I even know?"

My voice blurs, eclipsed by an encroaching wail. I collapse as if my bones have melted, lost all integrity. Elizabeth catches me easily by the elbows, maneuvers my weak form into her arms.

"Hush, Anna," she croons as I weep abysmally into her shoulder, clinging to her as if a great flood seeks to sweep me away and drown me. "Be still, my little sage, and do not be afraid. You are not alone in this. Whatever has befallen you, we will fix it together. You have my word."

Chapter Sixteen

The Shade and the Flower

Despite Elizabeth's reassurances, Ferenc's unquiet shade does not let me rest.

Though I have often navigated my way by the light of omens, those temporary stars meant to lead one onward before winking out, I have never truly believed in spirits. And yet now I feel his oily specter lingering all around me. It is as if Ferenc's restless soul has steeped into the keep's already malign stones; the castle seems to exhale malevolence into the air, curdling my every breath. Its miasma fosters my guilt as wet air nurtures mold, and my insides fester with it, my every nook and cranny teeming with its invading tendrils.

Until I am riddled with it like a fallen fruit. Veined with rot, on the brink of collapse, my whole self soft with putrefaction.

And if I was not deranged before, I have since succumbed.

Without sleep, my tempered disposition abandons me

completely, terror gripping me in its fist until I fear I will be crushed. My turmoil is such that my head aches incessantly, splitting my skull and distorting my sight. Every shadow caught from the corner of my eye nearly chases me out of my skin, and sometimes I swear I can even smell him, wafts of that loathsome scent he favored cloying in my nose.

Once, as I walk through the halls, I catch a hissing whisper that dogs my step. *Murderess*, it rasps at me like a beckoning as I round each corner, though there is nothing to be seen beyond. *Wicked murderess, deceitful bitch.* I seem to hear it emanating from all directions, even whistling on the wind that filters through the cracks in the timbered walls. I turn in a frantic circle, searching for its source, but it remains mockingly out of reach.

Whispering over my shoulder, high above my head, ricocheting off the walls.

"Stop," I hiss back through gritted teeth, clamping my palms desperately over my ears. "Begone, shade, hie you back to hell!"

The whisper rolls into peaks of derisive laughter, resounding so loudly in my head it's as though it has wormed directly into my brain. Breathless with panic, I pelt heedlessly through the halls, up and down stairs, until I thoroughly lose myself in an unlit part of the keep I've never seen before. Furniture looms ominously beneath the shrouds of dust cloths, and trailing cobwebs tack the rafters. Yet the susurrus only gains in volume the farther I run, until I press my back against the dusty wall and slide down, slumping against it with my wobbling knees drawn up to my chest. I am so full of fear and loathing I feel as though I may burst through my own skin, split its seams and shed it so at least my shambling skeleton may flee this place.

I'm still mumbling to Ferenc through tears, my eyes screwed tightly shut, when Elizabeth finds me hours later. "I'm sorry, I'm sorry, I didn't *want* to kill you, but I had to, I *had* to, *I'm sorry!*"

I only open my eyes when her warm hands steal over mine and lower them from my ears, her soft cheek pressing against my face. "My dearest dove," she whispers, her brow furrowing with distress, "what are you doing all the way up here? I couldn't find you anywhere, I was near driven to distraction!"

"It's Ferenc," I gasp, tumbling forward into her arms. I am shuddering like an animal, strange parts of my body twitching without reason. My left thumb, an eyebrow, a small muscle in my jaw. "He is—he is still here, Elizabeth! He haunts me, I swear it, he will not leave me be . . ."

Unable to restrain myself, I dissolve into sobs so wrenching they feel as though they might crack my rib cage open like a chestnut under a horse's hoof. Cooing under her breath, Elizabeth gathers me up against her and rocks me like a fretful babe.

"It is only your mind, my love," she murmurs. "You are merely overwrought, that is all. He is gone, dead and buried—far beyond the veil, if any stubborn part of him even persevered after death."

"Then why can I hear him, Elizabeth?" I keen against her neck. "Why can I *smell* him? No, he is still here inside these walls, hiding like a phantom. And he will not let me rest!"

I continue weeping as she helps me, stumbling, to my feet, and guides me to her bedroom. "You need sleep, my dove," she whispers, easing me into bed, lifting my feet off the floor one by one and tucking them beneath the covers with a pat. "I know you have barely rested for over a fortnight. Here, let me feed you a sip of the laudanum you gave me when it was I who ailed. All you need is proper sleep."

When she tips the spoon to my mouth like a mother bird feeding her young, I take it obediently, though the bitterness curls my tongue. I have resisted sleep remedies thus far, fearing that my mind could only conjure darker things behind the confines of my eyelids, but I agree with her. I cannot go on as I am without sleep, or I too will falter and die.

But perhaps death is sometimes kinder than the vengeance that lurks behind closed eyes.

And it is just as I fear. After the first blissful wave of somnolence breaks over my head, I find myself trapped in darkness. My dreams become a cruel land that may as well be the fairies' realm, populated by long-faced wraiths that caper about me and yank at my hair, gabbling nonsense in my ears. "Murderess," they kettle-shriek at me in a hellish cadence that mimics Ferenc's tone, "wicked, conniving witch!" As their voices blend into high-pitched titters, the black coalesces into a horde I recognize—the beetles that once ate me in my sleep, back when I lived down in the cellars.

"No," I scream at their onslaught, scrabbling backward in the shapeless dark, though there is nowhere to run. "Do not take me!"

But they pour over and engulf me, skittering down my throat and tearing my lungs with their needling legs. Stuffing me full with their bodies until I cannot breathe.

When I gasp myself awake, washed in sweat and shrieking, it is Elizabeth who coaxes me back to myself. "Come,
dearest, hush," she whispers to me as I cry, curling herself
around me. "It is all right, I promise. You are with me. We
will make you better."

But I do not get better.

After that I refuse any more laudanum, and none of my
own herbal remedies can guarantee a safer sleep. The nightmare seems to bleed over into my waking hours, uninvited.
Floods of beetles follow in my footsteps, skittering at the very
edges of my vision, dispersing into thin air whenever I wheel
around to catch them in the act. But I can hear the clicking of their shells against the floor even as they disappear,
and smell the musty reek of their great numbers. I even grow
fearful of my own reflection, reluctant to look at myself in any
mirror; my unfamiliarity terrifies me, as though I've become
my own haunt. I see a stranger with bleak eyes, sallow cheeks,
and limp skeins of hair like cobwebs. Worse yet, sometimes
there is a roiling somewhere behind me, reflected in the glass
like drifting smoke.

It disappears as soon as I round on it, leaving me with
nothing but a galloping heart.

Is any of it real? I wonder in my darkest moments. Or is it
as Elizabeth believes—a conjuring of my ill-used mind, broken on the wheel of my guilt like a martyred saint? Shattered
perhaps beyond repair?

And does it matter either way, if it will not grant me a
moment's reprieve?

"Nadasdy Castle wants me gone," I tell Elizabeth

miserably one night, sitting at her feet by the fireplace with my head in her lap. "I can feel it. It's Ferenc's, he's in its bones. And it seeks to cast me out."

Her long fingers stroke my hair, though how she can bear to touch its filthy mat is beyond me. "How can that be true, dearest, when this keep belongs to me—and there is nothing closer to my heart than you?"

I shake my head despondently against her knee. "Then make it stop plaguing me, Elizabeth," I whisper into her skirts. "Before it kills me just as I killed him."

When time brings no relief, Elizabeth decides to spirit me away to Csejthe, her honeymoon estate.

"You shall love it, you will see," she rhapsodizes as the rest of the household packs its bags. She will not allow me to lift a finger to help, as if I even could. The enormity of my relief at the imminent departure has only enervated me further, and I can barely lift my head from my hot bath. Instead, Margareta and Judit huff and puff sullenly about the chambers, stowing everything away for us while Elizabeth washes my hair. "The hills just around it are so lush and wooded, they leave the castle beautifully secluded. There is no press of humanity at the door. Only an idyll of quiet and peace, perfect for healing."

"That sounds wonderful," I whisper, barely daring to hope that such a haven truly exists. And that if it does, Ferenc will not be able to follow me there. "Thank you for taking me."

"Of course, my love," she murmurs into my ear, tipping a

ewer of water over my hair as I once did for her. "Did I not tell you I would take care of you?"

"You did. And I am so grateful for you."

We arrive a fortnight later after a tortuous carriage ride, the caravan of servants and covered wagons wending like a scraggling dragon's tail behind us. Though I am sure this diminished retinue would have far preferred to be left behind, they have little choice; they belong to Elizabeth as her chattel, and must go where their mistress goes. And perhaps there has been enough peace of late, since their master died, to settle their minds and keep them from running.

I find the estate even lovelier than described. Csejthe Castle sprawls upon a craggy cliff like a grand stone queen astride her throne, with rolling woods and farmland unfurling below. Unlike Nadasdy Castle with its white walls and red roofs, more of a sprawling manse than a castle proper, Csejthe is a keep exactly as a child might imagine, peeled from the pages of storybooks. Its pointed towers spear the sky, and massive ramparts hunch around the gatehouse and turrets. The forests below the keep are full of nightingales, the twilight alive with birdsong. The moon has risen early on the afternoon we arrive, a sharp crescent hooked in the bruised-plum sky. Though the air is still chilly, the year is creeping into April. I can already see the first few bold snowdrops nosing past the soil. And there is that sweet, wet smell of spring, budding green and newly fertile loam.

It is nothing like Nadasdy Castle, and I could not be more grateful.

I hang my head out of the closed carriage like an eager

hound, breathing the air in. It smells like exactly what I need. "You like it, I see," Elizabeth says, a smile restrained in her voice. "Is it as I promised?"

"Even better," I reply, closing my eyes as a breeze riffles through my eyelashes. "Perhaps it will be as you say. Perhaps I will be better here."

"You will," she assures me, reaching out to squeeze my hand with the warm ember of her own. "I know it."

Once we are settled in the keep, I walk through its clean stone corridors, gaining confidence as I find myself consistently alone. No longer bedeviled by bugs, whispers, or menacing phantom smells. These hallways are high-ceilinged and well lit, much airier than those of Nadasdy keep—and better yet, uninfested with Ferenc's taint.

In any case, Elizabeth does not allow me to languish indoors. For my sake, she has even become willing to expose herself to the day, though she makes sure to carry a broadbrimmed parasol. Each day after breakfast—now that I am able to eat again—I accompany her to the small orchard nestled against the west wall of the keep. The spindly apple, plum, and cherry trees are only just now budding with the lacy blossoms that precede fruit. At first our forays are brief. My limbs are weak, and I squint feebly at the sky like some subterranean creature unfamiliar with light. But soon, at Elizabeth's behest, I bring along a basket and my sickle knife, so I can show her which herbs are good to cut and brew into tonics. She has never seen them in their native forms, and each new specimen strikes her as a revelation.

"This one is agrimony," I say, indicating the spears of

clustered yellow flowers flourishing by a root. "Wonderful for so many things. My mother liked to use it for belly gripes, though it'll settle a sore gallbladder, too. You can even apply it to wounds and warts."

"Marvelous," she tells me, a smile lighting her eyes. I have been like a child for so long, dependent on her and struck dull by my distress, that I can see her take pleasure at even this tentative revival. "And this yellow one? Is it of the same family?"

"Not at all." I cut one of the flower heads and present it to her with a flourish, twirling it between my fingers. She plucks it from my hand with a coy smile, and tucks it behind her ear as I scramble clumsily up to my feet. It seems my former grace will need more time and coaxing to reappear. "Other than serving as an ornament for my lady, goat weed is a blessing for the constitution. It uplifts the spirits and banishes the doldrums."

"Well then, why don't we try it on you?" she exclaims, biting her lower lip with anticipation. "Surely there are others like it, are there not? Revitalizing herbs to bring you back to strength? If you show me, I could even make the brews for you!"

"You do not need to do that, after everything else you've done for me," I demur, though it reassures me to know that she is not weary of my unending weakness. "Look, my hands barely even shake anymore. I can make the tea myself perfectly well."

"But perhaps I *wish* to make them for you, as a gift," she counters, taking my proffered hands and placing them against her chest. My insides tighten at the delicate jut of her collarbone beneath my fingers, the satiny give of skin suspended above it, the softness of her bosom under my palms. We have not touched each other this way since before Ferenc died, but my skin remembers well.

It is my heart, I find, that is the trouble.

As she leans toward me slowly with parted lips, a vision of the infernal banquet brands itself across my mind—the memory of leaping firelight licking hungrily at the walls, Elizabeth's disheveled hair unraveling around her face, the exultant glee in her eyes as she laid into Orsolya's back with the bullwhip. My mouth turns abruptly dry as sand, my stomach clenching with revulsion.

As much as I long for the comfort of her closeness, I find I can no longer bear to let her touch me.

"I'm sorry," I say faintly, turning away from her so she cannot see the turmoil clouding my face. I cannot allow Elizabeth to know that I am rejecting her; I fear not even I would be safe from the retribution she would exact for such a grievous wound to her pride. "But I'm feeling a bit light-headed. Perhaps I'm more tired than I thought. Will you be terribly disappointed with me if we go back inside? I think I may need to lie down for a spell."

I hear the sharp intake of her breath, followed by the trace of a sigh. "Of course not," she says eventually, forcing cheer into her voice. When I turn back to her she is wearing a determined smile, though uncharacteristic uncertainty plays in her eyes, along with veiled speculation. "Rest is exactly what you need. After all, it's why we came here, is it not?"

"Yes," I say, weak with relief that she has not seen through my pretense. "Thank you, Elizabeth. Surely—certainly I'll be much better soon."

She loops her arm through mine, squeezing me to her side as we turn back to the keep. "You will, my dove, I know it. I will make it so."

Chapter Seventeen

The Poison and the Elixir

Though I walk on eggshells for the next few days, Elizabeth seems to have taken me at my word.

Following my instructions, she brews tonics for me, tisanes to soothe the mind and lift the spirits. I drink goat weed and golden root and cat's claw, augmented by tinctures of valerian and lemon balm. She has never made her own concoctions before, and the process of it delights her so thoroughly that her solar transforms into an apothecary's cabinet seemingly overnight, littered with vials of essentials and absolutes.

When the medicines leave me languid, prone to lengthy naps, Elizabeth diverts herself by charging out into the estate on horseback with her bow and a brace of arrows. She brings back squirrels and rabbits and sometimes geese—once even a tawny mountain lion speared right through its amber eye—proudly brandishing them at me before they're whisked off to be cleaned. She even has some of her prizes stuffed, and installed into the keep's cavernous great hall as ornaments above the marble mantel.

"You will empty the forests if you go on this way," I chide her gently, laughing, though the sheer number of them leaves me a touch uneasy. "Surely we don't need so many!"

She gives me a wide smile, almost a baring of the teeth. "Well, I must do *something* while you recover, mustn't I?" she retorts with just the slightest edge, dropping a quick kiss to my cheek before striding back off. "Quiet as it is here, sometimes I feel as if I will atrophy."

If anything, her restlessness spurs me more quickly back to health. I do not want Elizabeth to feel that her life with me is dreary, that her convalescing former lover has consigned her to this mountaintop. She assures me that such is not the case, that she could never be impatient with me. But with every new kill she brings in, I redouble my efforts to regain my strength. Now that my mind has cleared, a dark and slippery notion has come to plague me, darting in and out of the corners of my awareness like a silverfish—that I have unwittingly secured Elizabeth exactly the life she wants, all while keeping her hands clean of her husband's death. And giving her a noose to hang around my neck, should she ever have reason to take against me.

Which means I must take much greater care to pacify her than ever before.

I cannot afford to have her tire of my company, especially now that I can no longer imagine losing myself to her touch. If I turn away from her entreaties without diverting her in some other way, who am I to her, besides the once-deranged murderess responsible for her husband's death?

"Are you happy, my dearest dove?" she asks me on one of our walks through the orchard, when we have been in Csejthe for nearly two months. "You seem more yourself every day."

"I do seem to have found my footing again," I concur. "Thanks to you."

"And you have experienced . . . nothing unwonted here?" she asks, taking care to keep her voice light. "No nightmares, no whispers? Nothing like that?"

"Nothing at all," I reply frankly. Whether my madness was born of restless spirits or my own guilt, it has blown away into nothing in the clear mountain air. What is done is done, and though I will atone for it all my life I refuse to destroy myself over it any longer. And I have not failed to notice that not a single servant has suffered Elizabeth's wrath since Ferenc's death. I don't dare hope that having him gone has bled her entirely of the need to spread pain—all the game she fells is testament to the enduring nature of that need—but it does seem to have helped.

Perhaps my grievous sin has not been for naught.

"That's wonderful news," she effuses, squeezing my hand. "Then perhaps I might ask you for some help in my experiments."

"Experiments?" I ask doubtfully, the back of my neck prickling with foreboding.

"I am thinking of crafting potions to enhance not just beauty but vitality as well," she explains. "Inspired by the herbs we've gathered together and the tonics I've made for you. My face has begun to sag even worse of late, especially around the eyes. And you see how these frightful grooves have carved themselves around my mouth. I'd like to see how I might recapture the flush of youth—perhaps even to re-create the freshness I once shared with my son."

I glance over at her, find smooth skin with only the most cursory of creases from her smiles. I don't spot any semblance of this harpy that she seems to see within herself. "If you say so, Elizabeth, though you seem to me as beautiful as ever."

"Thank you, my dove," she replies with a tight-lipped smile. "But you do not know this face as I do, nor are you constantly reminded of its flaws whenever you chance across a mirror. Nor do you have a pressing need to fend off the ravages of age. And without this at its prime . . ." She gestures to her face, rolling her eyes. "How will I secure another husband?"

So it is the fear of losing the weapon of her beauty that dogs her still. That is no surprise, though the notion that she thinks to marry again rocks me with a squall of fear. If she finds another husband, where will that leave me? Her favor is all I have—all my family has. I cannot afford to have her discover that, with another, more suitable husband in hand, she no longer has any need of a pet sorceress. Or whatever else it is she thinks I am.

I realize with a bitter twist that I find myself in exactly the sort of cage I feared marriage to a man would bring. Except far, far worse—for Peter would have been unfailingly kind, never bending my talents to nefarious purposes known only to him.

"You plan to marry, then?" I ask, striving not to betray the fear. She has only just settled, laid her instruments of torture to the side. What if she finds a husband with his own sharp tastes to rile hers back to life? "I had thought it would be just the two of us for a while, at least."

"I am in no great rush, do not fret," she reassures me. "But yes, I will wed again. Being without a husband leaves all my holdings at risk of being plundered." Her face darkens at the thought. "Should they be stripped from me by greedy rivals, I shall be reduced to nothing, no one of account. Relegated to the nunnery to cluck prayers at the lord for the rest of my days. With all the other unwanted hens."

"Well, he shall be lucky to have you," I say warily. "Whoever he will be."

"He must be wealthy and highborn, of course, else why bother?" she muses, eyes turning inward, calculating. "Certainly more pliable than Ferenc, easier to mold—and so taken with me that *he* shall be the one pinned under my thumb. Though he will protect me and steward our estates, it will be only in name. In truth I will lead and he will follow." She flashes me a rakish smile, arching a brow. "To draw such a man, I must make myself irresistible. That's what the experiments are for."

"And what do you have in mind, exactly?"

"Oh, so you *will* help me, how lovely!" she crows, as if I have a choice. The familiar elation in her eyes sends a cold runnel of a chill sluicing down my spine. "I've been thinking a great deal about blood, you know. How that thorn's dirt sickened my own child's blood, how it nearly stole his life with a single prick."

"I see," I venture warily. "And what has that to do with preserving your face?"

"Well, if blood can sicken, it stands to reason that it can be purified. Made more robust than it already is," she theorizes, growing even more animated. "And since it is called 'lifeblood' for a reason, would that not exert a great effect on one's well-being as well? Perhaps it might grant a much longer span of life, and nurture the bloom of youth long past youthful years."

"It is an intriguing notion," I allow, my mind racing to grasp the implications. I have never been much concerned with blood for its own sake, beyond knowing how to call forth the flux or staunch its flow when needed. But blood sustains us, and sluggish circulation can lead to death. I suppose the opposite does have potential. "And how do you aim to achieve this effect?"

A slow smile blooms across her lips, both barbed and sweet. "I thought we might begin with arsenic."

While I was recovering, it seems Elizabeth had been reading of poisons.

"Have you any experience with arsenic, Anna?" she asks breathlessly once we are back inside, ensconced in her solar. She flits between the tables, laden with glass beakers, flasks, and tubes, books splayed open everywhere. From one she plucks a vial of silvery powder, sifting back and forth as she wiggles it in her grip. "See, look, here it is."

"I've never heard of it," I say. "Is it an herb of sorts?"

"No, it is a metallic substance, quite poisonous," she replies so cheerfully I almost think I've misheard her. "But only in large doses, according to my books. In smaller increments, it can be very healthful as well."

"Many herbs are such," I allow, as if my insides do not

already quake with trepidation. "Anything powerful enough to benefit can usually wreak harm as well."

She beams at me approvingly. "Exactly! I've read that it can be consumed with chalk and water to improve the complexion. I've also heard of ladies at court making it into a cream to rub on their arms and faces. It is meant to induce a very supple rosy glow."

"And are *you* thinking of using it for such a purpose?" I ask, alarmed.

"Not exactly. I was thinking that we could tinker with it a bit, you and I. If it brings about such a pleasing flush, I imagine it must have a benign effect on the blood. And perhaps, with some imagination, we could make an alchemy of this pursuit. Fashion it into a vitalizing and beautifying elixir." She clasps her hands together, peering into my eyes until her gaze bores into mine. "What do you think?"

"If we did this," I say slowly, "how would we test the efficacy?"

"Hence the experiments!" she proclaims, casting me a dazzling smile. "We shall first rely on your knowledge and mine to craft the tonic. Then we will find a volunteer."

"Like who?" I press, as delicately as I can, wondering who would be inclined to drink something unknown and likely poisonous.

"Oh, I'm sure we'll think of someone," she says breezily. "After all, what woman does not wish to enhance her beauty and extend her life? So, what do you say, now that you are recovered? Shall we begin today?"

Watching her glowing face, her unbridled eagerness to begin this endeavor, I sense that this is no true question.

"Of course, Elizabeth," I respond, deferential, though my stomach churns with dread—for myself, and for the future subjects of this experiment. "As soon as you like."

YYYYYYYYYYYYYYYYYYYYYYYYYYYYYYYYYYYYYYYYYYYYYYYYYY

She throws herself into the pursuit of this elixir with a single-minded resolve and passion unlike anything I've seen in her before. We work side by side through the night in the candlelit solar, while the sun swoops away and then alights upon us again. The tonic we produce contains an amount of arsenic that, neither of us having any real familiarity with the recommended dosage, could induce any effect from nothing at all to ghastly death. So I strive to counteract any ill effects with benign herbs, everything from bay leaf, clove, and basil, to nutmeg, foxglove, sage, and thyme. It also contains the most animating plants I could think of, bursting with magnolia berry, beetroot, oregano, and holy basil.

The resulting concoction is a vivid violet, and smells both herbaceous and spiced. As if it *should* be healthy, at any rate. Still, I myself would not be quick to drink it.

But our combined ignorance does not dissuade Elizabeth. "We must try it out at once!" she cries, though neither of us has slept nor eaten since the night before. Her eyes are glazed with sleeplessness, but her cheeks blaze with anticipation, as if she has already sampled the tonic herself. *"Judit!"*

A moment later, the disgraced former chambermaid rushes in. It is unclear what her station currently is, given that she has not been sent away even though she hasn't tended to Elizabeth in months. Now she is clearly torn between delight at being summoned and apprehension at what is needed. "Yes, my lady?" she says breathlessly, bobbing into a curtsy.

"Fetch me someone from the scullery!" Elizabeth orders, and my heart swoops toward my feet. Does she truly mean to test this unknown substance on one of my former friends?

I rack my mind and can think of no alternative, save for offering to drink it myself. Which I know she would not allow.

"Ah . . ." Judit hems, uncertain. "Who, my lady?"

"It doesn't really matter, but, someone plain, I suppose. Plain, but with *potential*. Ah!" She snaps her fingers with epiphany. "Don't we have a redhead down there? Very green eyes, freckles, a veritable mop of ginger hair?"

So Krisztina was right, I think fearfully. Even now, Elizabeth remembers her hair.

Judit licks her lips, fear flickering in her eyes. Elizabeth clearly does not know that Krisztina is her kin. "Yes, my lady, I—I think I know of whom you speak. But she's really quite plain, would someone with more classic color not suit better?"

"No, I want her," Elizabeth demands, adamant. I can see Judit deflate, her shoulders sagging. Though she does not know what's in store for her cousin, she knows it is unlikely to be good. "She is pale, but her coloring could be made vigorous. Fetch her, Judit." And, when Judit hesitates, dithering, she adds with a whip crack in her voice, "Do you not know better by now than to make me ask you twice?"

A quarter of an hour later, Krisztina stands in the solar with us, nervously tugging a stray lock of her springy hair. Judit was dismissed immediately after she brought her, which leaves Krisztina all alone, marooned in enemy land. Her gaze keeps flitting to me, and I can almost see the whirling of her mind. She is wondering if this is my doing, if I am intending to exact my vengeance for all her whisperings of "witch," the slantwise glances and baleful eyes always heavy on my back.

I wish to reassure her of my innocence—but how can I, when this elixir would likely not exist had I not piqued Elizabeth's interest with what I know of herbs?

"Yes," Elizabeth muses speculatively, circling Krisztina like a buyer examining the quality of a horse's flesh. "She will do quite well."

"Quite well for what, mistress?" Krisztina asks, a quaver in her voice despite her stalwart heart. I am so afraid for her that I can nearly taste my own heart at the base of my throat. It is all I can do to school myself when she looks at me, lest I frighten her further with my own barely restrained terror. "What would you have me do?"

"Drink," Elizabeth says simply, offering her the flask. "It is a tonic meant to induce vigor, to promote beauty. You would like that, wouldn't you? Brighter eyes, more color to your cheeks? If Anna and I have done well, it should even make you livelier. Better fit to carry out your duties."

Krisztina balks, shying away from the flask. "I would rather not, mistress, if it's all the same to you," she rejoins, her freckles a dense constellation of cinnamon pinpricks against her sudden pallor. "I was never much for tonics."

Elizabeth's face dims, darkening in a fearsomely familiar way. She surveys Krisztina with her lower lip snapped tight between her teeth. "It is *not* all the same to me," she spits. "You will drink it, as your mistress orders."

"No," Krisztina protests, and I can see panic beginning to flutter at the edges of her eyes. "No, my lady. I will work my fingers to the bone for you, but drink that purple mess without knowing what's in it? I've never drunk anything that color in my life, and I'll not start now."

"You will drink it!" Elizabeth grates out, thrusting the flask under her nose. "Or I will garnish the last six months of your wages for insubordination."

My hands have clenched into fists, nails biting into palms, because here she is again, resurfaced.

Dark Elizabeth, the shadow twin fueled by a furnace of choler. The other face that I have come to fear so well. Ferenc's death should have expunged her, scoured her out, but she persists even without him. Capricious and unpredictable as ever—and still just as ravenous for blood.

And what a terrible fool I was, to think it could ever be otherwise.

"But . . ." Krisztina flails, blinking rapidly, her hands twisting into her coarse skirts. "But I don't have those wages! I, I send most of my coin back to my family, they'll have spent them—"

"Why should I care what your greedy kin do with my money?" Elizabeth retorts icily, her voice so cold I half expect to hear a gale howling outside. Winter clawing at the solar's windows, summoned by her tone. "I am within my rights to do so, for a servant remiss in their duties. And then where will you be, you insolent chit?"

Krisztina stares back at her, eyes hollowing with fear. She knows this would drive her family to the poorhouse, if not to starvation and death. That coin is long since gone and cannot be gotten back. I can see the terrible moment when she makes her decision, the bleak hopelessness that descends to quell the remaining spirit in her eyes. She knows what she is doing. That she is likely condemning herself to die.

And she is willing, for her family's sake.

"All right, my lady," she says dully, taking up the flask. "I will drink."

"Yes," Elizabeth whispers, her rage subsiding like a watered flame, appeased. "You certainly will."

Before Krisztina swallows, she flashes one last look at me, so steeped with anger, hatred, and betrayal that I nearly stumble as if I have been struck. Because she is right to hate me, I think blackly, barely able to watch her throat work as she drinks.

For all I delude myself as to my own good intentions, at the end of the day, everything I have done has helped Elizabeth alone.

And Elizabeth, for all my misguided love, is a far worse devil than her husband ever was.

Chapter Eighteen

The Book and the Whip

As we brew more batches of Elizabeth's potion, I dwell feverishly on all I've given up, not least my sense of what is right.

And all for this thing I falsely took for love—the way her touch made my skin leap, my spirit surge toward her like a compass needle—though I know it now to be nothing more than the basest, simplest lust. The kind that even the most mindless of beasts may feel for each other. I can still conjure faint memories of that deceptive passion in our quieter moments, as I watch her slip into slumber with the small smile she always carries down with her into sleep.

But now I know the scarlet fury of the dreams that must surely play behind those eyelids. And I am terrified of her, of who she truly is, more than I have ever been.

Because now there is no more Ferenc, no catalyst to her cruelty, no one else to blame for her misdeeds.

Now her rampant darkness merely is.

For the first few days, as if by miracle, Krisztina actually flourishes. I do not know whether it's due to all the good I've instilled into the tonic, or to her own stubbornly resilient disposition. Or perhaps the arsenic itself truly does provide some benefit, unlikely as this seems to me. But when she comes to the solar to be examined and Elizabeth quizzes her on how she's fairing, she reports a sharp, whetted mind and buoyant spirits.

"I am quite well, mistress," she mumbles, looking as surprised as I am. "Nothing amiss."

"And look at her, Anna!" Elizabeth enthuses, smoothing the girl's hair from her face with something close to fondness. She's so rapturous over the results that she can barely contain herself, seems ready to burst into a jig. "Does her skin not glow, with such roses in her cheeks? And see how luminous her eyes are, like lanterns! We must be on the right track, don't you think?"

"Perhaps we are," I reply, struggling for equanimity. It is still so early that I am terribly afraid to hope, though Krisztina drinks this new dose readily. Is it possible that we have actually struck upon something good?

It is only three days later that she turns up listless, her cheeks still mottled with flush but her temples sweaty, her eyes more glazed than bright. "My stomach gripes," she complains through gritted teeth. "Something awful."

"Well, perhaps you ate something that does not agree with you," Elizabeth says dismissively, waving her concern away. "Or overtaxed yourself with work. Whatever the case, we must keep at it. Perhaps the tonic will cleanse you, do you good."

It does not.

Though Elizabeth perseveres with dogged conviction, Krisztina's belly only worsens over the next few days, until she cannot work, taking to her bed. Elizabeth has her pallet brought up into the solar so she can circle over her like a vulture, keeping tabs on her state. All I can think of is how lonely she must be, how she must miss her friends.

"I'm so sorry, Krisztina," I whisper to her, sitting on the edge of the pallet and folding her hand in mine as she sleeps fitfully. The worst of it is, I know that I could help her. Elizabeth still sleeps beside me every night, trusting as a babe; it would take so little to slide a knife between her ribs. But even if I escaped the castle alive I would hang for it, no mistake, or be drawn and quartered. A commoner cannot dream of laying a finger on a noble without courting such a grisly death. Perhaps it would even be worth it, ceding my life to extinguish hers, guilty by association as I am of her misdeeds. But I cannot consign my family to such a dismal fate, being kin to a murderess. For all I know they would be clapped in irons, too, and they asked for none of this. Even now, Elizabeth continues to pay me a salary beyond my family's wildest dreams, and all of it I send to them—so that at least someone may benefit from this malignant, sprawling madness.

As if she can hear my thoughts, Krisztina stirs just for long enough to yank her fingers free, shooting me an accusing look before she sinks back into sleep.

"Perhaps we miss this dose, give her a chance to recover?" I suggest the next morning as Krisztina writhes, curled into an agonized apostrophe. She is deathly white save for those roses Elizabeth chases after with such grim determination, and she hasn't managed to eat in days. Instead she vomits on the hour and lets loose a watery stool, like some dread echo of Ferenc's torment come to haunt me again. When I sweep my hand through her hair to comfort her, great hanks of it come out in my grip. For whatever foolish reason, that devastates me more than anything else—this ruination of her beauty, the evidence of how we are destroying her.

Yet again, Elizabeth is stealing my old friend's coveted hair.

"It does no good to ply her with it if she continues to sicken," I continue, desperate to sway her. "It will—it will skew the results."

"To the contrary," Elizabeth grumbles, flicking me a disgruntled glance. "We must stay the course. Otherwise how will we know what to change, how to improve our work?"

"But . . ." I pitch my voice lower, though Krisztina is in such agony she isn't likely to hear me. "She will surely die, if we keep on."

"And what of it?" Elizabeth snaps, lifting her chin. "What's one lazy scull, in the face of our progress?"

"She isn't lazy," I mumble under my breath, turning away from her. "And she is a *person*, just as you are."

"What was that?" There it is again, that subtle hiss, the sound of the snake coiling up within her. Surging up with its black, blank eyes, testing the air with its tongue. "I'm not sure that I heard you, Anna."

"Nothing, my lady Elizabeth," I say, lifting my voice to hide the bitterness. "Nothing at all."

Krisztina dies later that night.

I insist on helping Janos bury her body in the orchard. There, at least, what remains of her may one day become trees, live anew as their leaves and flowers and fruit.

It is cold comfort, the bitterest dregs of consolation. I weep silently as we dig the hole, lower her shrouded body into it. Not a single member of her family is here to see her off, nor a priest or any of her friends. I know better than to count myself among the latter anymore. Not when I couldn't stave off her death.

Not her death—her murder, at Elizabeth's hand. And my own.

"How many like this have you buried in unmarked graves?" I ask Janos, knuckling sweat off my forehead, thinking of all the girls who "disappeared" from Nadasdy Castle overnight, allegedly sent home to recover after a punishment. The seamstress with stitched-together fingers and the chambermaid with the crushed ribs are only two that I can think of. Perhaps Krisztina has always been right. "Do you even care to remember?"

"Not while the lady lines my pocket with heavy coin, I don't," he retorts, shrugging his broad shoulders. "And you should strive to do the same."

It is too much to hope that her death might have dissuaded Elizabeth. Instead, she jots down the course of Krisztina's demise in a black leather-bound book, hunched over it with a frantically scratching quill.

"It will be different next time," she mutters abstractedly, more to herself than me. "It worked to begin with, so perhaps we merely overwhelmed her. A smaller dose should do for our next try."

For a mercy, our next subject is not a former friend, though I recognize her face; she is one of the kitchen servants. Alida flourishes at first just like her predecessor, and even longer, for a full fortnight.

She dies much slower, too. Languishing for so long that I begin to think slitting her throat would be a kindness.

I have barely helped Janos bury her before Elizabeth requests another victim.

This time, she thinks, we should triple the dosage. "We have learned what does not work, haven't we? Perhaps their bodies must push through the poison, by seizing upon that first flush of vitality and riding it forward," she insists, her eyes bright with renewed zeal. Now that she has latched upon this pursuit, nothing seems to subdue her. The sleeplessness is playing havoc with her face, painting lurid blue stains of fatigue under her eyes, turning her skin wan and hair lank.

Sometimes I wonder what she would do if I told her that this frenzied pursuit of youth and beauty seems to be stealing her own. But I am much too afraid to test her.

"Well?" she urges, impatient. "What do you think?"

"I think she will die faster," I answer, not even attempting to hide my despair. "And in more pain. I think that we must *stop*, Elizabeth."

The fire tempers into a smoldering anger, tinged with disappointment. "Do you truly give up so easily, Anna?" she demands, glowering. "I thought you were made of much sterner stuff. Has your fabled, stony heart deserted you so soon?"

"Because it's weak, not to wish to cause death?" I retort, unable to restrain myself. "It's unbecoming to save others from inhuman torment?"

"If you have such sympathy for them," she rejoins, her eyes cooling and lips thinning into nothing, "perhaps you would like to take their place, hmm? Be the next experiment yourself?"

A cold panic, like a sheath of ice laid over my body, tightens around me. Would she truly do it? I wonder, looking into her familiar dark eyes, as lovely as they always were, but no longer beguiling in the least. Would she sacrifice me so easily? Perhaps even a few months ago, I might have said she never would. But I have seen far too much since to entertain such a pretty delusion.

I no longer believe that she ever truly cared for me at all. I have been no more than a plaything to her—an amusing diversion, perhaps even an experiment myself. I can imagine her thinking about me in those early days, her mind aflame with plots and schemes with me trapped in their very center. *How far will this foolish girl go for me?* she must have wondered, so gleefully. *What can I make her do, now that she is so helpless, trapped by my coin and wrapped around my finger?*

If she did not think she needed my wisdom for her own

alchemy, I would likely be dead already. And as soon as I fail to amuse her, she will hunt me down like another stag.

She doesn't waver, doesn't even blink, holding me fast with her dread gaze. When the tension intensifies until I cannot stand it, I move toward her and wrap her hands in mine, terrified that she will recoil from me.

"Please, Elizabeth," I entreat as sincerely as I can, though I can feel my heart beating so savagely that she must surely see its imprint against my skin. "It is only that I am worried for you. You have not been eating as you should, or resting enough. Perhaps we should take some time. Recalibrate our plans." It is not just my own life I fight for in this moment of playacting. As the air grows even more taut and delicate between us, thin-skinned as an expanding bubble, I know that my family's lives hang in the balance, too. My heart fists miserably at the thought of my sweet dandelion Klara, who would blow away so easily without me to shield her.

Elizabeth surveys me for a moment longer with that brittle, tempered gaze. Then her face thaws, softens into a mimicry of warmth; I know now that she is no more capable of true warmth than a chill-hearted lizard clinging to castle stones, sucking in the sun. "Of course you are worried," she concedes. "I have been pushing us both so very hard. You know I didn't mean it, don't you? That I would never give up my dearest dove?"

The relief is so great it turns my knees to water. "Of course," I say softly, struggling to keep my jittering voice even, because I know no such thing. All the certainty I have is this temporary reprieve.

"Then you must know, also, that *I* will not give up," she

replies, sweeping her thumb over my knuckles. I grit my teeth at the feigned fondness in her touch. "I am dwindling by the day. No, do not deny it, you said so yourself, and I can see as much. And I need it, Anna, do you understand? I need this face, I need my spirits high. Without my beauty and my choler to sustain me, I am *nothing*. And that is something I cannot tolerate."

"I understand," I say numbly, though I understand nothing save that this is lunacy, the worst kind of calculated madness. She is prepared to sacrifice them all for the sake of something so inconsequential as beauty. Which is fleeting by nature and design, meant to desert us all. Even a longer life cannot possibly be worth the expense of so many others.

But I can do nothing save rack my head feverishly for some desperate stratagem—and stand aside until I can think my way out of this murderous maze.

Try anything rash and I will be the next to die.

Dorottya follows in Alida's footsteps, and then Angyalka, Borbala, Fanni, Jazmin, and Iren. I learn all their names so that someone might remember them. Elizabeth certainly doesn't bother with such trifles, beyond her obsessive recording of the "results" in that accursed black book. With each new death, she tweaks the potion in some way, but always the arsenic does its foul work. Yet she remains monstrously unswayed, her conviction seemingly impervious to doubt.

With every new death, I grow increasingly convinced that I have made a graver mistake than I could have imagined in ridding us of Ferenc. The more I consider it, the more I believe that their relationship was more complex than I could readily understand. While he may have been a blight of a man, the only servants that died during his reign were the three he gave to Elizabeth as gifts, the night of their demonic banquet—and that was an olive branch, an indulgence, a tip of the hat. He was the ice to her fire, the cold, quelling gale, always tempering and holding her back. And that was why she hated him and chafed so, maddened by his restraint. Pinned under his thumb such that she could not kill at whim, whenever the choler moved her.

Had I not murdered him, all the women marked in her accursed black book might still be alive.

Too long, I have clung to the notion that her love for her son—and her passion for me—somehow tips her balance toward good, even if only slightly. But I can no longer deny what she is. A blade is a blade, cold and ruthless, forged only to draw blood. No matter how enticing its gleam in a certain light.

When she tests the potion on a little girl—the tiny, doe-eyed daughter of the head cook, only seven years at most—my heart breaks clean through. I again consider killing her myself, so vividly that when I am able to steal a snatch of sleep, I dream of little else. But Janos would not have it—my death would be certain, and my family's demise along with it.

After the little girl dies like the rest, something vital seems to snap in Elizabeth. Some twisted offshoot of repressed guilt, perhaps, turning in on itself. Though I suspect even that may allot her far too much credit. More likely it is simple frustration at being thwarted, denied what she wants.

"What am I doing wrong?" she rages, pacing back and forth in the solar. At every step she seeks to destroy something—tip a glass beaker off a table, rip a book page in two. Her fury is insatiable, a devouring maw that sucks everything into itself. "I have tried everything, everything I can think. And still these accursed wretches fail to live, much less to thrive! How much am I expected to bear? *What else am I to do?*"

When I keep quiet, terrified that she will turn her wrath on me, she wheels around to glare at me, teeth bared. She has grown much thinner in her frenzy, her skin drawn taut over strong bones, and there is something fearfully stark and vulpine about her aspect. Even her teeth seem larger and sharper, though that is just because her lips have lost their plumpness. It is as if the bloodthirsty predator within her is rising to the fore, molding her flesh to match its own dread shape.

"Must you insist on standing there like some bedamned statue?" she spits through her teeth. "Do you truly have nothing to say for yourself, for your part in this abysmal failure? Is herb work not meant to be *your* province?"

I lick my lips, my heart beating so fiercely it feels mad in my chest, like a trapped hummingbird. "I am sorry to have disappointed you," I murmur through numb lips, though of course it is a lie—for what I wish for most fervently is to kill her for what she has done, drive a stake through her monstrous heart. I quash the mutinous thought as quickly as I can, terrified that she will somehow read it in my eyes. "I do not know what else to say or do, my lady, save for keep trying."

"*Then try harder*," she roars at me, spittle flying from her lips. With a furious sweep of her arm, the glassware on the table comes crashing to the floor, shattering into a glittering shower of shards.

When there is nothing else left to smash or tear, she yanks

at her own hair and shrieks up at the ceiling like a wolf, baying out her rage. It ripples my skin in gooseflesh from toes to temples, until I am so afraid I dare not approach her, fearing that she might slash at me with her nails.

My instinct is right, though it is not me she chooses to rend—at least, not yet, though I have no way of knowing how long her forbearance will last. Once she is through with the potions for good, that will spell my own end.

The next day, she has Janos string up three more maidservants in the courtyard. It is a wonder that any are even left, but we are so secluded up here, in Elizabeth's aerie, that there is nowhere to run. Under the remorseless single eye of the sun, with the whole keep gathered to watch, she flogs and whips them ruthlessly for a list of invented misdemeanors. Their screams and sobs tear the balmy air, and every time a breeze blows by my nose, smelling incongruously both of blood and summer peaches, it is all I can do not to gag.

By the time she exhausts herself, they have no backs left to speak of. Only I stay to watch until the bitter end. When Janos takes them down to bury them, I must make sure that I am there to bear witness.

It is the very least that I can do for them, now that I have failed them in every other respect.

Chapter Nineteen

The Runes and the Peddler

After that, we have a brief, strange snatch of peace.

I use the time to think myself in circles, plotting how I might flee this place and keep my head. Each avenue leads me to the same dead end. But there *must* be some path leading out from this thorned thicket of a predicament, I tell myself. Even if I cannot see it yet.

Elizabeth leaves me to my own devices for the first time since I became her chambermaid. For there is a new presence in the keep, a skulking crow of a man whom she has hired as valet—though why she should need him, I have no idea, when Janos would gladly bury the whole world in the orchard if she paid him to do so. This Thorko has a pale, repellent face, gleaming as if coated with a scrim of oil, with fleshy red lips like a woman's exaggerated pout. She does not tell me who he is, and I am too grateful for my reprieve to ask. I sleep in the solar while she sequesters herself in her chambers with him. Odd, rhythmic chants and shrill cries emanate from behind the closed doors, until I begin to wonder if she has taken him for a lover.

What feels like a very long time ago, it would have pained me beyond anguish to think that she had chosen to share her bed with someone else. Now, heartbroken and devastated as I am, I am merely relieved that I need not pretend that she does not revolt me.

And when I am summoned to attend to her late one night, I find that the truth is so much worse.

"My lady?" I call out, rapping on the heavy, bronze-hinged door. "May I come in?"

"Yes, my dove," her voice trails out, with a silky note to it that immediately suffuses me with terror. She does not mean that endearment any more than I consider her to be a lady, and I know she uses it now only to toy with me, like a spider playfully dangling a fly over its maw. I have learned that Elizabeth is to be especially feared when she sounds like this. Like some lounging wildcat, her muzzle bloodied with her kill. "Go on, come in."

I crack the door open and slip through—only to nearly stumble at the force of the reek. The room stinks of frankincense, such that I am first reminded of my village church. Though our holy house never smelled of charnel like this, as though it had been ransacked by janissaries. It is so dark I can barely discern the outlines of Elizabeth's deep copper tub, illuminated by the faint light from a circle of candles ringed around it. They are rendered from black tallow, something I have never seen before. The darkness of their bases somehow dims the light even as it's cast.

Elizabeth lounges in the tub, with Thorko behind her where I once used to kneel, his face shrouded by a heavy cowl. Her head rests against the rim, tipped back to let him paint her face and chest with his fingertips, leaving strange, angular markings like chicken scratch. The sigils seem to dance unsettlingly in the dim light, blurring and doubling when I peer at them too hard. The air above her coils with wreaths of incense smoke like dragon's breath, and the dark water in the tub glistens with an oily sheen.

With a stuttering heart, I abruptly realize what it really is—followed by the even more sickening thought of how many people she must have killed in order to fill it to the brim. I have not seen Margareta or Judit in days; they both must have fallen to her blade.

"Elizabeth," I manage to whisper, swallowing a ragged whimper, my hand floating to my mouth like a ghost. "Oh, Elizabeth, what have you done?"

Elizabeth smiles beatifically at me, reaching up to smear more blood through her hair. "I should think it obvious to you, of all people," she croons, turning to cast a conspiratorial look at Thorko. "I am working witchcraft, of course. Making magic with Thorko's help. He is a teacher, a renowned priest of the occult. And a longtime family friend as well."

"You flatter me, my lady," Thorko says with false modesty, inclining his cowled head. His voice is low and dulcet, jarringly pleasant in comparison to his face, grotesque and striped by flickering shadow. "I am merely a guide. Any accomplishment is entirely your own."

My heart shudders in revolt. Everything she's done so far has been depraved enough, but this?

This is a transgression on an unfathomable scale.

"But—Elizabeth, this is Lucifer's own work!" I force through quivering lips. My voice is high and hysterical, sure to madden her, but I cannot help myself. "How can you do this, entreat the adversary himself—"

She rolls her eyes, pursing blood-smeared lips. "Hardly the devil," she replies airily. "We are calling upon the maiden Szepassony to bless me with beauty to match her own. Just as my mother used to do when I was young, with Thorko's guidance. I thought it foolish at the time, but now that sciences and ciphers have failed me . . ." She shrugs a shoulder, pulling a helpless face. "My mother was a beauty until the day she died. What harm is there in trying, if it worked for her?"

"What harm?" I repeat, incredulous, crossing myself. How can she toy so casually with the profane, the forbidden and obscene? When she shied away from me as if terrified of possession, of specters lurking behind my eyes? "Szepassony is a demon herself! She is the white lady, seducer of men, abjured by the church! She lures children away and feeds them frozen death at her breast. She . . . She is *wicked*, Elizabeth—and you have killed for her!"

"Oh, what does wicked even mean, other than that she knew her mind? And the *church*," Elizabeth scoffs, turning and spitting demonstratively over one shoulder. "That is what I think of the church and its mealymouthed priests, yet more sanctimonious men breathing down my neck. Long before Szepassony was named a demon, she was a goddess of beauty, a deity of storms, a wild maiden dancing in the rain. Does that sound like something to loathe or fear?"

"If that is true," I counter, keeping my eyes trained on her, unable to bear Thorko's smirk twitching under the candles' writhing light, "why would she demand the blood of innocents from you?"

"Everything has a price," she concedes with another infuriating shrug. As if that is all those women's lives are worth, a heedless flick of the shoulders. "Especially a goddess's favor. And blood is worth more than the finest gem."

"Elizabeth, please," I attempt desperately, one last time. "This is wrong, do you not see? Worse than wrong. This is infernal."

"So you will not join me, then," she murmurs with a furrowed brow and a pout, sighing gustily. "A terrible pity, though I'm afraid I suspected as much. I see that I have misjudged you badly, Anna, just as Thorko says." Of course he does, I think with a surge of pure terror, catching the smug glint in his eye as he turns away from us to refresh the censer. He craves her favor entirely for himself, and what better way to secure it than by ensuring the demise of the lady's disgraced former favorite? "You are merely clay where I thought you to be stone. And what is clay but something to be molded by another's hand, with no native shape of its own?"

With that she turns away from me, shifting in that awful crimson tide to receive a goblet from Thorko's hands. When she drinks, it overflows her lips, cascading down her chest as if her own throat has been slit.

"What is that, Elizabeth?" I ask in a warbling voice that does not even sound like my own. "What are you drinking?"

A blade-edged grin splits her face, revealing teeth streaked with glistening red. "My new elixir, of course," she replies. "We had the crucial ingredient wrong after all, you and I. How could we both have been so blind? What better to maintain one's own blood than the blood of the freshly dead, mingled with the finest of life-giving herbs? And that is where *you* come in. For whatever else has broken between us, you are still my little sage—and if anyone can marry magic and medicine, even if reluctantly, I have faith that it is you."

I stumble back a step, awash with disgust that she should enlist my help with this obscene alchemy. "No," I manage. "Never. I will not help you, not in this travesty."

Her smile somehow widens, whetting itself, sharpening at the edges. "No?" she repeats delicately, savoring the word. "And what if I should send for your mother, your sweet sister, your fat little brothers? Do not forget that I know where they may be found, nor should you doubt my resolve. From a certain angle, it would almost be a kindness to you. As you have told me, your brothers may be little louts, but just think—would they not be veritable fonts of lifeblood for my use? I would merely be repurposing them!"

She blinks at me, self-satisfied as a fox with a sparrow in its jaws. I stand petrified, my heart more trembling than beating, my mind churning like a maelstrom. She will do it, I know better than to doubt her. Refusing her means certain death for my family—and I cannot bring myself to condemn them, not even if it means that many others must die in their place.

But perhaps there is another, subtler way to resist. For too long I truly have been nothing but her clay, warmed easily between her hands—but even clay hardens when exposed to too much heat.

And I am no stranger to poisons.

"Very well, my lady," I say, inclining my head to hide the intention in my eyes. "I will assist in your endeavor as best I may."

"Oh, I am so pleased to hear it," she purrs, drawing her lip slowly between her teeth. "And should you think to perhaps offer me some *sharper* medicine, as you did my husband, do not forget that I have Thorko with me." She arches her back and flings her arms above her head, allowing Thorko to paint her throat with more bloody sigils when he returns to kneel behind her. When she squirms under his trailing touch, I swallow another gout of disgust. How can she not see the lust playing in his gaze, nor divine his true intent? "Be assured that he is quite equipped to carry out my vengeance, should any ill befall me from your brews."

"I would never consider it," I force through clenched teeth, though of course that was precisely what I intended.

"Then we are decided!" she exclaims. "Thorko will fetch you when we are ready to incorporate your knowledge. For now, you are dismissed."

Her gaze slides easily away from me. I can hear him murmuring to her, a trill of her laughter as I turn my back on them and leave, roiling with revulsion.

⋀⋀⋀⋀⋀⋀⋀⋀⋀⋀⋀⋀⋀⋀⋀⋀⋀⋀⋀⋀⋀⋀⋀⋀⋀⋀⋀⋀⋀⋀⋀⋀⋀⋀⋀⋀⋀⋀

The two of them barely surface from her chambers, wallowing in their den of iniquity. They might as well be lovers for all the heed they pay to the outside world, save for plundering it for the victims Janos readily provides, and pestering me for different combinations of herbs every few days.

When I am not grinding herbs for them, I spend my time storming around the keep, lost in thought. The castle is already so empty, with so many fallen to Elizabeth's whip and knife, that the corridors fairly echo. Only the cornerstones of Elizabeth's household, Master Aurel and Mistress Magda and their handpicked favorites, seem safe from her depredations. The rest of the lower-ranked servants would have long since run, were there anywhere to go. But the castle perches upon its jutting peak, the drop-offs on either side sheer enough to preclude escape by anything but the main road, and that remains guarded day and night by Elizabeth's sentries. Whether or not they are loyal to her, they are certainly faithful to her coin; I know as much from the unfortunate laundress who attempted to flee a fortnight ago. Once she was dragged back, Elizabeth had her beheaded to discourage the rest from growing so bold.

But though I still cannot think of how to run without imperiling my kin, perhaps I can be of some little good while I languish here.

The next time the wine peddler makes his visit to the kitchens, I approach him when he's done bartering with Mistress Magda.

"May I speak with you?" I ask softly, laying my hand on his linen sleeve. "Just for a moment? There is coin in it for you."

"Certainly, mistress," he replies, casting me a wary look. I still wear one of the finer gowns Elizabeth commissioned for me, after gleefully disposing of my simple smocks. Though

I'm sure he has noticed the eerie silence of the keep, I look like someone of consequence. Someone he cannot easily brush off. "What can I do for you?"

I take him by the elbow and guide him to an alcove off the kitchens. "Do you know Peter Erdelyi of Sarvar?" I ask, my insides clenched tight with hope and impatience. "Son of Adorjan Erdelyi, the vintner?"

"Why, of course I do!" he says, his amiable face splitting into a grin. "Salt of the earth, is Adorjan, and could tease wine from water like the good lord's son himself, beg pardon for the blasphemy. His son's a fine, steady lad, too. Who are they to you?"

"Peter and I are fast friends, reared together. And if you hold him and his father in esteem, I would ask that you do something for me. A paid favor." My voice quavers when I speak, trembling with held tears. "Please—it's very important. I—I can give you good coin to see the task through."

The man's kind, brown gaze shifts between my eyes, heavy with such sympathy and warmth that my knees nearly buckle to see it. It feels an ashen eternity since I have seen a friendly face.

"Whatever it is, mistress, I am happy to do it for your own sake," he says, taking me by the shoulders. "But tell me, and I mean no insult—are you well? You look peaked, and I'll tell you, this place is damnably strange. I'm like to jump out of my skin since I arrived. If there's aught I can do to help . . ."

I bite the inside of my cheek, fighting back a tide of tears. I'm terrified, unspeakably afraid, but I cannot let this chance pass me by. "Then here is what I would have you do."

Come dusk, when the wine peddler's covered cart rattles down the steep road leading away from the keep, the three remaining sculls go with it. I yearned to go with them myself, so badly I could nearly taste the freedom of the mountain wind scouring that open road. But while Elizabeth will likely not chase these poor girls down once she discovers they are gone—even her influence only extends so far—I know she would hunt me to the ends of the earth.

For the rest of the day, I sit at a window and nervously watch the empty road winding down the hill, my jaw clenched so hard it nearly cracks under the strain. I even pray under my breath, though it is not my wont, wishing them fleet-footed steeds and many miles of distance. It is only when the moon tears a hole in night's black fabric, letting in the light, that I relax a little and allow myself to breathe. Perhaps I have done it, achieved some small measure of good. Even then I keep my vigil long, as though my presence in the window has become a good-luck token ushering the escapees to safety.

Midnight finds me dozing against the sill, jarred roughly into wakefulness by a sudden racket below. Bleary with sleep, I stumble to my feet and trip down the corridor, following the sounds of commotion to the keep's great hall.

The sight that meets me robs me of my breath.

The escaped sculls stand with hands bound behind their backs, one restrained by Janos and the other two by Elizabeth's guards. Elizabeth looms before them in her plum-and-gold dressing gown, her neck and face still rosy from where she must have hastily scrubbed herself clean.

"Your doing, I suppose?" she snaps off, barely curling the end into a question. Under Thorko's tutelage she hasn't left her room in weeks, and her eyes look fearfully huge against her sun-starved face. Like pits that might yawn open and swallow me at any moment. I see nothing left of her but dark Elizabeth, the rest scorched away and fallen like a husk. "The wine merchant swore up and down that he did not know of his clandestine cargo, but these meek simps hardly burrowed amongst his barrels of their own accord. This one . . ."

She strides over to the oldest of the bunch, a spirited brunette who was one of Ilona's better friends. She takes the girl casually by the hair and rattles her head about. "Terezia here was more than ready to give you up in exchange for her life. Weren't you, you shrew?"

Terezia is so petrified she can barely summon the courage to swallow. "Yes, mistress," she chokes out desperately, her eyes flitting to me. "We didn't want to, but she—she made us go! Said she would ensorcell us if we went against her wishes!"

Those implacable dark eyes slide back to me, and I can nearly see the flames licking in their depths. "Well, is it true? Did you turn on me, Anna, like some treacherous trull? Bite the hand that loved and fed you?"

"I did," I say readily, inclining my head. If she truly believes that this was all my design, she might let them live. "I—I have been sorely irked by the loss of your favor, Elizabeth, and—"

She cocks her head sharply, like a hawk. "Did you truly just say 'Elizabeth,' you traitorous bitch? Even now you presume to refer to your own mistress, the lady you so baldly tossed over, by her given name?"

"Forgive me, my lady," I eke out. "I will not forget myself again."

"And do you truly expect me to believe that you freed these chits, *my* property, solely to gall me? Come now, Anna. Do you think me such a fool?" Her face turns saccharine, lower lip jutting in a pout. "You did it to save their worthless little lives, didn't you? Out of the tenderness of your pathetic heart. Go on, admit it—tell me you did, and I may even let them live."

"Forgive me, my lady," I repeat, trembling so hard I can feel my flesh tugging minutely at my bones. "But it's as you say."

She watches me keenly, shaking her head in tiny, almost involuntary movements. "How could I have thought you to be so different than you are?" she wonders in a tone of genuine curiosity. "You know why I require them—and yet you value their paltry, meaningless lives over my needs. How can you say you ever loved me and not make yourself a liar?"

"I did love you, my lady," I say simply, my voice hoarse with grief. "At first, when I knew no better. But whatever guise you choose to take, you kill for sheer pleasure just as much as any gain beyond it. Because you *like* it, revel in their pain."

"And what if I do?" she demands, blazing with fury. "They are *mine*, to do with as I will. How dare you judge me for it?"

I shake my head, so awash in devastation I can barely stand. "I do not know whether you have always been so—or whether it is this woman's life that cages your spirit, that has twisted you into a creature so misshapen by choler. But whichever it is, it does not excuse you in my eyes."

She is across the room like an arrow, my ear ringing from her slap almost before I register that she has moved. The crack of her palm against my face echoes through the room.

With that first blow, the only time she has laid a hand on me in anger, she shatters even the memory of any fondness between us.

"How can you be such an ungrateful bitch, after all the good I've done you?" she hisses into my face, spittle flying between us and flecking my cheeks. "Lifted you from that village's godforsaken muck? Wrested you out from your father's grip when he would have crushed you to death?"

"But . . ." My lips have gone so numb I can barely feel the words escape through them. "What do you mean? My father died, else I could have never—"

"Oh, don't be such an imbecile," she spits, rolling her eyes. "Of course he did not die by accident. What, you think the cosmos revolves around you, caters to your whims such that it would strike him dead *the very day* you needed him to be so?"

"You killed him." The truth of it tolls inside me, undeniable as church bells. "To get to me."

"Not with my own hands, but yes, of course I did. Thorko was in my employ even then—he accompanied Janos to fetch you, should there be any trouble. When that blasted ruffian wouldn't yield you to me . . ." She shrugs elaborately. "Well. Stirring a horse into pique can be a simple thing, and Thorko is a man of many talents. From what I am told, the world did not much mourn your father's passing. You certainly did not."

I glance over at Thorko, where he skulks in the shadows

by the hearth. As if feeling my regard, he looks over at me slyly, a glimmer of satisfaction flashing across his face. My father's murderer—or the hand that slayed him, anyway.

"That may be true," I say, marveling at the breadth of her depravity. That she would so blithely kill a man just to win possession of a person, as if I were no more than a coveted toy. "But you are worse, far, far worse than he ever was. You *did* mean for me to kill your husband. And you never truly believed me to be deranged, did you? All of it—just a ploy to hide your intentions, and your own true nature from me."

"And if that is true, does it really matter?" she murmurs, her dark gaze still locked on mine. She reaches out and draws a strand of my hair through her fingers, twirling it around her knuckle. "You cannot deny that I also treated you like a queen, like my own equal. Festooned you with finery, elevated your mind, tended to you when you ailed. Why can you not simply set aside your useless scruples, let things be as they were?"

"That is impossible, my lady," I say, shaking my head, though it tightens her grip on my hair, sets my scalp to prickling. "Because we are not equals. Unlike you, I have never killed or maimed for pleasure."

Her face twists, contorts into that draconic visage that haunts my days and dreams. She whips me tight against her, my back to her front, and I freeze when I feel the icy edge of a blade beneath my chin. "Then perhaps it has come time for you to serve me better, little traitor," she hisses into my ear, breath rushing through her gritted teeth. I can feel her heart battering against my back, and I don't dare move a muscle for fear of provoking her. "Silently, for once, with your blood rather than your tiresome mind."

Thorko materializes beside us as though from the ether, his hand alighting on her shoulder. "Do not forget that we still need her, my lady," he mutters to her, even as I tremble in her grip. "To work her magic with the herbs. And perhaps beyond that as well . . ."

She holds me tight for an endless, agonizing moment, shuddering with indecision—then releases me abruptly and steps back, twitching her head at her men. As one, they unsheathe their knives and twist the women to face them—plunging the blades into their bellies.

I stifle a gasp as they crumple, falling to their knees before collapsing onto the unforgiving stones.

"It is a terrible death, you know," she whispers, moving to stand beside me, her lips hovering near my ear. My skin crawls in revulsion, stirring in response to the warm fan of her breath. "To be run through the gut. Hours of agony. And you will sit here and watch it all unfold, and not move so much as a finger to ease their suffering. Or I will have Janos make you wish you were in their place."

I stand like a stone while she sweeps out of the room, two of the men trailing after her. Janos sprawls his bulk into a chair, blithely unconcerned.

I do not allow myself to weep until I'm sure she cannot hear me—then I sink to the floor myself and dissolve into sobs like I have never known.

It takes the women hours to shuffle off this mortal coil, just as she said. By the time their pitiful moans whittle away to nothing, I have drained myself dry of water, shed all my salt. The sky is fracturing with dawn when I come to my feet, rising reborn and newly forged. No longer caring if she kills me, nor what miserable end I shall come to once she's finished with her games.

As long as I can somehow take her with me at the end.

Wrestle her, screaming, into the deepest pit of hell.

PART THREE: Sundered

Chapter Twenty

The School and the Sister

Ihaunt Csejthe's corridors, drifting through them like a specter through fog, unable to sit still. Tormented by the relentless torrent of my thoughts. Nobody disturbs my wandering; Elizabeth must be either distracted or still too wroth to summon me for any herb work. And I am content to keep out of her sight for as long as she will allow it.

But I cannot stop thinking of her schemes, her many machinations, wondering how far back they stem, winding into the loam of our shared past like spidery rivers. Did she plan all this, I ask myself, in the held-breath moment when our eyes first met? When she saw me snared like a fish on the hook of her beauty, did a vision rush over her in the space of a breath—all the ways in which a pet witch could be put to use? Did she think even then to seduce me, beguile me into killing her husband for her? Was she already dreaming of the elixirs I might devise and brew?

Though it makes me shudder with mortification and self-loathing, I begin to believe that our lovemaking was always for some other gain. Feigned from the very inception.

I would not put any of it past her.

A few days later, the insistent rumble of carriage wheels from the road draws me to a window. We are visited by merchants whenever the keep's supplies run low, but I've never heard such a sustained rattle, one carriage after another like a processional. I lean on my forearms and crane out the window, to see a young woman's shining head catch the sun as she alights from her carriage with a footman's help. As soon as it pulls away, a new carriage draws up, disgorging another girl.

They continue to arrive all day. The carriages each bear a different crest; these young women must be of noble birth, though from what I can gather from my perch, none of their gowns are so fine as Elizabeth's. Which means all of them must hold some lesser status.

What is this new perfidy? I wonder to myself, my stomach assailed with misgiving. What does she want of them, when she cannot possibly need so many ladies-in-waiting?

I watch the parade anxiously, nibbling on my knuckles, until night falls and music strikes up in the great hall, wreathing faintly through the corridors. I make my way there with dragging, leaden feet, at odds with the lighthearted music emanating from within. Margareta and Judit are long dead, I think grimly. One of the new arrivals must be similarly gifted.

As I step over the threshold, my heart lifts reflexively at the bright chatter of conversation—it's been so long since I heard anything like it here. The keep has been about as lively as a crypt, but now my gaze skims over a dozen gathered girls, ranging from young womanhood to twelve or thirteen. They sit on chairs or lounge on pillows, as Margareta and Judit used to do—with Elizabeth by the hearth, occupying the center of the room. She looks gorgeous, jubilant, more effervescent than I've seen her since we first met. Scrubbed clean and clad in one of her finest ruby-colored gowns, its snowy ruffles cascading beneath her chin.

One of the new girls stands behind her, painstakingly dressing her hair. She's small, clearly much younger than the rest, her dress coarse and a bit tattered. At first my eyes nearly drift over her, distracted by the hubbub and the crowd.

Then I see the achingly familiar, buttery hue of her hair.

"Klara?!" I cry, despair wrenching my fist against my stomach. My heart feels like a battering ram inside my chest.

The girl's head flicks up, and there can be no mistake.

My sister's face breaks open like the sun bursting through clouds, and she abandons her post to dash across the room toward me, dancing nimbly between the gathered girls. In a moment she has flung her little arms around my waist, pressed her head into my chest. She is a great deal more solid than I remember, more robust girl and less will-o'-the-wisp.

At least I've managed that much for her, before failing her so utterly.

"Annacska," she squeals into my bosom, nestling so tightly against me I can feel the hammering of her own heart, though I know hers beats with joy. "Surprise!"

"What," I manage, the edges of my sight blackening like something being burned. "What is my sister doing here, Elizabeth?"

I am so distraught, so far beyond my own grasp, that I do

not even remember to call her "my lady." She doesn't seem to mind, crossing her arms loosely over her chest. A smile slinks across her face, her eyes gleaming bright with spite above it.

"Welcome to my new finishing school, Anna," she says, the smile widening into a toothy grin. "The silence was becoming so stifling, wouldn't you agree? And of late, we've had such undue difficulty procuring good help." She shrugs, as though bewildered, though I can see that she nearly overflows with self-satisfaction. "One would almost think the poor have no true desire to uplift themselves by seeking good, honest work under my roof."

Because you killed most of your household, I want to scream. *And no one in their right mind will come work for you any longer.*

"So, a while ago, I thought to myself," she continues, laying a pensive finger against her cheek. "What better time than now to fulfill a long-held dream? You see, I've always wished to mentor the daughters of noble families less fortunate than my own. Give them the opportunity to grow, open their minds to new things."

New things like flogs and whips and blades, no doubt.

"But . . ." My voice emerges as an airless rasp, as if I am already entombed. "But my sister, she's no noble, just a commoner . . ."

"I thought I would extend the invitation to her, regardless, as a *very special* favor." She draws her lower lip between her teeth, releasing it with excruciating slowness. Savoring this victory over me like a cat licking blood off its whiskers. "Given that I hold you, her elder sister, in such high esteem. Your mother was only too happy to hand her over, I'm told."

"The lady's man left her such a large bag of coin, Anna!" Klara pipes up happily, grinning at me. "And Mama said I would be even better here, with so much more to eat. She said I would be with you!"

Of course she did, I think bleakly. What choice did she have, when faced with the countess's men?

"What was it that you told me about Klara, Anna? That she was like your mirror?" Elizabeth continues. "But sweeter, even more obliging, more tractable than you?"

Great wings of panic beat inside me, overwhelming me with their buffeting force. How could I have ever trusted this slouching monster with the knowledge of my sister? Because all this is my fault, the punishment for my faithlessness, for betraying Elizabeth by attempting to rescue those girls from her. Now they are dead, and my dandelion clutched in the palm of her ruthless hand, soon to be crushed between her fingers along with all the rest.

I should have known she would never stop finding ways to make me sorry.

My next mad thought is to simply spirit Klara away, but I can see Elizabeth's men in every corner of the room.

There is no escape, not unless I wish to cost both of us our heads.

"Please," I manage, clutching Klara so tightly against me she gives a surprised yelp, squirming in my grip. "Elizabeth—my lady—do not do this. She, she has done *nothing* to you!"

"Nothing besides being born of the same blood as you, my dearest dove," she rejoins with a sarcastic twist to the last words, her voice winking with a vicious edge. "Which renders her exquisitely suited to serve as my chambermaid, just as you once did."

"Send her back, *please*," I wail, clutching her against me. "You do not need her, not when you have me. I will do anything, I swear it, whatever you require . . ."

Frightened by my terror and the desperate force of my grip, Klara tugs away from me, peering up with huge, unsettled eyes.

"Nővér?" she whispers uncertainly, her pale lashes fluttering with confusion. "Why are you yelling at the lady?"

"Come, pet," Elizabeth calls, snapping her fingers as if my sister is a dog. Klara breaks away from me before I can snatch her back, pelting straight into the murderess's arms. "That's right, come to me! Very good! Yes, Anna, she is rather younger than is ideal—but perhaps that's for the best. She will take so quickly to service, with fewer bad habits to unlearn."

She winds a hand around Klara's thin neck and draws her close, stroking my sister's collarbone. Klara allows herself to be enfolded, lets the countess press their cheeks together. "We shall have a very lovely time, shan't we?" the wicked bitch murmurs into my sister's hair. "I will feed you cherry bonbons and stuffed partridges, and barely watered wine. Would you like that, pet?"

"Yes!" Klara exclaims giddily, overcome with the lavish attention, the sheer, bludgeoning force of Elizabeth's personality. And who would not be swayed by the thought of rich food and drink, and even more by the beckoning grasp of those eyes?

"Oh, you would? Truly?" Elizabeth tickles her delicately, pinching at her sides and cheeks until Klara is helpless with laughter, so limp she allows herself to be drawn onto my enemy's lap. "I am delighted to hear it, pet. And I think we shall get on very well indeed." She gazes at me pointedly over my sister's shoulder, tipping me a wink. "Perhaps even better than your big sister and I ever did."

The wings inside me buffet ever harder, raining feathers as my sight continues to blacken. Curling at the edges like a scroll.

She will kill her.

She will kill her.

She will kill her.

It does not stop tolling in my head even once I hit the floor, darkness stitching itself closed around me like a winding cloth.

The last thing I hear is my sister's voice calling my name—drowned out by the bright peals of Elizabeth's mocking laughter.

Chapter Twenty-one

The Flight and the Sentence

I awake from the faint as if someone has doused me with icy water.

"Klara," I gasp, bolting upright and looking wildly around before I realize where I am. I'm no longer in the great hall but in the solar, deposited clumsily on my bed. Whoever carried me here clearly paid no great mind to my state. I might have choked on my own vomit, for all they cared to arrange me comfortably. One of my legs dangles so awkwardly off the edge that it has gone corpse-numb, shattering into agonizing pins and needles when I try to move it.

As soon as I can stand, I begin to pace.

I have been oblivious through the night, waking just before dawn. There is no sound of music, nor, blessedly, of screams or pleas. Elizabeth must be holding back for once, practicing restraint. I have no doubt that she will kill these girls, noble or no, just as she did the servants. But perhaps she means to take her time, knowing that more won't be procured quite so easily once this crop is gone.

And if I know her at all, she will save Klara for last. Milking my torment until the very last drop, supping on my tears.

Which means I have a chance to make Elizabeth's crimes known to the world.

To save my sister, if not myself.

^^

I steal Elizabeth's black journal. And then I steal a horse.

Both are easier feats than expected. In her haste to take up with Thorko, Elizabeth didn't bother to hide the book in which she recorded her macabre results. Once she was done with her murderous experiments, I doubt she ever even gave it a second thought; my former mistress is nothing if not mercurial, given to passions that burn off like early-morning mist. I find it after an only cursory search of the solar, which I never bothered to properly clean after her last outburst. The book had been swept into one of the corners, in a pile of shattered glass and other debris.

I tuck it into the small satchel I plan to take with me, then set out for the stables.

The castle is quiet, nothing but silent stone and dusty air swirling in the pallid, early light. In the absence of sculls, it has been a long while since anything has been thoroughly cleaned; cobwebs cling to every rafter, reminding me of the one I trod through the day my father died. As I creep through the halls I maintain my vigilance, watching for servants, but there are so few left that our paths are not likely to cross.

I see none of the new arrivals, either. Untroubled by Elizabeth's dark diversions, the new girls must be sleeping off the excitement of the previous day, my sister among them. Every time I think of her in the castle, sick wells up my throat, until I'm forced to banish thoughts of her to keep myself steady.

When I reach the stables, I unsheathe my trusty little knife and prod the stable boy, curled up in the backmost corner, awake with my foot. He opens his eyes groggily, fairly leaping to his feet when he finds me looming over him, grim-faced as a banshee.

"Saddle a horse for me," I order once he's upright, barely recognizing the terse steeliness of my voice. This time, I don't even have to strive to intimidate. It comes naturally. "The fleetest one you have. Or I swear I will send you straight to hell, with a death curse dogging your heels."

"Y-yes, mistress," he stammers without hesitation, bolting to carry out my command. I almost wish he had resisted, even if nominally. But the way he looked at me was just as we all look at Elizabeth. Like peering into the jeering face of death itself.

Ten minutes later, I am riding hell-for-leather down the path. I slipped by the gatekeeper readily, as I had hoped I would, unbolting the great doors for myself. No one has chanced to flee from the castle in months, and the man likes his drink well; even back in Sarvar, where we had many more visitors, he was often deep in his cups soon after midnight.

By the time the sentries rouse themselves and think to scramble for their horses, I am already well past the most winding of the road's hairpin curves, disappearing into the woods that surround the foot of the hill—where I can conceal myself easily behind a hanging tapestry of vines and shrubs. I nicker under my breath to keep the horse quiet when Elizabeth's men thunder past, calling to each other. Though my heart swells at the base of my throat, their bleary eyes barely graze over our hiding place. I doubt they've ever had to chase after anyone fortunate enough to be on horseback; they must think I am long gone already.

Once I'm sure they've moved on, I spur my horse into a brisk canter, returning to the main road. For the remainder of the morning I ride from village to village, sweltering under the summer heat, searching for one large enough to house a magistrate. I know where one was to be found in Sarvar, but this place is strange to me, and more sprawling. By the time I plod into a modest township, complete with a sizable church, central square, and meeting hall, the horse has worked up a lather and the sun marks nearly noon.

"I'll take care of you as soon as I'm done," I soothe the horse as I tie him to one of the stakes outside the hall. One of his eyes rolls dubiously at me; he must be parched as well as hungry. "I promise."

Inside, one of the scurrying clerks points me to the magistrate's chambers, casting a supercilious eye over my flushed cheeks and sweaty hair.

"Master Horvath is busy with another complainant," he informs me, pulling a sour face. "You will have to wait, over by the benches."

"I don't mind waiting," I assure him hastily. "I have time."

I collapse gratefully on a bench, tilting my head back against the wall. The hall, though well kept, is nowhere near as grand as Nadasdy Castle, but I am reminded of the day I waited for an audience with Master Aurel. My eagerness to enter Elizabeth's service feels like it must have happened to someone else, a different Anna I've long since abandoned. My patience deserts me much more quickly this time, and my feet tap spastically against the floorboards, beating out my fear and nervousness. I cannot stop thinking of Klara, left to Elizabeth's mercy. Surely the countess knows by now that I have deserted her, is already seething. I can only imagine the fearsome expanse of her rage.

At least, in my absence, Elizabeth has no audience—less of a reason to torment my sister when I cannot see it.

Fortunately, no one else is waiting for Master Horvath's attention. When the polished mahogany door swings open and a couple hurries out, the woman in tears with the man's arm slung around her shoulders, I scramble to my feet and slip past them.

"Master Horvath?" I call out, knocking on the frame. "May I come in?"

A long-suffering sigh billows out, followed by a begrudging "Go on, then." I step gingerly into his chambers, musty and windowless, the walls lined with towering shelves of books. The magistrate sits behind an imposing desk, massaging the wattle beneath his chin and peering at me narrowly through lopsided spectacles. He has gray hair in kinky curls, clumsily clubbed back, and the florid look of someone given to gout.

"But you're only a girl!" he half bellows incredulously, gawping at me. "Have you no father with you? No chaperone?"

I shake my head stiffly, dipping into a quick curtsy. "No, master. It's just me."

A bushy eyebrow shoots up over the spectacles' frame, and he twists his lips from side to the side. "And what grievance have you to report?"

"Murder, sir," I say, taking a deep, shaking breath. "More than one. And torture, and witchcraft. I . . . I have a great deal to tell."

His face blanches into a grayish pallor, like a decomposing mushroom. "More than one, you say," he replies faintly, gesturing me to the chair across from his desk. "In that case, I suppose you'd better sit."

Half an hour later, I finally catch my first proper breath. Master Horvath hunches over Elizabeth's black journal, running his stubby thumb down the pages. He listened impassively, barely twitching his tufty brows, while I described Elizabeth's atrocities, all the deaths I witnessed at her hand. I told him of the demonic banquet before Ferenc died, the girls that succumbed to arsenic, and the ones she bled dry for her rituals.

The ominous blandness of his regard makes me feel like a vole scurrying across a field, with the shadow of a bird of prey circling above.

"To recap," he says crisply, smacking his lips with obvious skepticism. "You claim the countess—that is the Lady Báthory, so that we are clear—is not only a poisoner, sadist, the devil's own consort, and an adulteress who bore a peasant's child, but that she murdered her own husband as well?"

"Yes, sir," I reply, swallowing hard. I left out my own part in Ferenc's death, fearing to muddy the waters by implicating myself. "She, she had him poisoned."

"And these entries . . ." He looks up at me, fixing me with a gimlet gaze. "According to you, they are somehow proof of your outlandish claims? The records of some unnatural experiment?"

"The countess wishes to preserve her youth and beauty at any price," I explain, moistening my lips. "She was testing an elixir on these women, one that she wished to eventually take herself. What you are reading is the record of her failures, the pain she inflicted in pursuit of that folly."

"The folly of a poisonous elixir *you* helped her devise," he rumbles, eyes narrowing even further. "By your own admission."

"I had no choice in the matter," I protest. "She was my mistress. And I'm a midwife's daughter, with some knowledge of herbs and medicine. That was why she enlisted my help in that endeavor."

"A midwife's daughter," he repeats, his eyes sharpening into twin bores. "What did you say your name was again?"

"Anna Darvulia, sir," I supply, heart suddenly knocking against my ribs. Shouldn't my name be of the least interest, in comparison to everything else I've told him?

"Anna Darvulia," he mutters. "Not a common name, yet a familiar one. Tell me, what cause would I have to know it?"

"I'm—I'm not sure, sir," I stumble, taken aback. "I have been the lady's chambermaid for nearly a year, both here and back home in Sarvar. Always by her side. Everything that she has done, I have witnessed. And she . . ." My courage deserts me, and suddenly I feel like no more than what I am. Just a sixteen-year-old girl without anyone to help her. "Sir, she has my sister. Unless you do something, she plans to kill her—along with the daughters of nobles, a dozen girls she has lured to the keep. She is a monster, a black-hearted devil, she must be stopped—"

"Yes, yes, I think I have the gist," he says abruptly, rising and maneuvering his ungainly bulk around the desk. "Why don't you wait here? I must consult . . . one of my colleagues on the protocol, see how justice might best be served. The countess is a powerful woman. This matter is sure to be a delicate one."

A clamor of hope rises up inside me like a belling chorus, and I clutch the chair arms with bloodless fingers. "Oh, thank you, sir! I am so grateful, I—"

He waves off my thanks irritably, bustling out the door behind me. I am so engorged with the possibility of Klara's freedom and Elizabeth's demise that it takes a few moments for the metallic rattle behind me to sink in.

"What . . ." I whisper to myself, rising and rushing to the door. The handle will not give under my hand, and when I tug at it the door does not budge an inch.

Despair cinches my throat like a drawstring purse. The bastard of a magistrate has locked me in.

I fall upon the door, beating it with my fists. "Let me out, God damn you," I sob, pressing my cheek against the wood. "Let me go, I have done *nothing* . . ."

Though I pound and beg until I exhaust myself, my

entreaties are met by nothing but echoing silence. When the door finally opens some time later, it reveals the magistrate, flanked by two grim-faced men. And I understand at once what is happening. I can practically hear Elizabeth's derisive laughter, swooping about some hidden belfry in my mind, flapping and squeaking like a horde of maddened bats.

The magistrate knew my name. Which means that this trap, too, she has devised for me. Perhaps this is what Thorko meant, when he stayed her hand from killing me, cautioning her that she might need me even beyond my skill for herbs. And she has been calling me a witch where others could hear since I tended to her son—could she truly have been plotting even then to cast the blame for her misdeeds on me?

Of course she could have.

Of course she *has*.

"No," I whisper, shying back. "Please . . ."

"Anna Darvulia," he intones as the men surge forward and wrest me between them, dragging me out into the hall while the magistrate keeps pace. "Also known as Anna the Cunning, the witch of Sarvar. You are hereby under arrest, for the foul, unnatural murder of Lord Ferenc Nadasdy."

"Please," I cry as they drag me down the hall. "Please, at least go see for yourself! Ask the remaining servants, search the orchards! There are bodies everywhere!"

"Do not presume to tell us our work, you murderess!" he roars at me, spittle flying. "You shall await your trial in gaol with the rest of the scum, and we will investigate in due course—*as we see fit.*"

They will find nothing, I think bitterly as I am dragged

along, so violently that my toes barely graze the floor. Because they will hardly bother to look.

Why investigate a highborn lady, one of the most powerful nobles in the land, when you can burn a common witch in her stead?

Chapter Twenty-two

The Gaol and the Stratagem

By the time Peter comes to visit me, I have been moldering in my gaol cell for nearly a month.

It feels like much longer, here where natural light does not exist and even torchlight is mean and scarce, but I have been marking my imprisonment by the frequency of the meager meals they give me. The food is putrid, so rank I can barely choke it down, and my ribs stand stark beneath my skin. The water is befouled as well. When I first arrived, I spent several days violently emptying my guts out in the corner, but what I drink tastes somewhat fresher now. The grizzled turnkey who tends to me either took pity on my misery, or grew tired of the constant stench of my pooled vomit.

Given the way he looks at me, with dour suspicion, spitting over his shoulder and crossing himself every time he nears the bars, I suspect it was the latter.

At least it isn't cold down here, I tell myself. Though

perhaps the reek would be less in winter, and my cell not so rife with fleas. I often wake myself from fitful sleep by scratching so hard I draw blood.

If nothing else, my captivity has given me plenty of time to think. At first, I dwelled incessantly on Klara's fate, sometimes growing so helplessly furious that I would tear my own hair just as Elizabeth once did, wailing and pounding the walls until my knuckles seeped with blood. The reservoir of rage inside me never seemed to empty, nor did my rumination on other possibilities. Other lives my sister and I might have lived. If only I had never found that kitten, nor caught Elizabeth's eye with my accursed face and healer's hands. If only I had been unwilling or unable to save her son. If only I had been accosted on my way to her, and now lay rotting in some ditch along the road with buzzards picking at my bones. If only I had not killed Ferenc.

If only, if only, if only. If only I had died before I met that twisted bitch, my sister would be safe.

The turnkey did not approve of my displays. After a particularly impassioned bout of cursing my lot, he conquered his fear of me long enough to venture into my cell and beat me so brutally I feared a splinter of rib might have pierced my lung. I quieted after that, allowed my wrath to fester into a seething rage instead.

When Peter arrives, I have begun thinking of something else.

I can hear him coming long before I see him. The abiding dark has sharpened my ears, and I recognize the steady tone of his voice even before he draws close enough to my cell that I can see his anguished face. At the welcome sight of him, tears surge up in an instant, and I strain against my shackles, scrabbling to come closer to the bars. Beside him, the turnkey casts me a grim look.

"Careful not to touch the witch, nor give her nothing," he cautions Peter. "Anything you leave with her, she can use to ensorcell you or harm herself. And the magistrate would be wroth were she found hanged before her trial."

"She's not a witch!" Peter grinds out. "And she's hurt, look at her! Have you *struck* her, you lout? A defenseless girl in your care?"

"Just the once!" he replies, indignant. "She was ranting and raving, calling on demons and the like. Raising an unholy racket. And whether she's a witch or no isn't mine to say, but I don't like the look of her eyes. Like I said—mind that you not touch her."

"How much time do we have?"

"For what you gave me? Ten minutes." A crafty look oozes over his pockmarked face. "But could be a quarter of an hour, for another thaler."

Fuming, Peter rummages in his coin purse and tosses the man another coin. The turnkey snatches it out of the air like a snapping dog. He favors me with another contemptuous glare, then strides back into the dark, leaving us alone.

"Bee," Peter exhales, surging forward and wrapping his hands around the bars. The sincere concern on his face is almost unfamiliar, after the morass of malevolence, suspicion, and deceit I've inhabited for so long. I've almost forgotten what it looks like to have someone simply care for me. "What have they done to you?"

"I'm all right," I reassure him through a hot wash of tears, though the groan that wheezes out of me when I try to scoot closer to the bars proves me a liar. I'm manacled to the wall anyway. Despite the turnkey's fears, Peter couldn't touch me if he tried. "They've done nothing worse than beat me. Oh, Peter, thank you for coming, it's so *good* to see you, I thought I might die in this hell without ever seeing . . ."

I dissolve into tears, and for a moment I simply slump and sob, while Peter watches me helplessly, his own eyes glossed. "How did you know to look for me here?" I manage when I can speak again.

"A fortnight ago we heard news that you had been arrested, accused of witchcraft and the murder of Lord Nadasdy. Your mother came to beg me to watch your brothers while she came to you." His face warms with tenderness. "As if I would not have gone to you at once myself, as soon as I knew."

"Mama?" Hope flares painfully inside me, alongside a childish yearning for my mother. "Is she here, too, then?"

He shakes his head, brow furrowed. "I convinced her to let me come alone so she might stay back with your brothers. And I promised to fetch Klara for her, bring her back with me."

My shoulders hunch at the mention of my sister, my stomach fisting.

"The countess won't let her go so easily," I whisper brokenly. "She's a monster, Peter. A devil, a beast. I barely escaped her myself, and then the damned magistrate wouldn't even believe me. I don't think they've so much as searched the keep. She's poisoned the well so thoroughly against me, made me into her scapegoat. Implicated me from the start."

"So it's all true?" he asks. His eyes are unreadable in the flickering torchlight, his tone almost wary. "She is truly a murderer and devil worshipper? She has killed and tortured her own servants for leisure? Murdered her husband?"

"Peti . . ." Trepidation closes my throat like a vise. "You—you believe me, don't you?"

"That you are no witch?" he scoffs. "Of course I believe that, bee. You've one of the purest hearts I know."

I look away from him, my insides clenching. "I'm not sure you'd still think so, if you knew all that I've done for her. *With* her."

"Bee, look at me." When I meet his eyes with an effort, I find them wary but receptive. "I already know she has a son—your mother told me that much was surely true, so why would I doubt your word on the rest? But it is said the lord died of poison. And I know you know poisons like any other midwife, just as you know life-giving herbs."

"That part is complicated," I admit, heaving a painful sigh that strains my aching lungs. "The countess asked me to kill him, and I . . . I made a terrible mistake. He was a cruel man, given to violence. I thought I was doing good, keeping others safe from him. I didn't realize that it was always her. That she was the rotted root."

Peter's regard shifts between my eyes. He slides down the bars, gingerly sits on the soiled floor with an arm draped over his knee. "I'm not sure I understand. Will you explain?"

I tell him everything, casting back to my first days with the countess and how she tested my commitment, by setting obstacle after obstacle in my path before she even allowed me to become her chambermaid. Though my gorge rises at the retelling of all the torture, especially the poor women who fell to arsenic and the ones skinned and bled dry for Elizabeth's spells, I spare him no details. It is crucial, more important than anything I have ever done, that I make him not just believe me but understand the full measure of the threat.

By the time I am done, my placid friend is beside himself with wrath. He stumbles to his feet, pacing back and forth in front of the cell.

"That *fiend,*" he rages, hands balled into fists. "That, that depraved, barbaric ghoul! I will go immediately to the keep and wrest your sister from her hands."

"Peter, no," I hiss ardently, scrabbling to edge nearer to the bars though my manacles bite into my skin. "She will not simply give you Klara; she will set her men on you, and I have seen them kill without a second thought at her command. And even if you succeed against all odds, what then? You may save Klara, but I will still go to the rope or stake—and what of all the others who will fall victim to her? We must be careful in this, more clever than she is. We must trap her, just as she trapped me."

"How?" he questions, his face suffused with fear and uncertainty. "When she is a countess, and we are common? How are we to fight her?"

"Listen to me, Peti," I instruct, fixing my gaze on his. "Here is what we must do."

Once he is gone, I settle in for the wait. With an end in sight—or at least, some kind of purpose beyond merely languishing in this squalor—the days seem even more interminable.

But in a fortnight, my plans bear fruit. I have another visitor.

Elizabeth does not come in as quietly as Peter did, but rather streaks in like a feral cat.

"Where is he, you conniving bitch?" she screeches through the bars, lips peeled back from her teeth. Her eyes flare with a firestorm of wrath and terror, and a surprising scrim of tears. My heart swells at the sight of her emotion, expanding with hope. Perhaps I have judged her aright for once; perhaps my desperate, foolhardy scheme actually has some scant chance of success. "What have you done with my son?"

"What have *I* done?" I lift my eyebrows innocently, cocking my head to the side. "Mistress, I mistake your meaning. As you can see . . ." I sweep my hand to encompass my cell, the rotted straw, slimed stone, and the carcasses of the rats whose necks I snapped for their presumption to gnaw at me. "I have been somewhat indisposed."

"You know what I mean," she grinds out, gnashing her teeth together. She looks a fright, her hair tumbling tangled over her shoulders, her corset mislaced and awkwardly bulging under her gown. Her cheeks are streaked with the dried salt of tears, and it pleases me savagely to see that her fabled beauty has deserted her. "I'm well aware it was your lackey who spirited him away, at your urging."

A trill of misgiving sours my rising triumph. "My lackey?"

"Your *Peter*," she snarls, eyes flashing. "Your best friend, so clearly, pathetically enamored of you. He said to tell you that he hopes you will still love him. Though he has somewhat less skin now to call his own."

"Wh-what?" I fumble, my heart beginning to race. "What are you talking about?"

"Oh, was his capture not part of your *stratagem*?" She snaps, sucking frantic breaths through her nose, her nostrils flared like a bull's. "He barged into my keep, the very face of insolence, to announce that he had stolen away my son, stashed him somewhere known only to himself—and you. He demanded that I give him your sister in return. And that I turn myself in and answer for your accused crimes, like some common criminal." She spits over her shoulder, her jaw grinding. "The bloody cheek of him."

Why would he have gone to Csejthe Castle, I think desperately, when I urged him not to? The plan had been for him to send a letter to the countess, making those same demands anonymously—enclosed with a lock of her son's distinctive hair, so she would know beyond a doubt that he was in our keeping. I never meant for him to strut into her stronghold and declare himself her enemy. He may as well have slit his own veins open himself.

I slump against the clammy stone, reeling with despair, castigating myself. I should have known Peter would be unable to restrain himself from charging in for the rescue as soon as he had Gabor hidden. He loves Klara like his own blood, and he does not know Elizabeth, perhaps cannot even fathom the confounding reality of her even after all I told him. He would have believed she might be reasonable when faced with the loss of her son, open to making the exchange.

Even after all I said, he does not know her vicious, shift-less heart as I do. That even her mother-love for her own child is no certain thing.

"Though I will say he has remarkable fortitude," she remarks, clicking her nails against the bars, her composure slipping back into place at the scent of my burgeoning distress. "Thorko has a way with needles—an affinity, one might say. He applies them to particular places to tease out rather exquisitely agonizing pain. And yet your gray-eyed boy would not let anything slip. Not even when Thorko thrust them under his fingernails."

I flinch at that, as if I have been needled myself. "He is a good man," I reply quietly, as though I am not quaking within. "Better than you will ever understand."

"He is not a man, but a mutton-headed imbecile!" she bursts out, smacking a fist against the bars. "And I swear I will kill him, make him rue the day his parents rutted him into existence, if you do not tell me where to find my son! And don't forget, I still have your sister, too." She clasps her hands under her chin, purses her lips, flashing in an instant from rage to snide mockery. "Precious little darling that she is. Every bit as sweet and pliant as you say. I haven't touched a single hair on her head, you know. Not yet."

Her face hardens, and she presses her forehead hard against the bars, spearing me with her eyes. "But I will," she says darkly, low and hoarse. "You *know* I will. Oh, how I shall hurt her, once I have made her watch me pluck out your boy's pretty gray eyes."

"You won't," I counter, struggling to contain the manic

thumping of my heart. "Because if you do, I will have your son killed."

This is a tremendous gamble on my part, the biggest of my life. While I doubt that Elizabeth is capable of any sentiment verging on genuine love, I also know she prizes her son for what he represents—the very distillation of the youth and beauty she fears is sieving through her hands. The physical perfection she equates with power and respects above all else.

But how far does this esteem extend? What is she willing to give up for him? I am betting my life, and Klara's—and now Peter's as well—that she would yield her own to save her son. It makes me ill to gamble thus, downright sick with fear, when I have no assurance that this is true, and colossal misgivings that it will not be enough.

But it is the only hope we have, the last hand left for me to play.

"I will snuff him out, Elizabeth," I continue, purposely testing her with the familiar use of her proscribed name. "Your living legacy will die and be forgotten."

Her eyes narrow, shifting between mine. Assessing my own fortitude. I do not let myself so much as blink. "You would never kill a child," she finally pronounces. "Not even to save another, nor yourself. That is not your way."

"Do you really know me so well as that, my lady?" I ask glibly, marshalling every muscle to keep calm. If my coolness deserts me now, all is lost. I must summon every fiber of fortitude still left to me, apply them all at once. "I'm not sure that you do. Perhaps that might be true, were we speaking of some other child, a true innocent. But he is your son, with your foul blood surging through his veins. He is destined to grow into an abomination, and the world will be better for being rid of him. And don't forget . . ." I lean forward, trap her in my wintry gaze. "I am a quick study, my lady, and I have learned a thing or two from you. And you know I have killed before, when I thought it for the greater good."

"I don't believe you." It's a dry whisper, a leaf skittering over the ground. She stares at me unblinking, and even in the faltering light I can see how her pupils have expanded to consume her eyes. "You wouldn't dare, and what's more, you couldn't manage such a murder. Do you not remember how you suffered even after Ferenc, who deserved the death you gave him a thousand times over? And a child? No, you would not. It is not how you are built."

"I assure you that I would. And even if mercy got the better of me, can you be sure my accomplices, his jailors, will be so soft of heart?" I shake my head a trifle, as if ruefully. "You cannot imagine the force I have already had to exert to encourage them into restraint. Instead of that lock of hair? You would have received your sweet boy's ears, had they been allowed their way."

In truth, her son is imprisoned in a cave near our lake, watched over by some of Peter's cousins. My mother brings him food every day, and knowing her, rocks him to sleep in her lap.

But Elizabeth cannot imagine such mercy in another, not when she is incapable of it herself.

She sways in place, all the blood draining from her face,

as the thorn I've planted under her skin twists its way toward her heart.

"It's over, Elizabeth," I continue, drilling down. "If you do not free my sister and my friend, and confess to Ferenc's murder in my place, your son will die. And you along with him—for what good will you be, already so old and pale, when the best part of you is gone?"

She crumples to the floor at that, sinking down with something close to grace. On her knees, she nods mutely, her hair slipping forward to hide her face. Relief begins to unfurl cautious tendrils inside me, though I am still too afraid to hope that I have won.

"Well, you have done it," she says tiredly, after a long moment, massaging the bridge of her nose. "You clever, clever girl. Gotten the best of me. I hope it brings you joy, Anna, to have achieved something no one else ever has."

"It doesn't," I answer, though I still keep my face composed and back straight, unwilling to reveal the enormity of relief finally coursing through me. She cannot know I ever doubted that I would triumph, or that alone may convince her to retract. And yet it seems that I truly have prevailed, bored my way down to the core of her and struck upon the only friable fault line that she has. "But it will bring me peace, knowing you are not free to have your way with the world. Brutal as it is, it is no match for you."

She exhales a dry husk of a laugh. "I should have known you would be my undoing, the first time I looked into your eyes," she breathes, leaning against the bars. "I knew you were a danger to me even then, useful though you could be.

Too alive, too single-minded, too much yourself. It was part of why I loved you."

I scoff under my breath, shaking my head. "Come now, my lady. It is much too late for such dissembling. We both know there was never any real love between us."

"Well, I didn't loathe you, at any rate," she says tartly, rolling her eyes with a shade of her old spirit. "Which is much more than I can say for anyone, save my son."

"In that case . . ." I incline my head and allow my lips to quirk. "I did not loathe you either. At least, not to start. I have since rectified my regrettable lapse in judgment."

She snares my gaze with hers, and I feel an implacable flicker of the old compulsion when her lips curve faintly, her fingers curling around the bars. "Oh, I know that you did not loathe me, Anna. Though it may be well snuffed, I do not doubt that your love for me was true once. Just as *you* should never doubt how truly I enjoyed you."

I recoil a little, surprised that she should offer me such an unselfish assurance that at least what we shared between our bodies was genuine. "That is good to know, I suppose," I say stiffly, loath to reveal how much the admission means to me, or how much I believed in my early love for her.

Surely another shoe is left to drop.

Her gaze shifts, liquid, between my eyes, an eyebrow lifting. "And for whatever that is worth, will you make me a promise? Grant me one final favor?"

And there it is, landing me back on solid ground. "What would you have me do?"

"Will you bring Gabor to see me?" she asks, her face shattering, threading through with cracks like that porcelain vase Ilona once broke. Slow, glistening tears begin rolling down her cheeks, and I realize with a shock that this is the first time I have ever seen her cry. Though it is always possible that even this display is for my benefit. "Just, just one last time, when I am in here instead of you? I wish to look upon him, see what I shall leave behind."

"I will," I say. "I swear it."

"Good," she replies thickly. "That is all I can ask."

With an effort, she lurches up to her feet and dusts off her dress, neatly swallowing the last of her tears.

"Guard," she calls out in her imperious tone, as if she were not about to condemn herself to death. "I need to see the magistrate."

Before she leaves, she turns to cast one last look at me over her shoulder, her clean profile limned with firelight. Though I could not swear it, I almost think I see one eyelid drop.

A parting glimmer of a wink.

A final secret shared between us, like a swallow of wine passed from mouth to mouth.

Epilogue

Would like to say I never think of her.

But how could I tell such a lie, when I see echoes of her not only in Gabor's face, but in the face of the squalling, black-eyed babe my sister bore only six months ago? Gabor and Klara have been wed for a year now; Peter's family kept him with them once everything was done, and he grew up loving my sister. Elizabeth's bloody tapestry unraveled quickly once she confessed. Emboldened, even her most loyal servants turned against her, and the orchards readily yielded the yellowed skeletons of her secrets. Csejthe's tallest turret was made into her prison; she was locked into it, sealed away with bricks.

Trapped where she could no longer carve her will into the world.

Though I have tried not to paint the son with the brush of his mother's crimes, I have also found it near impossible not to watch him for some sign of her. A flicker of deviousness, a touch of heedless cruelty, a subtle reveling in another's pain.

But I see none of that in him. He was a lovable child, clever and sweet-tempered and far brighter than my own brothers, reluctant to so much as pull Zsuzsi's tail; our cat loved him so well she now purrs in his son's crib, watching over him like a sentinel. And now Gabor is a dear husband to my sister, as loving and devoted as Peter would have been to me. But I would not wed him, even after all he suffered for my sake, not when I know myself incapable of such a love.

And I have vowed that no one will ever own me again. The sweet girl Peter married from a neighboring village makes him a much better wife than I would have.

I was not made to be anyone's wife. Not when I am Anna the Cunning, midwife of Sarvar, and its former, reformed witch. Not even Elizabeth Báthory, for all her wiles and malice, could keep a hold of me.

But at the very least, when the messenger arrives with the note, I can honestly say I have not thought of Elizabeth in months. Yet when I unroll and read the letter, her face seems to float before me like a specter. Those sly, winking eyes, the scarlet lip fastened between her teeth, the inky sweep of her hair.

And when I read that, in dying, she has split her fortune between me and her son, I cannot suppress the tears that spring to my eyes.

Goodbye, my lady, I think, my nose filling with the faint, spiced ghost of her perfume. *Though this world is well rid of you, my curse is to remember.*

Acknowledgments

When I first started writing YA, I thought I had a pretty firm sense of the space I wanted to occupy. Contemporary fantasy was prime territory—and the more witches the better, generally, for obvious reasons. Horror could be really compelling, too, and I could see how elements of science fiction might be intriguing if liberally plied with magic. Under the right circumstances and star alignment, I might even consider venturing into stone-cold contemporary realism, though the idea was a little daunting—because how does one even plot without supernatural shenanigans?!

Historical fiction, on the other hand, was pretty much off the table. I remember reading Mackenzi Lee's *The Gentlemen's Guide to Vice and Virtue* a few years ago and feeling staggered by the breadth, vigor, and intricacy of the long-dead era she evoked so seemingly effortlessly on the page. But knowing the work it takes to construct even a contemporary world convincingly rooted in our own, I balked at the idea of such a historical deep dive, the heavy lifting required to become so intimately acquainted and conversant with a bygone age. It just sounded really *hard*, when, you know, I could stick with modern sassy witches.

But, it turns out, being a little obsessed with your subject totally changes the game.

Growing up in eastern Europe, I encountered Elizabeth Báthory over and over in my cultural studies classes at the various American international schools I attended. Her story is so blood-curdlingly infamous, so wickedly twisted, beguiling, and confounding, that a number of nations lay claim to her as a colorful part of their own history. I met her in Hungary, Romania, and even in Bulgaria, though as far as I know, the diabolical countess never actually set foot there. As my fascination with Elizabeth grew, I sought out accounts of her life, both fictionalized and historical; in writing this story, I leaned heavily on *Infamous Lady* by Kimberly L. Craft and *The Countess* by Rebecca Johns, both of which I highly recommend.

Despite the intrigue she inspires, there are gaping voids in our knowledge and understanding of Elizabeth's life. There's no book, letter, or HBO miniseries out there that can really shed light on why a noblewoman who spoke five languages, and often interceded on the behalf of lowborn women in her care, would so heedlessly commit such atrocities against her own gender. What drove her on, spurred this unslakable bloodlust? Was she deranged, evil, somehow tormented . . . or something even darker and more unfathomable than that?

This absence leaves ample room for the imagination—and it gave me the precious and ridiculously fun real estate in which to take my own stab at portraying this monstrous lady's psyche.

Still, even with all my enthusiasm, Elizabeth and Anna's story could never have existed without Anne Heltzel's patience, warm wisdom, killer e-mail game, and editorial genius. In so many ways, this book is her baby just as much as mine; I'm forever indebted to her for giving me the opportunity and freedom to play with it. I'm also deeply grateful to Andrew Smith for taking this gamble, and to the whole team at Abrams/Amulet for their unflagging support.

I'm also, and always, grateful to Taylor Haggerty, lovely friend, agent extraordinaire, and the dark and twisty star to whom this book is dedicated. This writing thing has been a wild ride and about a gazillion times more fun than it would have been without you.

To all my dear friends, especially Claire Schulz and Jilly Gagnon, stalwart confidantes and mainstays in g-chat land— I'm so lucky to have you in my life.

I'm also grateful to my family, especially for their unwavering support even when I'm staking my claim in some admittedly bloody territory. I promise, this book is *not* your fault.

And finally, all my love and gratitude to my husband and heart, Caleb, for never batting an eye at my ridiculously ample non sequiturs, loving me so well even when I'm freaking out, and generally not being too creeped out to sleep next to me at night. You will always be my favorite.

Stay tuned for

POISON PRIESTESS

A Lady Slayers Novel

COMING IN EARLY 2021